D0042393

THINGS WE LOST IN THE WATER

For Mikey

THIS IS A BORZOI BOOK
PUBLISHED BY ALFRED A. KNOPF

Published in the United States by Alfred A. Knopf,
a division of Penguin Random House LLC, New York, and distributed
in Canada by Penguin Random House Canada Limited, Toronto.

www.aaknopf.com

Library of Congress Cataloging-in-Publication Data
Names: Nguyen, Eric, 1988– author.
Title: Things we lost to the water : a novel / Eric Nguyen.
Description: First edition. | New York : Alfred A. Knopf, 2021. | "This is a Borzoi Book"
Identifiers: LCCN 2020033323 (print) | LCCN 2020033324 (ebook) |
ISBN 9780593317952 (hardcover) | ISBN 9780593311035 (paperback) |
ISBN 9780593317969 (ebook)
Classification: LCC PS3614.G864 T48 2021 (print) | LCC PS3614.G864 (ebook) |
DDC 813/.6—dc23
LC record available at https://lccn.loc.gov/2020033323
LC ebook record available at https://lccn.loc.gov/2020033324

Jacket photograph by Maki Studio / Alamy
Jacket design by Chip Kidd

Manufactured in the United States of America
First Edition

THINGS WE LOST TO THE WATER

a *novel*

ERIC NGUYEN

ALFRED A. KNOPF · NEW YORK · 2021

August 1979

New Orleans is at war. The long howl in the sky; what else can it mean?

Hương drops the dishes into the sink and grabs the baby before he starts crying. She begins running toward the door—but then remembers: this time, another son. She forgets his name temporarily, the howl is so loud. What's important is to find him.

Is he under the bed? No, he is not under the bed. Is he hiding in the closet? No, he is not in the closet. Is he in the bathroom, then, behind the plastic curtains, sitting scared in the tub? He is not in the bathroom, behind the plastic curtains, sitting scared in the tub. And as she turns around he's at the door, holding on to the frame, his eyes watering, his cheeks red.

"Mẹ," he cries. *Mom.* The word reminds Hương of everything she needs to know. In the next moment she grabs his hand and pulls him toward her chest.

With this precious cargo, these two sons, she darts across the apartment, an arrow flying away from its bow, a bullet away from its gun. She's racing toward the door and leaping down the steps—but she can't move fast enough. The air is like water, it's like running through water. Through an ocean. She feels the wetness on her legs and the water rising. And the sky, the early evening sky, with its spotting of stars already, is streaked red and orange like a fire, like an explosion suspended midair in that moment before the crush, the shattering, the death she's always imagined until someone yells *Stop*, someone tells her to *Stop*.

And just like that, the sirens hush and the silence is violent: it slices, it cuts.

"Hurricane alarm," Bà Giang says. The old woman drops her cigarette. "Just a hurricane alarm. A test. Nothing to be afraid of." She reaches over and cups Hương's cheek.

"What do you mean?" Hương asks.

"A test. They're doing a test. In case something happens," Bà Giang says. "Go home now, cưng ơi. Go home. Get some rest. It's getting late."

Home.

Late.

Getting.

There.

"Late." Hương understands, or maybe she does not. A thousand thoughts are still settling in her mind. Where were the sounds from before? Not the alarm, but the grating calls of the grackles in the trees, the whistling breeze, a car speeding past—where are they now?

She notices Tuấn at the gates. Her eyes light up.

"Tuấn ơi," she calls.

Tuấn holds on to the bars of the gate and watches three boys riding past on bicycles. One stands on his pedals. Another rides

without hands but only for a second before grabbing—in a pan-
icked motion—the handlebars. A younger one tries to keep up on
training wheels. Three boys. Three brothers.

"Tuấn ơi," Hương calls again.

Tuấn waves as the boys ride leisurely past. When they're gone,
he returns, and Hương feels a mixture of pure happiness, comfort,
and relief.

Up the dirt road. A mother and her sons. Hand in hand.

Hương

Hương and her sons had been in the country for only a month, but already they were having problems.

Their sponsor, a white Catholic priest, paired them with the Minhs. "Both thirty-two," he said while driving. "You will like them."

The priest—she never remembered his name—was old and serious and restrained. He walked with his hands behind his back as he took long, sweeping strides and had a habit of keeping his head slightly bent forward as if he were listening to something everyone else could not hear, giving him a look of arrogant superiority. He reminded her of the priests who came to her childhood village with hard European candies and boxes of Bibles in hopes of converting someone in their bad Vietnamese. She remembered one priest who couldn't pronounce bạn and instead said bàn, and they made fun of him behind his back, calling him Father Table. Still, Hương did not not like this New Orleans priest. She was lucky, she told herself. She was alive. She made it to America.

The priest took an exit onto another highway. He didn't use his blinker.

They had been on and off highways all morning, dropping off other "refugees"—the word still felt strange in her mouth, in her mind—at temporary homes. Earlier that morning, the priest dropped off a couple from Vũng Tàu at a tall building. Then a single Saigonese girl at a short house painted pink. Another family of three was given to an American fisherman and his wife, and they greeted each other with hugs as if they had known each other all their lives; the wife gave their son a pink stuffed elephant. Hương and her boys were the last to be dropped off.

Bình slept in an infant seat as Tuấn kneeled by the window and watched as the world slipped by, pointing and calling out the names of everything he saw: xe hơi, xe đạp, cây, nhà. What Hương noticed the most was the concrete—the buildings, the roads, the sidewalks, the fountains, the statues. *So much concrete,* she thought. She imagined them rubbing against her, scraping her knees and hands, leaving bruises and scrapes and marks. She was thinking that way nowadays: what can hurt her, what can leave a scar.

The priest turned onto a road, and just like that, the hardness of the city disappeared, replaced by flat plots of parched grass and a traffic light. Beyond that, a billboard advertised a deep red sausage with rice grains inside.

As they waited, the priest glanced up into his rearview mirror and smiled. "Gần tới rồi," he said, *Almost there,* in an accent Hương found oddly charming, like the way the Australian English teachers at the refugee camp spoke, and that gave her something to latch on to, a type of comfort. The van continued down the long stretch of road for another five minutes before slowing down into a turn. In front of a house, a fat Vietnamese man waited.

"Mr. Minh!" the priest chuckled. Mr. Minh waved when he saw them.

"Welcome to America!" Mr. Minh shouted as the priest parked

the car. He pulled the door open and bowed extravagantly, making a show of the gesture. His large hands came at her next and grabbed her wrists. He shook them furiously. "Chị will like it here very much!" he said. "It's America! We're all friends here!" His face glowed red. How unlike her husband he was. Công was thin and suave, bookish and reserved, and, above all, neat; this man was chubby and rude, drunk and loud—above all, loud. She could have pictured Mr. Minh spending his time at bars and his poor wife coming to get him at three in the morning. She thought, not without bitterness, that they never would have been friends in Vietnam. They were two different types of people; a friendship had little chance.

"We're all friends here!" Mr. Minh repeated, confidently, caressing her sloppily, stupidly. It made Hương feel little, like a bug waiting to be squashed. She held on to her baby boy and motioned for her other son to stand closer. The wife—Hương noticed her now—stood aside as if this were the regular order of things.

"He used to be a police officer," the wife said in her scratchy voice. "Now, he drinks!" She laughed and Hương didn't know if she was supposed to laugh out of courtesy or just nod sadly in agreement. She decided on doing neither and stayed silent and stiff.

"Very well," the wife said. Then, in English, she said something to the priest, shook his hand, and grabbed Hương's suitcase. The priest drove away.

"This way," she said.

Hương walked up the porch steps and crossed the threshold. Right away, she smelled the rotting wood, disarming at first but only because it came so suddenly. The lights were off, and in the darkness, the room felt vast and empty. As her eyes adjusted, she realized the room was small and arranged at its center were a floral fabric sofa, a white plastic chair, and a small television. A fan spun lazily above.

The wife told Hương it was called a "shotgun house." Ngôi nhà súng, she clarified. "See?" she said. She placed the suitcase down and mimed the shape of a gun with one hand. With her other, she held her wrist. Closing one eye, she looked through an invisible scope and the appearance of intense concentration fell onto her face. For a few seconds, she stood silently, so focused on something in the distance that Hương looked toward where the wife stared, too. Then "Psssh!"—the imitated sound of gunfire. It was so unexpected but also so childish. Hương jumped back and felt stupid for doing so. Like a child tricked in a schoolyard, she immediately hated the Minhs, their poverty, their obnoxiousness, their immaturity.

"See?" the wife said. "A house for guns." She made the motion of dusting off her hands. "But you don't have to worry about that here. No war, not here, not ever."

"Of course," said Hương, composing herself.

"That's all in the past now," the wife said.

"Yes," said Hương, "the past."

"Just stay out of the doorways to be on the safe side." She broke out into a cackle, though Hương didn't find any of it funny. Nothing in America was funny. Mrs. Minh's tricks weren't funny, their situation as người Việt wasn't funny, and Hương felt outraged that people like the Minhs should even think about laughing.

"Let me show you more," said the wife. She led Hương through the doorways and into the kitchen and the couple's bedroom in the back. "You'll sleep up front. The phòng khách," said Mrs. Minh.

The next morning, the priest arrived to take Hương downtown, dropping her off at the church. Before coming to America, Hương had never been inside a church. In Mỹ Tho there was none. In Saigon, only a handful. But here they were everywhere, and all the other Vietnamese seemed grateful for that. The first few weeks, as they slept in the pews, they seemed at peace. Hương, for her part, slept uneasily under the watch of the statue of Jesus on the cross.

His sad, pleading eyes made her want to cross herself like all the other Catholics did. She knew Công would have laughed at her for it, so she didn't.

"Here," the priest said before letting her go. He tore out a sheet of yellow paper from a legal pad he carried everywhere. For the last week they had been finding her a job. "Because you need money to survive in New Orleans," he said as if he thought life in other countries were any different. They had often gone out in groups, but today was her first day alone. *Franklin's Seafood,* said one line, followed by an address. *Poydras Street Dry Cleaners,* said another.

"Franklin's looking for cashiers," he said, "and Poydras a clothes folder. Oh, and . . ." He wrote something else down and gave another sheet to Hương. "Be on the lookout for signs that say HIRING." She held the loose sheet of paper and sounded out the word with her lips.

"Hi-Ring," she whispered.

"Hi-er-ing," he said.

"Hi-yering."

"Hi-er-ing." Hương mouthed the words and folded the paper away. The priest gave her directions and she was on her way, pushing the stroller she'd borrowed from the church for Bình with one hand and leading Tuấn with the other. By the time she was on Magazine Street, she looked up and wondered how a city could be so empty. Down one way, a driver had parked his school bus and was reading the newspaper and eating a doughnut. Down another, two women talked to each other in smart business skirts.

As she walked, Hương reached into her purse for a pocket-sized notebook, a gift from the church. Từ vựng căn bản, she had written at the top of the first page, followed by the phrases she had remembered from her English lessons:

Hello.

How are you?

I am fine.

Thank you.

She practiced the words aloud, repeating them in whispers, analyzing the pronunciation, the tones. English was such a strange language. Whereas in Vietnamese, the words told you how they wanted to be pronounced, in English the words remained shrouded in mystery.

She scanned the priest's list, then returned to the notebook. So many words, so many ideas, so many meanings. If only Công could see her now! She imagined that she spoke English the way he spoke French, like he was born there. She saw them sitting together on a porch looking out on a garden—maybe like one of the gardens she'd passed here in New Orleans, with immaculate flower beds and sprinklers and birdbaths—and she's holding up the words, helping him pronounce them. What she would tell him then, when they were settled, successful, American, reminiscing of all that life threw at them, the improbability of their survival, and yet nonetheless . . .

Suddenly, Tuấn pulled her arm.

"Look!" he said. "A cat!"

"Tuấn!" Hương grabbed him before he stepped into the street. A car passed by. A horn sounded.

"But it was a cat," her son said, "and it wasn't like any other cat. Didn't you see it?"

"Stay with mẹ," she said.

They walked two more blocks before finding the first address on the list. A cartoon fish with huge eyes stared back at her from a tin sign. Leaning her forehead against the glass, she peered inside and imagined herself holding a tray of drinks and chatting with customers.

A girl at the front counter waved at Hương to get her attention. When Hương didn't come in, the girl came to the door and asked her something she couldn't understand. Hương reached for the notebook in her purse then, but it was gone. A sense of panic came over her. After emptying everything into her hands, she realized she must have dropped it while Tuấn was running into the street. She found the note the priest gave her—there at the bottom of her purse, a piece of shining gold—and handed it over.

"Please," Hương said in an almost whisper, unsure if it meant làm ơn. Surely, it meant làm ơn! She forced a smile and hoped it didn't appear too eager. Then she stopped smiling altogether to avoid any possibility of looking desperate. She remembered the women in their business suits. How confident they were. How successful.

The girl looked at the word, then at Hương. She did this several times, confused. "No," the girl said. "No," she said again, this time more forceful, like the word was a pebble and she was flicking it toward what must have been a strange Vietnamese woman, a woman who did not belong here, a foreigner. "Do you want to *eat?*" the girl continued, slow and loud. "We serve *food.* Do you want to *eat?*"

"Eat?" Hương asked. She didn't know what that meant. It sounded like a hiccup, one that you tried to suppress. *Eat! Eat! Eat!* What was the girl talking about?

The girl became impatient, angry even, pointing inside, where people were enjoying their grotesquely large meals.

"I am sorry," Hương said, giving up, using the phrase she knew by heart: *I am sorry.* It was a good phrase to know. This was what the Australian English teachers taught her at the refugee camp. *I am sorry for what happened.*

Before the girl could say anything else, Hương turned around and walked away with a steady stride. She didn't know what had just happened, but she felt, in the pit of her stomach, that she had done something wrong. The last thing she saw on the girl's face was a grimace. She was being told, she was sure, that she had done something rude, against the country's laws. They would arrest her. They would arrest a woman and her children for not knowing the rules. Would they even let her stay because she was arrested? What would happen to them all then? They crossed the street and took another corner. She walked faster.

"Mẹ, what's wrong?" Tuấn asked. He looked back toward where they had come from.

"Don't look back," said Hương. She pushed the stroller and led Tuấn away. "Don't you look."

Suddenly, she noticed, all around her people were talking. There were couples talking, groups talking, children talking, a woman held a dog in her arms and she, too, was talking to that small animal. Yet the words they were saying didn't make any sense. She repeated the words she knew in her head, a chaotic mantra of foreign sounds that contorted her mouth comically, strangely, like a puppet's—*Yes, no, thank you, please, yes, no, sorry, hello, goodbye, no, sorry.* The important part was to keep moving. She knew that much. She saw a fenced-in and empty park across the street and without looking ran toward it, but before she reached the gate, a man with beads around his neck and oversized sunglasses bumped into her. She could smell the alcohol on him. All of a sudden, the whole city smelled of alcohol and everyone everywhere was drinking and smiling and laughing. What was wrong with these people? What was wrong with this place?

She turned back and was stepping into the street, pushing the stroller with both hands, when a car slammed its brakes and the driver pressed down on his horn. It stopped before hitting her or the stroller. She looked down at her shaking hands: she had let go. In the surprise of the car coming and its horn sounding, so suddenly and so loudly—she had let go. The first sign of danger and her first instinct was to let go and she'd nearly killed her son and the man pressed down on his horn again and she realized she was still in the middle of the street and she felt ashamed, the most shame she'd ever felt in her life. She held back tears, but Bình cried. She clasped the handlebar of the stroller more tightly.

"Stupid fucking lady!" the driver screamed.

"What did he say?" Tuấn asked.

"Let's go home," she replied. "He said we should go home." They crossed the street and headed down another.

"But home is so far away," said her son. "I'm tired."

"What?" She had forgotten what she told him. She looked around for anything that might have been familiar.

"Home is far away," her son repeated.

"I know," she said, more to herself than to him. "I know."

The Minhs were home when Hương returned. After dinner, Mrs. Minh left for a job cleaning at a university. Hương's sons slept peacefully. She kept a watchful eye on Bình. Did he understand that he'd nearly died today? Did he know he had a horrible, reckless mother? She would have to tell Công, wouldn't she, about all that had happened? She would confess it to him, everything she'd ever done—if only she were given the chance, an opportunity to talk to him, to learn what had happened, to get him to America and plan a way forward. For that she would confess it all.

At the camp, she had written him and mailed the letter to their home in Mỹ Tho. When she received no answer, she wrote to their old home in Saigon. She wrote as soon as she was able to. She must have sent a letter every day. Noticing how many letters she had been sending off, another woman at the camp reprimanded her.

"Are you so stupid?" the woman asked.

"What do you mean?"

"The Communists, when they see the letters, they'll know you escaped and they'll know who to punish: your husband!" Hương stopped writing then.

As the sun rose, Mrs. Minh arrived home, smelling of detergent and rubber gloves. Without a word, she joined Hương on the couch and watched TV, which Hương had turned on for its soft glow. From her seat, Mrs. Minh would glance at her temporary guest every few minutes as if to say something important but ended up talking only about the shows. In this show, a witch causes havoc by her misunderstandings but her husband loves her anyway. In this one, there's a magical talking horse. Here, a group of Americans are shipwrecked.

They settled on the shipwreck show, or at least Mrs. Minh did. In black and white, it looked far away, a different place, a different time. Even if it was a different language, it was easy to laugh at, easily understood.

Except Hương wasn't laughing. It didn't even look like she was paying attention. The light on the screen bounced off her eyes.

This would happen multiple nights: Hương staring blankly at the screen in the dark while Mrs. Minh sat on the edge of the couch in contemplation. It made the air heavy, both of them knew, but neither one knew how to fix it.

Then one night Mrs. Minh asked, "What do you think of America?"

"Dạ thích," Hương said. "It's not Vietnam, but it's not bad, either." She coughed to clear her throat. All day she hadn't been talking to anyone in Vietnamese except her sons. It felt so strange after so much silence, and the words came out muddy and sticky.

"The priest said you left on a boat," the wife continued. "Is that true?"

"Vâng." Hương wanted to tell the wife about the way the water moved, how you never got used to it, about the men on the boat and their constant fighting, about the uneasy sense of knowing only water, knowing that it connected the entire world—one shore to another—yet not knowing when you might see land. There were so many things to say, and finally she decided to ask a question, the most important question she could ask, the only one that mattered—"Do you know how to get a message back to Vietnam? I have a husband. He was left behind . . ."—but Hương stopped short of finishing when there was shuffling noise in the bedroom, the rustling of sheets, the bouncing of bedsprings.

She bit her lips and held her breath. Something was coming; she could feel it. Mrs. Minh's eyes wandered to the back of the house. Then came a scream and the sound of glass hitting wall, one clash of impact followed by the rainlike sound of hundreds of shards falling. The baby woke with a cry and Hương got up to calm him. Tuấn stirred from his corner of the couch and asked what was going on.

"Nothing," she told him. "Nothing to be afraid of." She bounced the baby as footsteps made their way across the hardwood floor and the bathroom door closed and the shower turned on. The baby leaned his head on her chest and quieted.

"I'll go check on him," Mrs. Minh said, standing up. "Yes. I'll go do that."

The couple would fight into the morning. Something else would break. At one point, Hương thought she heard a smack on skin but she wasn't sure.

By eight, Mr. Minh had left, slamming the door so hard Hương was sure the house would fall down. Mrs. Minh mumbled as she prepared breakfast, "Damn that man. Worthless . . ."

The next afternoon, Hương left the Minhs. With Bình in her arms and Tuấn following behind, she walked several blocks until she saw a *motel*. The word, she remembered, meant *place to stay*. She would stay at the motel for a week, find a way to get in touch with Công, and get him here to New Orleans. No one told her how to, but, she decided, no more waiting. It was time for action. She paid in cash. The room was twenty-five dollars. She put the thirty dollars she had left in her front pocket, holding her hand over it to make sure it was secure.

After she called him, the priest arrived the next morning. He sat in his van as Hương led the boys out. The radio played gospel hymns, but he turned it off as they made their journey downtown.

He had been searching for her all morning, he said when they were on the highway. The window was down and the wind was more hot than cool. The Minhs had told him she *"just up and left,"* without telling them where she was heading. She hadn't even left a note about where she was going, how to reach her, or what her intentions were. She could have *"dropped off the face of the earth"*— she had no idea what that could possibly have meant.

"I nearly had a heart attack," the priest said. *Did she know New Orleans could be a dangerous place?* he went on. People get murdered here. Robbed. Beaten. She was a recent immigrant, and people could have taken advantage of her. Why did she leave?

She didn't answer him right away. It could have been a rhetorical question. But he didn't have to live with them. He didn't have to live with Mr. Minh's night terrors or his drunkenness. Or the couple's arguments. He didn't have to live as if in a nightmare, where everywhere she turned something was strange, askew, incoherent. That was what her time in New Orleans had been like. He couldn't have understood any of this. His life wasn't complicated. He was a priest, for God's sake! He didn't know a thing about suffering.

At the church, they filed into his office. The priest turned on the air-conditioning and searched through the mess on his desk.

"They don't like us," she said finally. She didn't know what she expected him to say or do. Anger bubbled inside her. "You don't understand," she managed to say before taking a seat.

The walls of the room were lined with certificates with fancy writing and gold seals; crosses, some plain wood, others decorated with gold; and there were photos, mostly of him—here with a group of nuns, there with a youth baseball team, another a group portrait with other priests. And among all this, a framed cream-colored piece of paper. An emblem sat in the middle and below it, a motto: IN SERVICE TO ONE, IN SERVICE TO ALL.

Finally the priest said, "I've been a priest for ten years." He took off his glasses, rubbed them with a cloth, and put them back on.

"And I don't think I've ever taken on more than I have this year."
He went on to talk about God, bringing up Bible stories about tests
and hardships. God was testing him, he told her.

For the first time since she'd met him, she realized she was less of
a person and more of a test to this man. She was a puzzle to figure
out, a jigsaw, a number among other numbers. He lived to serve
not humanity but his ideas and career. In that way, she thought,
Catholics were not too dissimilar from the Communists. She had
been hoping this man was different. How foolish she was to put
her life in his hands.

"Don't you understand?" he asked, rhetorically. He smiled
dumbly, as if he had reached an epiphany.

She breathed in and exhaled. She was exhausted. "Yes," she said
and left.

As she closed the door, a woman's voice, somewhere, squealed,
"Trời ơi!"

Hương looked up. She scanned the pews to see if anyone was
there, and her eyes stopped at a closet door left ajar, a thin strip
of light streaming out. She paused at the threshold. Inside, Thủy,
a girl younger than Hương whom she knew from the church, was
bent over a table.

"Chị Hương!" Thủy opened the door and cried out her name
again. The girl jumped up and down and reached out for Hương's
hands. "Come! You have to hear this!" she said. Hương didn't
know how to react as Thủy moved aside and showed her the cassette player on the table. She pressed a button and it began to click.
Soon, through the static, a man spoke.

"Thủy ơi!" said the grainy voice. "How I miss you so! It is raining here again, my love. Can you hear the water? The heavens cry."
The voice quieted to the sound of water pelting against mud.

The man was probably a young boy Thủy's age. Hương wanted
to laugh at their young, naïve love. Instead, she took a step closer,
inspecting the cassette player—the spinning of the tape reel, the

clicking of the movement, the smooth buttons with their colorful symbols on top. She focused on the spinning of the wheels.
For a moment, there was no other sound except that clicking as it
echoed in that small closet.

"Thủy?" the man's voice came on again. Hương stepped back.

"There he is!" Thủy squealed and clapped her hands in excitement. She hugged Hương, and then, embarrassed, restrained herself.

"Thủy, when you return home, we should get married! I know
that's not what your parents want, but . . ."

Thủy turned down the volume and Hương left the girl to her
tape message.

Walking down Camp Street, Hương thought about the ease of
making a cassette. Unlike the letter, its content wasn't obvious;
instead, it was hidden, unless the tape was played. But people
would play it only if it looked suspicious. If she were to label it
"Uncle Hồ's Teachings" or maybe just "Communism," they would
not even bother looking any further into the matter. Yet there
was the cost of sending it. And would she mail it to their Mỹ Tho
address or their Saigon one? Would Công still be there? Was Công
safe? What if the Communists captured him? No, she had to wipe
those uncertainties from her mind. She needed to think positively;
it was the only way. She would have to ask the priest about the
tape recorder. After apologizing for her behavior that morning,
she would say politely, "Cha, cho con mượn cái này." Coyly, she
would add, "I will return it, I swear. Just one night."

Công would be reached. They would be reunited. New Orleans
looked brighter and happier then. She smiled. It was the first time
in weeks. Perhaps even months.

At the motel, she set the tape recorder on the desk. She tested it,
and the sound of her voice surprised her. She sounded young and
immature, a little bit needy. Did she always sound like that? She

tested it again, changing her voice and the pitch of the words. She wanted to make a good impression. When she was happy with her test recording, she cleaned up and dressed the boys as if the recorder could see what they looked like.

"I don't like this," Tuấn complained. He pulled at his shirt. "Itchy."

"It's only for a little bit," she told him. "It's important. We dress up for important things." She told this to herself and changed into an áo dài, the one luxury she had packed. After they were ready, she pressed the button and the machine began recording.

"A lô, anh Công? Hương đây." She paused. Where to start?

It felt odd speaking to a machine now. She had practiced so much, but now it meant something. She had to pick the correct words to get her meaning across clearly, to describe her situation correctly, to express her emotions so that there were no questions about how she felt. Her lungs became heavy and her cheeks flushed red. She turned off the machine and then turned it back on.

"We made it to America," she started. She turned the recorder off and took another breath, then started it again. "But before, we were in Singapore in a camp full of other boat people. That's what they call us: *boat people.*"

She wanted to stop, but the words just kept coming. She had so much to say and none of it would make sense to Công.

They spent a week on a boat, she and Tuấn, and, somewhere within her, their baby. The only food they brought were a small bag of cooked rice and another bag of bananas. (Công knew that already.) A few days in, this was split among the twenty or so people on the boat. (She had lost count of how many there were.) She remembered that at one point the entire boat ran out of water, and all the babies, including her son, were crying and screaming of thirst. Then it rained, the sky turning black, and water droplets fell down. They lifted their plastic bottles and bags to the air as the children opened their mouths. Soon came the lightning and thunder and everyone crouched down, huddled in the mass of skin and bones as if the act of clutching on to one another was enough to save them if the boat were to topple over.

The next day a ship found them, and their greetings were friendly. The ship sailed them to a camp in Singapore, where they stayed for several months, long enough for her to have the child, which she was surprised survived at all after the cruelties of the sea. Finally, they were told to get on a plane and that plane took the three of them—a mother and two sons—to New Orleans, a place she never heard of before and still couldn't place on a map.

She held up Bình and the baby cooed into the recorder. She should have told Công about him first. Why didn't she? "This is our son, Công. I named him Bình. Isn't he đẹp trai? He was born at the camp. I thought I wouldn't have been healthy enough and that if he came he wouldn't be healthy, either, but here he is. He's healthy and he's strong! He's a miracle." She held the baby up higher and he laughed as if tickled. "That's your father," she said and pointed to the recorder. She waved his little hand and he laughed louder. She wished he hadn't. This was a serious moment. They, all of them, should be serious.

"Công, are you safe?" she asked now. "Where are you now? Are you coming over? How is our house? What are the Communists doing? Is it safe there? Are you safe?" There were so many questions. She opened her mouth, but nothing came out except a weak whimper. She stood up to get a tissue.

The last night in Mỹ Tho they packed an old suitcase. They had used it years earlier—before Tuấn, before there was talk of family—on a trip to Đà Lạt. Hương remembered the rolling hills, covered in morning mist and looking like giants: tall and sturdy, mysterious and unknowable. She told Công that this was where she would want to spend the rest of her life. Công, on the other hand, didn't like Đà Lạt. He didn't like traveling. He had left the North with his family when he was a child. A refugee, he associated movement with loss. Since then, he had looked for a place to put down his roots—to stay. In the days before Saigon was lost, everyone was trying to leave, but Công was adamant about staying. They had just moved from Mỹ Tho to the city for Công's job at the university. He had worked his entire life for this, he had said, and now they were letting him teach literature—to talk about not only the great Vietnamese poets but about the great French ones he loved, too, like Rimbaud, Verlaine, Gautier, Apollinaire, and Hugo. At the age of two, Tuấn knew these names better than those of the other kids, and he sang them wherever he went: Rim-baud, Ver-laine, Gau-tier. Công was proud of all he'd accomplished, even if teaching was, at times, difficult. More often than not, he came home with two or three full folders of papers to grade, along with stories of troublesome students. He struggled with the ones who were closed-minded, the ones who were stuck to their small-town ideologies and resisted being educated. The worst, he would tell her (looking around as if he were disclosing a secret), were the students who joined the Communist clubs. They were so set in their ideologies there was no teaching them. ("You would sooner teach a horse to fly," he would say.) Still, his life was coming together the way he had planned. The look in his eyes said "hãy tin anh." *Trust me.* And Hương did.

They were finally getting used to Saigon, the loud vendors, the littered streets, the overbearing smell of motor exhaust. They had fallen into a comfortable domestic routine.

Mornings, Công and Hương would wake up early. The day would start with morning stretches in their small backyard as the sun rose and their coffee dripped into warm perfection. After, they'd cook breakfast together, often rice with nước tương and eggs. By the time the city woke up—with people walking to work and motorbikes taking to the streets—Tuấn was awake, and they got him ready for school. She'd walk him there as Công biked to the university. They'd arrive before classes started and she'd hand him over to his friends—three other little boys—and they'd play with a soccer ball. Hương would sit under the shade of the tree and watch until the teachers came to collect their students.

During the day, she'd clean the house and settle the family accounts. Công brought in the money, but it was because of her know-how with numbers that they could survive. Công appreciated her for this and often told her she should have gone to school and studied math. But that idea only called to mind abstract theories discussed in front of dusty chalkboards. And why would she want that when she could calculate numbers with the sun streaming in through the window, a light breeze blowing now and then? No, that life wasn't for her. She knew her life and what she wanted, and having had it, there as if in the palms of her hands, she felt happy.

In the afternoon, she would pick Tuấn up and they'd go to the market to buy ingredients for dinner that night. It was the best time to buy because the sellers were tired by then and easy to bargain with. Though, of course, it meant not getting the best picks of produce and meat. Still, it saved them money; their country was at war, after all (though, in Hương's mind, the war was always over there—someplace she'd only ever heard of). Công, if he wasn't busy, would be home by the time they returned.

They'd cook as a family, discussing their day. If Công had a particularly good day or if he left his office early, he would bring home a treat for his son, the catch being he had to answer one of his riddles. But, of course, their son was so smart—the professor's son—that he answered everything right and claimed his prize with a kiss and a smile. Theirs was a house of love, Hương was sure. It was all they ever needed—love. And with love, they would survive. She believed this with all her heart.

When the city fell, Công didn't anticipate things changing dramatically. The Communists had won the entire country; what else did they want? The war was over, after all. Life would resume. He had a new class to prepare for. The week Saigon fell, he said he was dreaming about his syllabus and wondering if he could fit the works of Musset in there somehow. The peaceful shift of power and how easily everything returned to normal—the school schedule, the bustling market—seemed to confirm what Công said.

That was May 1975.

But soon the curfews came. Tanks and soldiers with guns patrolled the streets as everyone else went about their daily business. Hương remembered how young the soldiers were. She had assumed they would all be older men, but they were all younger than she was. She saw the soldiers eating at restaurants, playing catch in the park, wooing girls. Surely these Communists could not have been bad. They could not have conquered an entire country—these boys with bone fingers, hungry arms, optimistic smiles. They passed out pamphlets from the new government explaining how it existed to serve the people. She would grow to hate that phrase—*serve the people*—at first because it was ubiquitous, then later, much later, as it became sinister, prickly.

The next year, a letter came for Công, asking him to report to a military training camp in Lăng Cô. As a member of the University of Saigon faculty, the future of the new nation depended on him, said the letter. It was time for the teachers to be taught. Pack enough clothes for two weeks of reeducation. They held him for five months.

When he returned to Saigon, shirtless and shoeless and emaciated, Hương didn't even recognize him until he called her name— "Hương. Anh đây." She ran to him and held him gently. Nights after, the feel of bones would haunt her.

It took him a month to recover. When he was better, Công didn't talk about what happened at the reeducation center, but he decided they should leave Saigon. Immediately.

They packed the suitcase—and Công gathered his favorite books into a knapsack—and took a bus back to Mỹ Tho, where Hương had grown up, where they had met. She still had a plot of familial land out there and a small shack, both inherited after her mother died years ago. An hour outside the town, the bus was stopped by a group of military officers and they were questioned. What were they doing, going to Mỹ Tho? Did they have permission to go? Did they know they had to ask permission? Công told them they were visiting Hương's mother, who was very ill. The officers looked at the couple suspiciously. The couple was let go. They told Công he looked like an honest man.

Upon their arrival in Mỹ Tho, they stayed with a family friend for a few weeks before setting up a meager, quiet home. If asked, by villagers or military officers, they said Hương's mother had died and they had decided to stay in her maternal village where they would farm a small plot of land.

How life was different for them now. In Saigon, Hương was the young wife of a professor and they were a professor's family. Now she and Công rooted around in a country garden, the dirt getting under their nails, the scent of earth and insects and sun baking themselves into their clothes and skin. They had planned on planting all types of vegetables—cabbages and cucumbers and lettuce—but the only thing that grew were bitter melons. Why were they farming, she often asked, when Mỹ Tho was a fishing village? Safer and a better investment, was Công's answer with an anxious look in his eyes. Or perhaps it was something else. She didn't ask; the recent months had been so much. Yes, of course, she reasoned, safety. So they farmed, and when the harvest was ready, Công took it to market.

Having no school, Tuấn stayed home and became bored and listless. He complained about not having books or toys. He asked about school and his friends. Somehow, he had the idea they were just a short walk away and he wanted to go there. He became grumpy when Hương said he needed to stay on their property.

The change didn't sit well with Công, either, who, though still loving, was distracted and distant. It was as if he was always looking over his shoulder, expecting someone there. Tuấn must have sensed this, too. During the day, their son would find little gifts for his father to cheer him up—a particularly pretty rock or an interesting flower. Công would smile and ruffle his son's hair. But then, again, his gaze would return outside to the quiet village, which, soon, became impossibly quieter, emptier.

Men began to disappear. First here and there, but then more noticeably. Then some women. Then entire households were replaced with families with stale Northern accents and pale skin.

One night, in the dark of their bedroom, Công told her they should leave the country.

"Leave?" she asked. "Why? Where?" The proposition seemed absurd, more so coming from Công, a rational man who only ever wanted a home.

"We can go anywhere. Remember Cảnh?" he asked.

Cảnh was a fisherman. The village woke up one morning and his shack had disappeared, the wood walls gone, the plot of land empty like he had never existed. Everyone was sure he'd packed up and sailed away. Cảnh became a local legend: one was not condemned to the oppression of the new Socialist Republic of Vietnam as it eliminated its traitors, planted new seeds, grew a new society. One could leave.

"Công," she said, "go to sleep."

Công got out of bed. He took out his notebook. He consulted his books and wrote until the sun rose. He came to bed only to sleep for two hours before getting up again, acting as if nothing had happened.

The nights would continue the same way. He became erratic. He wrote in a mixture of French and Vietnamese, pages and pages of it. She couldn't understand anything. When one sentence started in Vietnamese, it ended in French. She never knew he had this in him, this paranoia. Sometimes his handwriting looked more like miniature drawings than words. And there were letters put together that surely couldn't have meant anything in any language.

Eventually, the government began a new economic program. They would buy from the country's workers—"the foundation of our new society"—and, to ensure everyone got what they needed, sold the crops back to the masses—"to serve the people."

One day, a government official came for their bitter melons. He laughed as his colleagues loaded up a truck. "Who eats mướp đắng anymore, sister?" he said, though he took a load of the crops anyway and handed her not money but a small book of vouchers. "Thank you for serving the people."

"Serve the people!" she scoffed after they left.

Hương felt belittled and betrayed. As the official went door-to-door, at times laughing at her neighbors, sometimes even yelling at them if they didn't produce enough, she began feeling angry more than anything else.

"Ungrateful," she said. "They're stealing our food and giving us vouchers that won't buy even a kilo of rice and then telling us we're heroes of the country, the backbone of society." It made her want to cry for the state of her country.

But Công saw an opportunity. "Classic communism by the book! Now aren't you glad we grew crops?" he told her. Công's plan went into motion. They grew more than they would sell to the government. The surplus they sold on the black market, mostly to traditional herbalists and of course to starving families. After several months, they had the money for an escape—for three seats on the boat, for the fuel for the boat, for the food they would have to bring along. The money they had left over Hương sewed into their clothes, along with whatever jewelry they could trade for what they needed.

When the time came to leave, Hương couldn't believe it. That night, an old man with a dirty beard arrived at the house. They packed the suitcase and Công paid the man. They followed him into the jungle.

The old man, who must have been at least fifty, ran like a teenager, and they tried to keep up with him through the thick, moist air that made it hard for Hương to breathe and run and carry Tuấn at the same time. A storm was coming; this was why it was so humid. Was it safe to go to the water now?

Tuấn cried and Hương had to cover his mouth.

"Please be quiet, Tuấn. Please!" she begged him.

He cried louder and she felt his hot breath on her palm. When there was a sudden noise, she nearly let go but didn't. They all stopped running. The insects stopped their singing. The birds stopped their calling. It was the first time she had ever heard complete silence in the jungle.

"It sounded like a gunshot," said Công after a lengthy pause. "Are they after us?" Then, in an accusatory tone, Công yelled at the old man. "Are you one of them, old man? Are you ambushing us?"

The yelling made Tuấn cry louder, and the old man yelled back that he would never do anything like that; he said he was a man of his word, that he'd served for years in the South Vietnamese Army. The two men argued as Hương tried to make out their figures. She began to walk toward a shadow she thought was Công, but, approaching it, she saw it was a tree with its top chopped off like it was struck by lightning. The loud, sudden noise repeated and everyone went quiet again.

"Anh Công?" she said, grasping out in the dark. "Anh Công?"

"This way," she heard Công say. He grabbed her hand and they continued running, rubbing against trees, stumbling over vines. Hương had to stop twice because her stomach ached. For a month she'd had the idea that she was pregnant, and the last four weeks of sickness confirmed it. When she gave Công the news, she said she could have it taken care of before the trip, but he was so ecstatic he wouldn't let her. "Why would we want to do that?" he asked and touched her belly. "Just let me name the baby," he added. She had chosen Tuấn's name; he could have this.

Then, there was the beach. Several boats waited ashore. There were more in the water—Hương could see flashlights in the distance—circles of light floating and bobbing up and down, then disappearing. A woman was screaming on the shore, pointing out to the water.

"My baby! My baby boy!" the woman screamed. "My baby is on that boat! Bring him back! My boy!"

The woman looked familiar, but it was too dark and Hương couldn't tell for sure. The woman ran into the water and disappeared.

Hương squeezed Công's hand. A sudden rush of energy came over her. All this time planning and here they were.

"Let's leave," she said. "It's time to go, Công." She pulled him, but he stopped to gaze back into the jungle. He paused. Eyes straight ahead, she pulled harder and they ran toward the boat. There, a man waved them forward. They were the last ones on before the boat was pushed out into the water.

"Quick, quick," said a man as the boat sputtered forward.

They were out at sea for ten days. Hương would stay sleepless for most of that, holding Tuấn in her arms, his head against her chest, buried there, away from the sea. *How had Công's hand slipped?* she kept asking herself. That was the only explanation. The only possible one.

After she recorded her message, she wrote "The Teachings of Uncle Hồ" on the tape and the address of their Mỹ Tho house on an envelope. In the morning, she would ask the priest to take her to the post office. The message would be sent. She would receive something back. They would be reunited. It was the best she could hope for. She could hope.

After dinner—instant noodles from a Styrofoam cup the church gave out—she cleaned up her sons and tucked them in. When she couldn't sleep, she turned on the TV and watched it with no sound. Images flashed on the screen: men in business suits signing papers and shaking hands; reporters laughing behind a desk and shuffling their papers; a man smiling in front of a map of America.

Deep into the night, Bình woke up crying. Hương rocked him in her arms and walked him around the room. Though the blinds were drawn, the lights from the streetlamps streamed in. In the glow, Bình looked angelic and she felt sorry he'd been through so much already. From the very first day, even. His birth took ten hours and two midwives. When he was finally out in the world, one of the midwives frowned. Something was wrong; he wasn't crying, he wasn't breathing. The other midwife took the baby and examined him. From where Hương lay, she could see the child in the midwife's hands. She was afraid he would be still, but his arms were waving frantically like he was drowning. "I know," the first midwife said. She took him and tapped him on the back, once, twice, three times before the baby started coughing and the first cry was heard as he took in a breath of air. Hương let out a sigh of relief along with the midwives. Thinking about that now, she wondered what hardships her children would have. What misfortunes? What heartaches? What wars?

"As long as I am here," she whispered, enclosing his small hands with hers, "nothing will happen to you. I promise. I will protect you. The both of you. I promise." She felt a certainty in this statement, in her ability to keep this promise. It was the most sure thing she'd ever uttered.

She took him in her lap and together they watched the evening news.

Any minute now, she was sure, they would talk about home.

Tuấn

The Versailles Arms apartments were new. That much Tuấn could tell. The white paint smelled fresh. The rooms had a crispness of touch to them, no dust, no staleness. When they moved in—after living at the church, the Minhs', the motel, and the cha xứ's house—everyone else was moving in as well. Rows of cars idled outside. One car's radio was tuned in to what sounded like a sports game, though Tuấn couldn't understand any of it and couldn't guess what was being played, either. It all reminded him of the motel they'd stayed at, where people moved in and out of rooms and sat in their cars waiting for someone to come out and meet them, or just sat with their windows down, smoking or eating hamburgers. Except here everyone looked like they meant to stay. That was the difference.

As men brought in boxes, women unpacked them. Tuấn and his family had only one suitcase and a few plastic bags of things they'd accumulated since getting here: a new pair of shoes for him,

Styrofoam cups of noodles, a blanket with baby animals on it for
Bình. They had so little. His mother must have seen him noticing,
because she placed her hand on his shoulder.

"We won't be here long anyway," she said.

"We won't?" He looked up. He couldn't read her face. What she
felt—for she must have felt something—was undetectable. She had
been like that since they left Vietnam, a silent mother. Sometimes
she cried, but most of the time she was quiet and her face stayed
serious.

"Yes," she said. "Once your father comes, we'll move someplace
else." She nudged him forward and he walked up the steps.

"Where?"

"Garden District, maybe, with a fence and a garden." She
smirked when she said that, and he knew everything was going to
be fine then. Sure of it.

Versailles was built on the eastern outskirts of New Orleans, across
the Industrial Canal, where the tall buildings were replaced by
swampland. Gated by a chain-link fence on the front and flush
against a bayou in the back, Versailles held ten apartment buildings, each with two homes, one on top of the other. The buildings
dotted the sides of an unpaved road that ran through the middle
of Versailles until it ended at the water.

For weeks, they didn't unpack. Everything stayed in their suitcase. It made Tuấn uneasy. None of this belonged to them; they
had to be careful not to break anything, dirty the carpet, mark the
walls—it was not theirs. His mother continued sending tapes to
their father. They sat on the floor in front of the cassette recorder,
talking into it as the spokes spun. She ended each message, "See
you soon," and Tuấn echoed: "See you soon, cha!" She'd tuck them
in after, and, though he knew it was impossible, he heard his voice
bouncing off the blank white walls: "See you . . . soon . . . cha!"

It wasn't until summer that his mother started decorating. From the church, they got a used couch and an old dinner table and a painting of a moss-covered tree. One day, Tuấn's mother thought flowers would be nice. Saying that, she emptied a pickle jar into a bowl and rinsed it out.

"Something nice," she said.

"What if cha came home and there was nothing nice!" Tuấn added.

She smiled.

Together, the three of them wandered the banks of the bayou, just outside their apartment since they were the last building in Versailles, searching for flowers. From a distance, as she held on to Baby Bình, Tuấn thought his mother looked younger, brighter, and his brother looked like a perfect toy, more of a doll than a real boy. He bet she picked flowers when she was a little girl, too, and made a note to ask her later. He picked up a fist full of the brightest ones he could find and ran up to her. She giggled and shook her head. She didn't like the yellow ones. The blues, she liked, and the purples and the whites, too. When they gathered a good bunch (even Bình managed to pluck a baby violet), they walked back inside. She threw the flowers in the jar and started on dinner.

Just then, someone knocked. They stopped what they were doing and eyed the door. All this time, they had lived alone. And when Tuấn thought about it, no one had ever knocked on their door before; no one visited. Who could it be? His mother cleared her throat and turned off the stove. She wiped her hands on a towel. Tuấn followed after. Maybe someone had seen them plucking flowers and they weren't supposed to. What if they were in trouble? The idea flashed in his mind. He wasn't so sure about opening the door. He wanted to tell his mother to stop, but her hand twisted the knob and the door popped open.

An old woman's weathered face greeted him when it did. He heard the sticky movement of her lips as she moved them into a smile. Slowly she shuffled in. In one hand, she held a cane and in the other, a box wrapped in shiny red paper. Tuấn watched in amazement. That such an ancient woman could do all of this without a cry for help caught his attention. She reminded him of an elderly water buffalo: her large flaring nostrils, the frowning lips, a lumbering gait.

"You must be Hương," the old woman said.

"Yes," his mother replied, "I'm Hương." She, too, seemed mesmerized. She wiped her hands on the towel again, though they were already clean and dry. Her mouth opened to say something but she was interrupted.

"Bùi Thị Minh Giang," the old woman said. "Or how they say it here, Giang Bùi, from downstairs," she added. She handed his mother the box. "Almond cookies," she said. "If you get the cà phê ready, we can get started on those!"

Tuấn sat with them while they talked about themselves (she was the wife of a businessman who died during the war) and New Orleans ("The coffee here is good, isn't it?") and Versailles ("Can you believe they call this place *Versailles*?"). At one point he stopped paying attention and she left.

They never invited her back, but she returned anyway. The next day before dinner and then the next and then the next, until Bà Giang's visits became so expected, a part of their regular lives, Tuấn couldn't imagine a day without them or her playful teasing.

At some point during her time there, she'd poke his arm or his belly and he'd jerk his body back. "You're getting so big now!" she'd say. "Chubby hands, chubby arms, and that tummy. As fat as an American!"

At the word *American*, Tuấn would spring up on his chair.

"I'm not American!" he would say, reciting from memory what they taught him in school. "I am người Việt Nam. My father teaches the great and honorable literature of our nation. My mother is the daughter of our beautiful countryside."

At the end of his speech, they would clap and he would bow.

"Good boy!" they'd cheer.

"My boy," his mother would say.

He'd blush. His whole body would feel warm and loved. It almost felt like home, or a type of home.

Because of her age, Bà Giang didn't work, or she couldn't find work. To make money she took in the children of Versailles, the ones who needed supervision when their parents were out.

Besides Tuấn and Bình, there were three other kids. Trúc was a girl and nine and the oldest. She didn't like watching TV—what Bà Giang told them to do most days—because it rotted the brain and made you stupid; she watched anyway. Ngọc was the second oldest, a skinny boy with long legs and a monkey's laugh. Then there was Đinh-Fredric, a boy of seven—two years older than Tuấn—who was lai, which meant his dad wasn't người Việt but no one knew what he was, either. It was why he had two names, one Vietnamese, another from somewhere else, or at least this was what Bà Giang told Tuấn's mother.

Đinh-Fredric never sat with them for *Sesame Street* or *The Electric Company* or *Rocky and Bullwinkle*. Instead, he stayed in Bà Giang's room with the door closed. What he did in there no one knew.

Once, during a commercial break, Trúc told them Đinh-Fredric wasn't người Việt at all: he was American, one-hundred-and-ten percent.

"Listen to his name," she said. "It doesn't even sound like người Việt. What kind of name is Fredric?" Ngọc nodded; what kind of name *was* Fredric?

Trúc continued, "Why does he stay by himself? He's planning something in there, right now. Against us! My dad says Americans are bad, bad, bad people, and my dad is always right." Tuấn tried to remember if his dad said anything about Americans or America. Before they left, he had talked about Australia and France. "Australians are friendly," Tuấn remembered him telling his mother when they thought he was asleep. "The French, at least we know some French." They never told him they were leaving, but he pieced it all together from their late-night conversations. The only shock was when they actually did, and, after that, the fact that his dad didn't come along.

"What makes them so bad?" Ngọc asked.

Trúc let out an angry puff of air. "What makes them so bad?" She leaned forward. "Remember the boat?"

Ngọc nodded. Tuấn remembered the boat, too, though it wasn't the same ones Ngọc or Trúc were on. They were all on different boats. He remembered his dad not being there and the waves and the sick feeling in his stomach like there was too much water in there. He remembered his mother telling him to go to sleep, always telling him to sleep, even if he just woke up. And when he asked where they were going, she just shook her head as if "No" was a place.

"The Americans made you do that," Trúc said. "They took your home. They made you get on that boat. And now your mom cooks their meals, your dad cleans their houses, even if he used to be top boss, and they both come home smelly. The Americans are the reason for everything bad that has ever happened. Do you understand?"

Ngọc nodded.

"What about you?" She looked at Tuấn pointedly. "Do you understand?"

"I don't know," he mumbled. All this talk confused him. He wanted to be alone and think it all through.

"What did you say?"

"Dạ, I said dạ."

For lunch, Bà Giang gave them store-bought cupcakes, her favorite. They were made of chocolate and had cream in the middle. Each plastic packet had two. As Trúc and Ngọc returned to the TV, Tuấn paused at the hallway leading to Bà Giang's room. Who was Đinh-Fredric? Could Trúc be right? Was he bad? Was he an American? It didn't seem likely. After all, there were no Americans in Versailles. Everyone was người Việt. It was a rule: you had to be người Việt to stay in Versailles.

Tuấn wrapped the second of his cupcakes in a paper towel and tiptoed down the hall. Outside the room, he tapped on the door. When no one answered, he tried again, whispering into the keyhole, "Đinh. Đinh-Free-rock."

To Tuấn, Đinh-Fredric was a ghost. He'd only ever seen glimpses of the boy, a bright shirt running through the halls. He didn't have any hair or a head or eyes or nose or body. He was just a shirt. At times, Tuấn wasn't even sure Đinh-Fredric existed. He was an idea, not a boy. "Đinh!" he whispered louder.

The door opened slightly and a smell like old perfume, stale but flowery, sprang forth. Between the door and its frame, Tuấn saw eyes gazing at him.

"Bánh!" Tuấn unwrapped the paper towel. The cupcake was falling apart and the white filling oozed out. Tuấn wiped a hand on his shirt. "It's still good even though it doesn't look like it. You can have it if you want."

The boy stared back. His eyes traveled down to Tuấn's bare feet then back to his face. The door squeaked nervously as it moved back and forth.

"What are you doing?" Trúc interrupted. Tuấn hadn't even heard her coming. Trúc crossed her arms. She looked at Tuấn then at Đinh-Fredric then back at Tuấn and her eyes lit up. "Are you American, too, Tuấn?" she asked, a smirk sprouting on her face.

"No!" Tuấn exclaimed. "No! I'm người Việt. I'm người Việt! My father . . . He . . ." He all of a sudden forgot what to say. The words were in his head, but they were in the wrong order. Trúc's eyes stared down at him and made him feel like hiding. He dropped the cupcake and ran back to the television, where Ngọc sat, not even hiding his eagerness. The TV volume was on low.

"Did you see him? Did you see the American?" he asked.

Tuấn remembered the shadow figure in the dark, its thinness and smallness. He could tell Đinh-Fredric's skin was dark, darker than his own. His hair was short, and to Tuấn's surprise, stiff-looking and curly. Đinh-Fredric wasn't a ghost. He wasn't a monster. He was just a boy.

The bedroom door opened and closed with a quick yet noticeable squeak and clap. Tuấn stretched his neck to see if Đinh had come out. The hallway was empty and the cupcake was gone. Tuấn imagined Đinh in the room, licking the sweetness from the paper towel happily. It made Tuấn smile. They would be friends. Good friends.

"Nothing," Tuấn said to Ngọc. "I saw nothing."

That night, his mother recorded another tape message. She sat on the floor by the glass sliding doors that looked out onto the bayou. Their apartment was on the second floor, and a metal railing stopped you from walking out and falling. Tuấn wondered why they even bothered putting a door there, but maybe that was the way things were in this country.

"I am in another country," he often whispered to himself to feel the heaviness of the words fall out. "Out there, far far away," he would go on but only in his head, "is a large piece of land called Vietnam with different people, different trees, different houses, and that is where cha is and he cannot just walk out of it. Vietnam is not like a room, it's like a school and you can't leave because there are different rules in school and you can't go until thầy giáo says so, so we are waiting for thầy giáo to say he can go or for cha to sneak out and not let thầy giáo know."

As his mother rewound the cassette tape and began addressing the envelope, Tuấn asked, "When is cha coming?"

"Soon," she said, sealing the envelope. She pressed her fingers against it to make sure it was tight. She crossed her legs and patted them. Tuấn climbed onto her lap.

"Would he like it here?" Tuấn asked.

"Sure he will," she replied. Her voice was certain. How could he ever doubt her?

"What do you think he will like the most here?" Outside, the moon shined onto the bayou and reflected there, a mirror image.

"Us."

On Tuesday the next week, Bà Giang let them play outside. Ngọc wanted to play hide-and-seek, but Trúc said it was a baby's game, so Ngọc didn't want to play it anymore.

Then Trúc said, "I have an idea! It's called 'I'm Not American.'"

"That's not a game," Tuấn said.

"We played it all the time back in Saigon," Trúc said. "You wouldn't know. You're from Mỹ Tho. Your family is all country bumpkins."

"Hey!" Tuấn hollered back.

"How do you play?" Ngọc asked.

Trúc reached into her pocket and pulled out a red ribbon. She held it up, and the sunlight made it shimmer. "Easy. If you wear this," she said, "you're the American."

"This is stupid," Tuấn said. "I'm not playing."

"If you're not playing, you're just ngu and we don't like you."

"Play, Tuấn!" Ngọc said. "He'll play! How do we play?"

"So," Trúc began, "if you're the American, you wear this. The only way not to be the American anymore is to tie it on someone else. So you chase us around. When you catch someone, you knock them to the ground and tie it around their wrist." She pulled Tuấn's arm and demonstrated. She tied a double knot. "Ta-da!" she said.

"Then what?" Ngọc asked.

"Then you run away, dummy." She gave Tuấn a shove. "You're It, dummy!"

Ngọc burst out laughing.

Trúc began running and yelling, "The Americans are killing our people! The Americans are killing our crops!"

"Not the Americans!" boomed Ngọc. "Not the Americans!"

"The Americans are killing our people! The Americans are killing our crops!" Trúc repeated.

"Not the Americans!" Ngọc boomed again, this time with more fake horror. "The Americans!"

They did this for several minutes, running around dumbly while Tuấn trailed behind. They'd run around Bà Giang's apartment when Tuấn saw Đinh at the window. He had been watching all along. Caught, the boy hid behind the curtains, but Tuấn had already seen him and saw him still watching from behind the thin fabric.

"What you doing, American?" Trúc tapped him on the shoulder. "Do you want to play or kiss your American friend over there?" She made kissing noises and pointed to the window. She stared down at Tuấn, her tall body casting a shadow.

"Stop calling me American!" He threw out his arms to push her, but Trúc was already ahead of him. In the next instant, he tumbled on the dirt and found himself facing the bayou.

It was then that he heard Ngọc screaming, "Stop, you guys! Stop it!" His high-pitched squeal pierced the air. "Stop it! Stop! You both ruined it. This isn't fun!" He stomped toward the apartment. Tuấn and Trúc stayed where they were until they heard the door slam.

"I'm not playing anymore," Tuấn said, untying the ribbon. He rubbed his cheek. There was no bruise, just dirt. "You can be the American." He flicked the ribbon toward her, but it fell slowly to the ground like a feather. He began walking away. His body ached. He felt that there should have been a bruise somewhere. He'd have to check when he got home. "I'm người Việt," he began muttering. "My father teaches the great, honorable literature of our nation. . . ."

"Your father's probably dead," Trúc yelled. "They probably killed him. He's probably gone."

Without thinking, Tuấn turned back and ran into Trúc. When he got to her, he kept on going until they reached the bayou and they fell into the water.

"He's not dead!" he screamed. "He's coming. He's coming for us. You don't know him. He's coming for us!"

He tried to slow his heavy breathing as Trúc stared back at him seriously. Whatever had just happened, he didn't know he had that in him. It made him feel powerful, until he heard Trúc laughing.

"American lover, American lover," she sang as if it was the nastiest thing anyone could call someone. "American lover."

"You're not my friend!" Tuấn screamed as he got up.

"I was never your friend," she said back, laughing. "Why would you even think that?"

It was the one-year anniversary of Versailles. They—or most of them—had been there for one full year. To celebrate, they had a party.

"Because we've been here one year," said the mustached man into the microphone. "Because our community is full of love. Because we are, all of us here, survivors." He stood on a crate in the middle of the road. "Today we celebrate Versailles! Today we celebrate the true Republic of Vietnam!" Everyone cheered. A gun was fired into the air. There was confetti. Tuấn heard it all from their apartment.

For the past week, everyone in Versailles decorated their homes as if it were Tết. Paper streamers hung like moss from trees. Pots of marigolds (because no one sold mai vàng plants in New Orleans) sat outside doors to invite good luck. Lanterns swung in the light breeze on laundry lines. Tuấn didn't know what an anniversary was, but he hoped there would be more in the future.

At noon, he changed into his swim trunks and, together with his mother and brother, walked toward the water, where the celebration had already started. Someone played Vietnamese music from a recording. A group of teenage boys played đá cầu in a wide circle, joking while the beanbag bounced off their shoes. The smaller kids splashed in the bayou. Trúc and Ngọc waded in by themselves, a cloud of mosquitoes and gnats swarming their heads.

Tuấn had just touched the bayou when Trúc bent down and splashed water into his face. "Hey, American!" she said. "What are you gonna to do, American?" She splashed him again.

Tuấn spat out the dirty water and coughed until the taste of mud and sticks was gone. "I'm not American," he said. "I'm not talking to you anymore, either. Get away." Turning toward the forest on the other side of the water, he saw a boy sitting by himself. Đinh, who else?

Trúc grabbed him by the arm. "But we'll forgive you," she said. "Just prove you're not American. Prove you're not like him." She pointed to Đinh. His back was turned to them. He didn't notice them.

"This is ngu," Tuấn said and tried to walk away, but Trúc pulled him back. He looked to the adults. They were talking and listening to music. His mother was sitting in a plastic lawn chair beside Bà Giang, who fanned herself with a newspaper. They wouldn't even hear him even if he wanted to cry for help.

"Listen," Trúc said, tapping Tuấn's cheek. They looked eye-to-eye. "You see Fredric over there? You see him all by himself?" She let go of Tuấn's arm and dipped her hands into the water. "Put this down his shirt," she said. A smirk lit up her face. A guppy swam in her hands.

"Give me your hands," Trúc said. "No, make it a bowl."

Tuấn looked into his hands. Surprisingly, he didn't feel much. The fish moved but didn't tickle. "I don't want to do this," he said. "I don't want to." He tried to sound firm and mean the way Trúc always did.

"Đi," Trúc commanded. "We'll watch you."

He walked out into the bayou toward the other shore. It surprised him that the water wasn't that deep, only up to his belly button at its deepest in the middle. Passing the lone tree that grew out of the water in the middle of the bayou, he looked up and expected to see a bird, but there was nothing. He remembered the boat they left Vietnam on and the water they sailed through. The water in New Orleans acted differently. Out on the shores of Vietnam and beyond, the water had been violent, shaking anything that lay atop it. But here, the water didn't move; it stayed still, lazy. In the distance, ducks floated without a single care in the world like they were on vacation.

He found himself just behind Đinh. He dropped the fish into the water and it swam away. He smiled. Back in school, in Vietnam, the teachers told him about releasing captured animals for karma. It was like helping out one small thing so that someday, perhaps in the next life, the universe would return that generosity. *Maybe if I let this go* . . . he thought, but didn't finish the sentence.

Tuấn took several more steps before Đinh turned around and saw him.

Their eyes met. They said nothing.

"It's okay," Tuấn said. "I'm your friend!" he added. He dusted some of the dirt off one side of the log and straddled it to take a seat. He inched his way toward Đinh but not too close. Đinh reminded him of a small animal, a butterfly, perhaps, that flies away when it's scared. He wiped his hands on his shorts. "I'm Tuấn," he whispered. Then, "I know your name. Your name's Đinh. Đinh-Fredric."

The sun sat high in the sky. In the evening, the sun would begin its descent behind the trees, making silhouettes out of them before turning them into shadows. But now it just sat there, the same way the two of them sat on the log, avoiding looking at anything for too long.

He heard his name being called in the distance. He looked back.

His mother had gotten up. With one arm she held Bình, with the other she held her hand above her eyes and looked out into the water. "Tuấn," she called.

"I don't like it here," Đinh interrupted.

It surprised Tuấn. The boy was barely audible. "My mother came here to find cha. He came here, she said. She said she had a letter from him. But she lied and he isn't here."

How funny, Tuấn thought, that he didn't have his father here, either. What a coincidence! They were the same! They were exactly alike!

"Tuấn," his mother called again.

Đinh picked up a twig and bent it, snapping it into two then throwing it away.

Tuấn wanted to tell Đinh about his own father, about the man who missed the boat, the man who they were waiting for. He wanted to tell him about the tape messages—in themselves, like letters—his mother made. And how they, too, were waiting. He imagined they could wait together.

"My cha," Tuấn started, but Đinh threw his twig down, turned around, and started walking toward the other shore.

"Whatever happened to your cha isn't going to happen to my cha," he said accusingly. "Mày không biết!" he said, almost yelling now, almost crying. "You don't know anything." He got up and walked through the water toward Versailles.

Tuấn watched him and saw his mother meet Đinh in the bayou. The boy pointed to the woods and continued on his way toward Versailles.

As she waded her way to him (Tuấn could hear the water splashing), he slid down the log until he settled onto the dirt.

"There you are!" said his mother when she was behind him. "You got your mother worried." Bình giggled in her arms. She sat down on the log beside Tuấn. The baby grabbed Tuấn's hair and stroked it playfully. "What you doing all the way out here?"

Tuấn looked up at his mother. The sun made her glow beautifully. He wiped his nose. He hadn't realized he was crying.

"Nothing," he replied, embarrassed.

"Don't lie to your mother," she said. "People don't go somewhere for no reason."

She looked out into the woods. For a few seconds, something caught her attention, and they, the three of them, sat in silence. Tuấn looked where his mother was looking and saw what she was seeing: white flowers on the top of a tree. There were no other flowers on the tree, but there was that bouquet, there, growing on the edge of a branch. Tuấn smiled.

"Did you pick flowers back in Vietnam," he asked, "when you were a little girl?"

She looked down at him, as if remembering he was there.

"Yes," she said with a smile. "Mẹ used to keep this flower book. I pressed flowers into it. Later, I wanted to know what flowers they were. So I went to the library, the small one in Mỹ Tho. I met your father there. He was a librarian and he helped me find a book about flowers not just in Vietnam but all over the world."

"Where's that flower book now?" Tuấn asked.

His mother stood up and let out a small sigh. When Tuấn looked up, she turned away to hide her frown. "Let's go home, Tuấn."

Tuấn jumped up with a smile, the widest and brightest he could make to make her smile again. "Let's go home!" he exclaimed.

They waded through the water toward shore.

Hương

A splash of water in the bayou shook Hương out of her thoughts. She looked out her window and a saw a light in the water, a small circular spot of yellow that must have been a flashlight. The light flicked off as if noticing Hương, and then, after a few seconds, it was back on again.

It was nearly midnight and no one should have been out there. She put away the letter she'd been reading, grabbed the keys, and walked out.

"A lô?" she called and the light began moving. She walked toward the water and tried to see who it was. She wondered if it was one of the teenagers. The light moved back and forth, as if whoever was holding it were trying to hide. It annoyed her. She had work in the morning, and here someone was making a ruckus. She hadn't been asleep, but if she were, she was sure it would have woken her up.

"Hello?" Hương called, this time in English. "Somebody there? Hello?"

When no one answered, she called out louder. The light dimmed as she approached the water. The bayou lapped against the shore steadily.

She took a step forward and there she saw the boy—Thanh's boy. The darkness made him look smaller than she remembered, but she saw him clearly, a half-Vietnamese, half-black boy about the age of Tuấn. He stared at her as if thinking he couldn't possibly be seen if only he didn't move. He reminded her of a bird, a small orphaned sparrow, perhaps, who fell out of its nest, and with that, her annoyance melted away into something else, a mix of relief and pity.

"Get out of there," she said. She'd forgotten his name and waved for him to come along. "Let's go. Your mother's probably worried sick."

"No, she's not," he said.

That he spoke back so sharply surprised her.

"She doesn't care at all," he added.

"Of course she does," she replied. "Come along, tối rồi."

Hesitantly, the boy dragged a cardboard box out of the water and walked to shore.

"It's a boat," he told her.

Hương didn't know what to say to that, so she nodded, then said "Come along" again, pointing for him to the lead the way.

They walked to his apartment near the main road. All the way, the boy dragged the cardboard box—bigger than he was—behind him. Seeing him struggle, Hương reached over, but he pulled the box closer to his body protectively. Hương let him have it and continued ahead of him, looking back every few feet as he stumbled across the dirt road that ran through Versailles.

When Hương knocked, a light came on and the door opened. The boy's mother shook her head. "You should know better," she said and opened the door wider for her son to come in. She let out a heavy, exhausted sigh.

Hương wanted to say something else, but she didn't know what. The door closed and was locked before she had a chance.

It was past midnight by the time she returned to her room. Though she was tired, she pulled out the letter.

The next morning, Kim-Anh went on and on. They were the only two Vietnamese working in the Coke factory in Gert Town and, because of that, were drawn together magnetically, inseparable because of circumstance.

Kim-Anh was a spritely twenty-one-year-old with fair skin and a boisterous laugh who had no business being in America, let alone New Orleans. She had left Vietnam on—of all things—a cruise ship.

"I was told we were going to Úc," she told Hương. "Turns out it was Hồng Kông. Turns out my parents were right. Saigon was going to fall any day and I left just in time. And I was only sixteen! Imagine, a girl so young on a cruise ship without even an older brother to protect her!"

In Vietnam, Kim-Anh would have a husband by now, and a child, too. The girl had neither of those. She shared a house in Metairie with an American man who was much older than she was.

"He has so much money!" Kim-Anh always said. "I don't have to work. That's the truth. I just work because I get so bored at home."

It was an absurd claim. The other factory workers called her Princess.

It was the second Friday of the month as they stood in line waiting for their paychecks when Kim-Anh paused whatever she was talking about—Hương had stopped paying attention—and exclaimed, "Have you ever been to Madame Beaumont?"

Hương said no.

"The American and I are going tonight," Kim-Anh went on.

THINGS WE LOST TO THE WATER

"The men who go there buy me drinks on Fridays." She giggled. *"Ladies' night,"* she said in English.

"I have children," Hương said. She had nearly said *responsibilities* but caught herself before telling Kim-Anh she had to pick them up from their babysitter. "It's not that I don't want to go, but I'd have to pay Bà Giang more and this paycheck's already going to rent."

"What you need, chị Hương, is an American," Kim-Anh told her. "When I came here, I was lost, confused. Then you know what happened?" She smiled excitedly, silently begging Hương to ask what happened. "I met the American! Americans are so wonderful," Kim-Anh blurted out. "They're ugly, but they have money, which is all that matters sometimes, though sometimes it doesn't at all."

When they walked outside, the sunlight struck Hương's eyes. She squinted at the factory gates. The sound of idling cars and radios filled the air. A lone cloud floated in the sky, a perfect white against blue.

Kim-Anh opened her purse and drew out a clutch wallet decorated in fleurs-de-lis. "Chị Hương, I'll pay your babysitter overtime. You've been here for so long, and you never have any fun. You work too hard!" She handed Hương two bills. Two twenties. The man on them, someone told her, was named Andrew Jackson. His face looked strong and determined. On his head, white and wavy hair grew thick as grass.

"I can't. I shouldn't." Hương tried to hand the money back, but Kim-Anh stuck a cigarette in her mouth. She lit it up and waved Hương away.

"You're young, too, chị Hương," Kim-Anh said, smoke blowing out of her delicate lips. "Enjoy yourself a bit. You deserve it. You've worked so hard. I know that. Everyone knows that. Look at those bags under your eyes. There's a cream I got at D. H. Holmes for that, you know."

Hương touched the space under her eyes.

After a few more casual puffs, Kim-Anh's eyes brightened and she rounded her lips. When she couldn't make any smoke rings, she clasped her hands together and laughed at the fun of failing.

Hương looked down at Andrew Jackson in her hands.

"Ông già Mỹ and I will pick you up later tonight. We'll head out around eight." She spoke with confidence, a quality Hương always envied.

"But—" Hương said.

Kim-Anh giggled and waved to a car. The American waited for her. "I won't take no for an answer, sister," she said. "*I am not that kind of lady,*" she added in English.

On the bus ride home, Hương reminded herself she wasn't old. Twenty-seven wasn't old. She was nearly Kim-Anh's age. And she had missed out on so much. When she was younger, she'd heard of tango lounges in Saigon, but she never visited. She became a wife. Then a mother. When the Americans came to Saigon, the city was a place no self-respecting woman would find herself going to day or night. And when the Americans left—that was another story.

The war made her miss her youth. She owed this to herself.

At Bà Giang's, the kids sat in front of the TV watching puppets, except Thanh's son. They were both strange, sad people, that mother and that son. No one knew where the father was, but everyone said—Bà Giang said—Thanh came to New Orleans to find him. Thanh let herself in behind Hương. Hương didn't even have to look behind her; she knew the peanut-oil smell of the fast-food restaurant where Thanh worked. While Hương talked to Bà Giang, Thanh went to the bedroom and knocked on the door. Of course her son was hiding! He was always doing that.

"I'm going out tonight," Hương said to Bà Giang.

"So you've met a man!" Bà Giang replied.

"No, no!" Hương laughed. "There's no other man for me, Bà Giang. Kim-Anh is taking me out to see this place. Madame something or other. I won't be long. I can't imagine staying out all night."

Hương gave Bà Giang one of the two twenties and went to her sons. Bình was sitting with the other kids watching TV. Tuấn was in the love seat by himself with one of Bà Giang's sets of playing cards. They were facing down. After a few seconds, her son picked one up, then another. Unsatisfied, he returned both cards.

"Tuấn," Hương called. She sat behind him and watched his game. "What about that one? I remember seeing a queen there."

"No," he said. "Can't be." He picked it up anyway. Four of diamonds. "Told you."

She rubbed his hair and leaned down to kiss him. "Mẹ will be out late tonight."

From across the room, Bình saw her and ran toward his mother. He tripped on the way and stayed where he fell, having decided staying on the floor was easier than getting up. She lifted him and patted his head. "Be vâng lời for Bà Giang, okay?"

"Dạ," he said with a nod.

When she set him down, he followed her to the door. She picked him up and set him back on the sofa. But this time, as she left, he burst into tears. She held him and cradled him.

"Be good for Mom," she said. "Be good for Bà Giang. Why are you always crying?"

Bà Giang ran to him then and took the two-year-old in her arms. "Mommy's coming back," she cooed. "Is that what you're afraid of? Don't be afraid. Don't cry. Mommy's coming back." Then to Hương, "Have fun tonight. Have a drink. You deserve it!"

Bình cried even louder. Hương was about to grab him but stopped herself. Yes, she told herself, she deserved it.

"Goodbye," she called out as she left. Thanh and her son followed after.

She settled on a modest dress, a teal piece with a fabric belt. Before New Orleans, she wore mostly black and white polyesters—simple clothes that were also lightweight, because Vietnam was hot and there was a war and you dressed for practicality. But in New Orleans, the weather was not as hot, and everything was colorful already. She thought of the houses in the Marginy, the cars that passed by as she rode the bus, the flowers in the parks, soda bottle labels. She told Công about the colors of New Orleans, how it shook her awake and made her feel alive, how she had grown fond of the place because of the colors.

"You would like it here," she often found herself repeating, "when you come here."

All in all, she sent dozens of tape messages to Công and several short letters. They all went unanswered. Some were returned with a rude stamp—RETURN TO SENDER—next to the postmark. Others came back damaged, packages ripped apart, as if inspected. (*By whom,* she would wonder.) She kept everything that came back. Yet she still hoped some of the messages found their way to Công. She could hope.

She could hope for a hundred years. She could hope for a thousand years. She imagined her body made of hope, made for hope. Until the day his first letter came.

It came in a thin aerogramme tucked in between a Kmart circular and a magazine of coupons. It said "Trần Văn Công" and had the address of their Saigon home. Her heart stopped. Then it quickened wildly. The letter fell from her hands and she went to get a glass of water. The image of their old house flashed in her mind. *It was saved,* was her immediate thought. Perhaps everything was fine now. Perhaps they would even move back. (She immediately admitted to herself that it was a silly thought.)

She waited until after dinner to open it. In the dim light of her room—she had only a floor lamp with a weak bulb—she peeled back the flap. She did it carefully, afraid one slight clumsy move might rip apart the thin paper, leaving the message unintelligible.

She saw the letter in her drawer as she grabbed her earrings. Kim-Anh rang the doorbell.

"Are you ready, chị Hương?" Kim-Anh asked. She stepped inside and looked around. When her eyes settled on Hương, she grabbed the fabric of the dress, handling it with a surprising roughness. "You're not wearing that, are you, chị Hương?" Kim-Anh announced.

"What do you mean?"

Kim-Anh, for her part, wore a flowing pink lace shirt with a matching skirt. "We're going to the Quarter. You can't wear this. You can't." Kim-Anh held the fabric higher and shook it to emphasize her meaning. "Maybe something shorter? This makes you look like a mom."

"What am I supposed to look like?" Hương asked.

"How long have you been in this country?"

"Long enough."

"Things are different here."

"I know that."

A car horn sounded and Kim-Anh glanced down at her watch. "No time," she said. "This will have to do." She walked down the stairs. Hương followed after.

Kim-Anh's American was not an unattractive man. He almost looked like Andrew Jackson—a strong face, wrinkles of wisdom, and rich white hair, which, from the backseat, looked like soft white fire.

"You're as pretty as Kim," he said as they drove toward downtown.

"Kim-Anh," Kim-Anh corrected him.

"Kimmie. My Kimmie," he replied. He reached over and rubbed her hand.

"Keem-On," she said, slower this time as she pulled away her arm.

"Kim-Anh," he repeated.

"I told her to change, but we running out of time," Kim-Anh said.

"No, she looks all right," he said. "She looks pretty. What's your name again?" He looked at Hương in the rearview mirror. His eyes were pale gray and kind.

"My name Hương," she answered.

At one point, they drove on an overpass looking out over the city. How different it all looked at night, how it felt—at least from the car—less messy. She imagined putting the city into neatly labeled boxes. In here would be the Business District. There, Mid-City. In a tiny box the French Quarter could fit, while Gentilly would need a big one.

Because of traffic, they slowed down to a creep. Kim-Anh fanned herself with her hands.

"Hot," Kim-Anh said.

Already, Kim-Anh must have forgotten the heat of Vietnam and those blistering days when you couldn't even touch the ground with your bare feet. Back then, Hương and Công didn't have cars, they had bicycles. On hotter days, he didn't want her to work hard pedaling, so he told her to climb on his seat and he would stand and pedal them instead. Everyone did that in those days, but riding down the avenue she felt self-conscious. Together they would ride to their favorite little bakery, where they served bánh cam and, according to Công, the best salted lemonade in all of South Vietnam. Her favorite memories were of Công and her there, eating and laughing, the world fading away from around them, the only world that mattered the one they made.

Those memories felt haunted now. In her mind, they appeared smoke-smudged, and, watching, she felt uncomfortable, as if she were an intruder—these weren't her memories, they were another woman's, from a different time and a different place.

In the Quarter, the American drove in circles to find parking. At one point he found a parking spot between two cars, but his was too large to fit. "It's the problem with a car like this on nights like these," the American said. "You know what I mean?"

"I take bus every day," Hương said.

"A beauty like you doesn't belong on a bus," the American said. Then, as if remembering, "Kim said you were married."

"Kim-Anh," Kim-Anh said.

"Kimmie."

"My husband," Hương said. "He coming soon. Really soon." She said the same thing at work when the other ladies saw her simple gold band. What else was she supposed to say? If she told the truth, she would have been embarrassed. They knew she had been wait- ing a long time. What could she tell them now? The letter Công sent said this much: that he could not follow after her. She had to go on without him. Please don't try to contact him again. Please have forgiveness.

The letter was very unlike Công. Even the handwriting was sloppier. Almost every night, she looked at it again before going to bed, convincing herself at times that this was a prank—a cruel prank from someone in Vietnam or even someone in Versailles. She'd eye the people outside. How could people be so mean? She felt like a schoolgirl again, and the other students were laughing at her, pointing and laughing. She wrote back: "What do you mean?"

Eventually, they found parking near Lafayette Square, seven blocks from Madame Beaumont. Kim-Anh took off her shoes and walked barefoot. After two blocks, Kim-Anh stopped. Hương stopped, too, but the American continued, not noticing.

"I can't walk for so long," Kim-Anh yelled after him.

The American came back. "You're a strong girl," he said. He rolled his tongue against the inside of his cheek and pressed his lips together like he was going to say something else but stopped himself. "Both of you are strong girls. All you've been through, the boat, the sea—"

"*Cruise ship*," Kim-Anh said.

"Yeah, that's right," he said. "A cruise ship. Of course. A cruise ship."

Kim-Anh rubbed her right foot and continued walking.

"Kimmie," the American called after her. He took off. "Kim-Anh."

Madame Beaumont sat on the corner of Chartres and Conti. Loud music played from outside speakers, and gaudy Halloween decorations spilled out from its doors: a plastic skeleton sitting on a rocking chair and holding a glass beer bottle; a table with unlit tea candles; a stained wooden board with old-fashioned letters printed on it. Kim-Anh shook the skeleton's empty hand.

"Every day is Halloween!" she sang. She tried to pull the bottle away from the skeleton's grip. When it didn't budge, she moved toward the neon lights inside, giggling all the while.

The girl was wilder outside of work. Hương wanted to say it aloud, but the American went after Kim-Anh and she followed him into the bar, where Kim-Anh was already sitting on a stool. The dance floor lay bare and the lights spun, illuminating graffiti here and there on the walls and the floor. The American massaged Kim-Anh's shoulder and pointed to a booth in the corner. She pulled away and waved at the bartender. He put down his rag and she talked into his ear as if she already knew him.

"Over there," said the American, leading Hương to the booth. "What do you want? How about a Coke with rum? My treat."

"I don't like Coke anymore," she said. "What they have?"

"They have everything. It's America. We have everything."

"Something sweet," Hương said. "No beer."

"I know just the thing," he said. "You stay here."

A glittery silver ball hung over the center of the dance floor, where Kim-Anh now danced alone with a beer bottle in hand. The song changed to something faster, but the lights spun around at the same pace. Kim-Anh flailed her arms and closed her eyes.

Was this what she and Công missed during the war years? If so, Hương wasn't very much impressed. Within minutes she felt bored and wanted to go home. She thought about the laundry she would have to do tomorrow and the trouble of going all the way to the Laundromat and sitting and waiting. She thought about what she should pick up from the grocery store. Would the bag of rice she had now last another week? She wondered about her boys. Her mind drifted to Bình crying. She'd felt terrible when Bà Giang swept in and he calmed down. As his mother, she should have comforted him, perhaps even stayed home. At times like this she wished Công were there. Parenting was hard enough; parenting alone and in a different country was something else altogether.

The American came back and handed Hương a tall glass of what looked like milk.

"What it is?" she asked.

"Piña colada," the American said. "Tropical. Thought it'd remind you of Vietnam." He sat down next to Hương. "It has several entire servings of fruit, believe it or not." He picked up the glass and pointed at it as he talked. "It has pineapple. It has coconut. It has rum, which is sugar, which comes from a plant, which should count for something."

Hương laughed. "You are funny man, Mister . . ."

"Just call me Frank."

"Mr. Frank, you are so funny!"

"No, just *Frank*."

"Mr. Frank."

"Anyway, you'll like it. Drink up." They knocked together their drinks, and Hương sipped from her straw as Frank drank from his bottle.

"She's beautiful, isn't she?" the American said as he watched Kim-Anh dance.

"Very," Hương replied.

Men were beginning to join Kim-Anh. She danced with several, never staying with just one. One minute she's dancing with a man with a goatee, and the next the man is shorter and wearing glasses.

It was then that Hương saw how the bar was full of white men and how the few women there were like her, if not Vietnamese then at least Asian. The men were different from the type of men Công would have acquainted himself with, the women different from those Hương would have known. It seemed as if they were a different species of human altogether, living different kinds of lives she couldn't imagine.

She wondered what Kim-Anh was like before she left Vietnam. She had a slack Saigonese accent. She was a Buddhist, because she wore a bodhi seed bracelet, which she refused to take off even on the assembly line, hiding her hands in her pockets as they entered and exited the factory floor. Once she thought she had lost it in the machine and somehow (through her charm or wit, for Hương would give her that much—Kim-Anh was charming) got the operator to stop it. She frantically searched the conveyor belt and stuck her head in a compartment where the gears were hidden at the bottom of the vast machine. She eventually found her bracelet— fallen on the floor—but Hương could not forget the image of Kim-Anh squatting, her legs splayed apart, her back hunched so she could get her head inside. She looked froglike. It was so different from the confident yet delicate way she always held herself. How much had Kim-Anh changed since she'd left Vietnam and how much effort was it? Who was Kim-Anh, really?

"I saved her, you know," the American said. He pressed the beer bottle to his lips. When he put the bottle back down, his hands wandered on the table and returned to the drink. "She was nothing, you know. Just some poor city girl. No mother, no father."

He paused as if he had finished, and a silence sat clumsily between them.

"She must love you. She love you very much," Hương said, not knowing what else to say, just wanting to say something, anything, so the air between them didn't feel so heavy anymore.

He continued, "In Saigon, she worked at a bar where she had

to dance with older men. She was so little, how could those men? Those men were disgusting. They touched her, gave her bruises. I'm not like those men.

"I saved her," he repeated. "I told them she was my fiancée. That we were going to marry, but then I was forced to leave. I gave her money. She left by herself, you see. It wasn't a cruise ship. Just a regular fishing boat. When she got to Hong Kong, she wrote to tell me she was safe. She said I wasn't like any other man she'd met. I was different, she said, and she couldn't wait to see me again. I asked my church to sponsor her. And that's how she came over. I am not a bad man, you see. I go to church. I'm a good man. I saved her."

"Which church?" Hương asked. Everyone in Versailles came through Saint Expeditus. She didn't know any other church in the area that did the same.

"What?" He looked confused. He took another drink of his beer.

"Which church?" she asked again.

He paused and swirled his bottle around. "Church? St. Mary's. In Metairie. You wouldn't know it," he said. "I'm not like the other men, Hương. You got to believe me. I saved her." He wiped the sweat from his forehead, which shined even in the dim light, and folded the napkin until it was too thick to continue.

The song changed again and now Kim-Anh became more audacious. She held on to a man and swayed as he rested his hands on her hips. He was more handsome and better dressed than Frank. He wore a metal watch that reflected the disco lights. Frank wore no watch. When Hương compared Frank to this man, he looked pitiful and nervous. He was becoming even sweatier despite the air-conditioning.

He wiped his hands on his pants and stood up. "And this is how she treats me," he said, more to himself than to anyone else.

When the man Kim-Anh danced with moved a hand away from her hips and latched on to her backside, Kim-Anh smiled and nodded. She seemed at ease, familiar with it all. Hương was sure Kim-Anh knew what song this was, the exact lyrics, and when it would end. Hương imagined her coming here every night after work—she knew the bartender by name, knew the happy-hour specials by heart. She had a calculating look in her eyes; Hương saw that now.

Frank grabbed Kim-Anh's wrist, and Hương heard him say "No" to the other man as he pushed him on the shoulder.

"What you doing?" Kim-Anh shrieked. "Why you like this?" She pulled away. "Why you don't go home?"

"We're going home, Kimmie. Let's go." He tried to steady his voice but couldn't. His fingers fidgeted.

Hương stayed in her seat. The next thing she knew, Kim-Anh raised her arm and slapped Frank's cheek. A crowd formed around the couple. Hương stood up to see what was happening, though everyone was in the way.

Yet even with the loud music, she heard it all. Kim-Anh was shouting, "Go home, Frank. Go home!" When he didn't answer, she continued, louder. "Poor man, go home! Go home, poor man!"

Hương left Kim-Anh and Frank at the bar, walked out of the Quarter, and found a bus stop on Canal. After the bus arrived in New Orleans East, Hương got off, walked the four blocks to Versailles, and stopped at Bà Giang's apartment before heading up to her own. She carried Tuấn while Bà Giang followed behind with Bình. They tucked them in and drank tea to end the night.

As Bà Giang began to leave, she asked, "Did you find a người đàn ông mỹ? Those kids need a father. Any father is better than no father."

Hương laughed, though she didn't know why. "They have a father," she said.

"The fates would have brought him here if they wanted him." She stopped talking until they got to the door. "Do you pray?" Bà Giang asked.

"I don't," Hương said.

"That's the problem. You don't pray. You need to pray."

"I don't believe in that. You know that. We believe in different things."

"It's worth a try," Bà Giang said. "Why don't you try? Have you forgotten about Công?"

Hương opened her mouth to say something but found herself grasping for words. For a moment, she wanted to confide in Bà Giang, to tell her everything. That Công had abandoned her. That he was staying in Vietnam. That he was living in their home in Saigon right now. That she was all alone in the world. All alone with two sons.

But none of this produced any words. In the silence, Bà Giang realized her mistake and reached out for Hương's hands. "I'm sorry," she said. "I shouldn't have. I'm sorry. I didn't mean it."

They told each other good night and Bà Giang left.

Outside, Hương sat on her steps and looked at the moon. How did she get into this situation—to be right here, right now? She weaved back through time and wondered if there were warning signs. Yet another part of herself was outside of her body, watching her and calling her a stupid woman. She had thought there was love—pure and simple love—and she was duped, tricked. Life was a shell game dealer, and under every cup what she thought was there or could have been there was not. She looked at herself with pity and shook her head. This wasn't the way it was supposed to be, she told herself, holding herself.

What kind of man would abandon his family? That was the question she tried desperately to answer. Not only abandon them but lead them out to sea. Did she ever really know Công? Did she know he could be so cold, so unkind? What were his thoughts all along?

That he could betray her was less upsetting than the fact that he would be hurting their children—*her* children. What if they learned their father had abandoned them, did not—in the end— love them? How would they take that piece of knowledge? How would it be imprinted in their minds? How fast would it break their hearts?

And what if everyone found out? Wasn't it the fatherless boys you were always told to be careful around? How did those father-less boys feel hearing this? Her body shuddered. She looked around and everything became unfamiliar and threatening. The world was cold and wild. A country could collapse. A father could disappear. She would have to protect her sons, she was thinking, protect them from all the cruelties of the world.

She decided what do then. She ran upstairs and headed for her room. All the returned cassette tapes she had left in a shoebox. She grabbed that and his letters and the last postcard he sent in reply to her confused message. On the front, a yellowed black-and-white photo of Paris's Latin Quarter, where he'd lived as a student study-ing abroad. She remembered they kept it in their desk in Saigon. It was a memento of the past, kept but never used until he had to write her back: *Please don't contact me again. It is the best for the both of us. Please understand. Love, Công.* She threw it into the shoebox and hid it in the closet. No one would ever see this, she was thinking.

If her sons asked about their father, she told herself, she would tell them some kind of truth, what she knew of it: their father would not be joining them in New Orleans; this was all beyond their control and they had to try their best, she would say, to move forward. She would keep from them the father who stayed behind, the family they could have been, the injustice of what they had lost. She could protect them, if only they'd forget. She would protect them, if only she'd forget. Forgetting, she was so sure, was easy, the easiest thing that could be done; we forget all the time—we forget names and addresses, the color a childhood dress, the name of a favorite song. We could forget anything and everything, if only we tried, if only we made the effort.

Tuấn

The year Tuấn turned eleven two things happened: he had to repeat sixth grade and his mother told him his father was dead.

It was late summer when she did, the last weekend before school started again. She borrowed Bà Giang's sedan and the three of them headed to Grand Isle Beach for the day. They woke up early. Bình was asleep when they left the city, and Tuấn stayed up front with the map in his lap.

"It's been a long time since we've been to the beach," she said as they got on the highway, and she nodded at him as if this was their secret.

Halfway into the two-hour drive, she stopped at a Gulf station for gas and snacks. She got him a Popsicle, though it wasn't even nine yet. *Is it for me?* he asked. *Of course it is,* she answered, *who else would it be for?* He unwrapped it and ate it happily.

When they got back on the road, she said she wanted to tell him something, something important.

He was still thinking of school. He didn't want to take the same classes again, especially Mr. Landowski's English class. Mr. Landowski was a tough grader, and the only reason Tuấn was repeating sixth grade was because Mr. Landowski—whose real name was Toby—didn't think he knew English, which was wrong because Tuấn did know English; it was what he heard every day, everywhere. He'd stopped thinking entirely in Vietnamese nowadays— his thoughts were half in English, half in Vietnamese. The other day he forgot the word for "orange"; he kept trying to think of it but all that came up was "orange." He wondered if his mom knew that, that he was held back not through any fault of his own, but because Mr. Landowski was a terrible teacher. It made Tuấn think of his own father, who was also a teacher. And whereas his father was kind and gentle and patient—all qualities of a good teacher—Mr. Landowski had a temper and was easily flustered and gave bad grades that no one deserved.

"Your father," she said after a brief pause. His ears perked up. He stopped thinking about Mr. Landowski. He stopped thinking about oranges. His father! Perhaps he was coming after all these years. Perhaps they were driving to him now. Cha, he thought, was the word for "father." Finally! They would have so much to catch up on. And maybe, he thought for a brief instant, his dad could have a stern talking-to with Mr. Landowski, teacher to teacher, and tell him how wrong he was for holding Tuấn back for a year.

"Your father," she said finally, "your father is dead." She let out a sigh and added, "He died a while ago, but I think you're a big boy now and you should know the truth."

"How?" was what he managed to say. "Why? What do you mean?"

Tuấn bit his lip and looked out the window and at the passing cypress trees, which became blurry, and he didn't know why until he realized he had tears in his eyes. His mother said something then about *Communists* and *punishment* and *attempted escape* and *this was why we left* and *understand that he loved you, loved you dearly . . . that he did what was best . . . for you . . . for us . . . died a hero . . .*

"Why?" he asked again.

"Things like this happen," his mother said. She said some more things, but he covered his ears because he didn't want to hear any of it. When his mother tried to touch him, to comfort him, he pulled away.

The rest of the day was a blur. As Bình played in the water, Tuấn realized it was true—it had been a while since they'd been to the beach. He had forgotten beaches existed and oceans, too, and how the water was so violent—how could he forget that? The entire day he was thirsty from looking at the water and tasting the salt air.

His father was not coming, he realized with a sudden, heavy finality. His father was no longer in this world—not here in Louisiana, not there in Vietnam, just nowhere.

Once, in Saigon, they were playing hide-and-seek, the three of them. He was the seeker and he counted all the way to thirty (the biggest number he knew back then). He found his mother easily; she was hiding in her wardrobe. But his father was nowhere to be found. Tuấn was sure he'd be in his library. When he got there, though, it was empty. He searched the kitchen after that, then the backyard. *Surely,* he thought, *he must be in the backyard.* It was the last place he could have run off to. But no one was there. He looked up their tree, stared up at its branches for a few seconds. Nothing. He began to head back toward the house. Sadness was not the feeling that came over him. It was something else entirely, something heavier, darker. He felt as if he had lost something and that he would never get it back, when suddenly his father ran through the gate, singing, "You haven't found me, you haven't found me!" and Tuấn ran to him and was happy again. But that feeling—that heavy, dark feeling of having lost something—he would always remember.

That feeling came back when they'd left on the boat. It came in the middle of the night when they were camped out on the island with all those strangers. And it came back now. It gave him shivers down his spine, made his hands shake and sweat. Then it made his head ache until it throbbed and he had to close his eyes really tight. As he lay on the beach, he became angry—angry at the beach for reminding him of Vietnam, angry at his mother for bringing him out here to tell him the horrible news, angry at his brother for being so happy through it all—*Had she even told him?* Tuấn wondered, which made him angry at his mother all over again. He clenched his fists and banged them against the sand. He screamed, and his mother told him to sit in the car. He stopped what he was doing and looked her straight in the eyes. Into the silence, he pounded his fists on the sand again and screamed even louder. His mother rushed to him, grabbed him by the arm, and carried him to the car as he cried *Help, help, this is not my mother, this is not my mother, this is not my mother!* She slammed the car door and stomped away. She left the AC and the radio on.

Through the windshield, he watched as his mother and brother collected seashells. The last time he went to the beach was back in Vietnam after they'd left the city for the countryside. His dad had been worried about something at the time, and his mom thought it was a good idea to take a break from farming. She said they were thirty minutes from a beach; perhaps they could make a day trip out to it. At first his dad said he didn't want to go, that he didn't even really like the beach. But then, one Sunday, the three of them took the bus to the shore. Though there were plenty of other people, they found a clear, quiet spot on the sand. Tuấn remembered how—after months of frowning—his dad was finally smiling and laughing as they built sandcastles. He hadn't smiled like that since Saigon, and Tuấn was glad he got his old dad back again. They even had a sandcastle-building contest, and though his parents' sandcastles were obviously better, they told Tuấn his was the best.

As he watched his mother and brother now—a brother Tuấn's father didn't even know about—Tuấn felt somehow let down. Dad wasn't here to enjoy any of this. Dad would never be here to enjoy anything ever again. *Who were they, any of them,* he thought, *to have fun?* He let out a scream, the loudest he could, pushing all the air he could out of his lungs until he felt his chest and throat hurt, until he felt like they were on fire and his eyes were watering. But no one heard him.

When it was time to head back to New Orleans, Tuấn stayed in the backseat. His brother sat back there, too. "Why didn't you play with us?" Bình kept asking. "Look! Shells!" A towel full of seashells lay between them. Bình picked one up and another, showing them to Tuấn.

"You're not paying attention!" Bình cried and threw a shell at his brother. The shell pricked his arm. Something in him snapped just then, a rubber band in the back of his head releasing a stone from a slingshot. In the next instant, he grabbed the towel of shells and threw it out the window. The shells spread out like wings before falling and scattering on the empty highway. And the towel, a faded blue, floated and followed them for a few seconds before giving up and falling, too.

The car stopped. Tuấn met his mother's eyes in the rearview mirror. They didn't look mad; they looked sorry. She opened the car door and walked toward where the shells and towel had dropped. Tuấn looked out and saw her scurrying down the highway, picking up the shells and the towel. A car came up from behind, slowed down, and drove around her and their car. When she was making her way back, Tuấn sat back down.

"Why'd you do that?" Bình asked. "What was that all about?"

"Dad died. That's what it's all about."

Bình looked at him a long time without saying anything. Then, "Died. What does that mean?"

The car door slammed shut. Their mother set the shells and the towel on the front seat. They drove in silence all the way home.

When school started back up again, his dreams returned him to Vietnam, their old house in the city, and his father dressed not in the ragged T-shirt and shorts of the day they left, but in his school clothes, a clean and stiff white button-up with black slacks, a brown briefcase by his side. The sound of the city—mopeds, bicycle bells, and the occasional car—drifted in from outside. Tuấn would stand on their front balcony eating a frozen banana and see his father coming home from around the corner, calling his name. *Tuấn . . . Tuấn . . .*

One night in the fall, he heard his name inside their apartment. Over and over again, his father was calling him the way he did when he had a surprise, a toy or a piece of candy. For one second, he wondered if it would be those soft, chewy durian candies, and his mouth watered. He hadn't had durian in forever. *Could durians grow here?* he wondered. He opened one eye and thought about asking his father, who would surely be in the kitchen right then. His father was a smart man and could answer that question: Did durians grow in New Orleans? But then he opened his other eye and realized the sound was nothing like his name at all. It was a dog, a dog barking in the distance. How could he be so stupid? And to dream of durians in a country where no one knew about durians!

He couldn't go back to sleep then. The dog just kept on going. Head tilted to one side, ear in the air, Tuấn listened until the bark became a yelp.

Quietly, because Bình was asleep on the other side of the room, Tuấn grabbed his pillow and left. In the kitchen, he opened the refrigerator and drank orange juice straight from the carton, something his mother would never let him do. A Payless shoebox sat on the table and an ancient tape recorder with the stickers for the buttons missing. He took a seat and opened the box to find cassette tapes and a whole bunch of papers. He fell asleep before he could make anything out of it. By morning, he found himself still sitting at the table, head on wood, drool puddling near his mouth, pillow at his feet. The orange juice carton was gone. So were the shoebox and tape recorder.

His mother nudged him awake. "You've been chasing ghosts again?" she said. The water from the teakettle boiled and whistled into the air. She yawned.

"I don't believe in ghosts," Tuấn said. "Ghosts don't exist."

Steam from her mug rose to her face. "It's just a saying. There are no ghosts. We know that." She looked around as if pointing out the evidence. No ghosts, not here.

She blinked her eyes and rubbed them. Her painted fingernails lit up the morning darkness. It was her new job in the Quarter: she painted nails. To show customers what the colors would look like, she used herself as a model and always forgot to clean off the paint. The rainbow of reds and blues and purples made Tuấn think about the women who stopped by her salon. Who could have worn such loud colors?

In the bathroom, Tuấn washed the gunk out of his eyes, brushed his teeth, and took a hard look at his hair. He hated his hair. There was too much of it, and he couldn't spike it up like the other boys in school. He splashed water onto his hands and combed his fingers through his hair. It didn't help.

"The bus!" his mother yelled from the kitchen. He ran out and she stood at the counter. "Mau! Lẹ đi!" She opened the door. Sunlight flooded in, and the shadows of the outside railing made prison bars on the floor. "And don't forget your lunch." She stuffed a container into his backpack, zipped it up, and pushed him along.

In the distance, a large vehicle squeaked to a halt. Before Tuấn ran down the steps, his mother pulled him back. "Forgetting something," she said. She handed him the house key tied around a shoelace into a necklace. Since starting her new job, she had given him that responsibility. "Your brother's too young to carry around a key," she had said. "Be home quick after school to let him in. Do this for mẹ. Please." He was her big boy, the man of the house, the keeper of the house key.

"Yeah," Tuấn replied. He took the key and ran toward the bus stop. He held it tight in his fist, the teeth of the metal pushing against his palm, the shoelace swinging in the air.

"Is that dog meat?" Donald asked, and his friends snickered. Lunch had barely started and already they were surrounding Tuấn's table.

Donald Richard lived outside the gates of Versailles at the corner, in a house that looked too old still to be standing, in the shadows of the apartments. Next to the large gates, Donald's house looked small and lonely, though Tuấn could never have pictured Donald being small or lonely. With fat arms, a potbelly, and a snout of a nose to match it all, Donald reminded Tuấn of an oversized pig.

Donald and his friends poked at the thịt nướng. "Ja-uan," Donald called him. Donald and his friends called him that—*Juan* or *Ja-uan*—though he had no idea how they came up with *that*. Juan was a Mexican name, and he was from Vietnam. "Which isn't even near Mexico," a teacher had pointed out. Still, the name stuck. He was Juan.

The kids at school were stupid like that. That was why he was there, he was sure. They put all the stupid kids in one school, where he had to take remedial English (for the extra dumb, like he was) with Donald, where they went over flashcards and read books that still had pictures in them.

"*Farmer Jim has two cows. Say,*" Mrs. Trahan, the remedial English teacher, would say, *"Fa-arm-er J-im. Say, too k-ows."* Tuấn couldn't help but feel like a baby in her class.

Now Tuấn smacked Donald's hands away. "Not for fat pig," he said. "Oink, oink!" he called out. "Oink, oink!"

They all laughed and Donald grabbed Tuấn's shirt, twisting the collar, but the sound of Ms. Swanson's heels clicking against the floor made him let go.

"He's not worth it," one of Donald's friends said.

"Yeah, leave him."

"For now."

As the others left, Donald leaned in and whispered, "Dog eater." He said it again, pausing between the words—"Dog. Eater."— before catching up with his friends.

"Are you sitting alone because they made you?" Ms. Swanson asked when she found him. Ms. Swanson was a tall woman, taller than any of the other adults. A permanent wrinkle marked her forehead, making her look angry or annoyed. She wore suit jackets with skirts, but they always looked small on her bulky, uneven body. The upper part of her body bulged against the fabric; the lower part seemed dainty. Tuấn thought that if she looked like that growing up, perhaps she understood what life was like for him. In his mind, he saw her standing in a line, waiting to be chosen for dodge ball or sitting alone during lunch. She placed her hand on her hip and frowned when he didn't answer. "Or do you like sitting by yourself?"

"Yes, ma'am," Tuấn answered.

"Well, which is it?"

"I like sitting myself," he said. He stuffed a spoonful of rice into his mouth and she walked away.

After the bell rang, everyone headed for class while Tuấn waited. It was the easiest way, he learned, to avoid the too-crowded hallways. When all the students were gone, Tuấn headed for the door. As he rounded the corner for Mrs. Trahan's class, Donald jumped out, his hands stuck in the air like a monster's.

"What you doing, Ja-uan?" he asked. "Don't you know the bell's gonna ring in a minute? You'll get in trouble if you're late, Ja-uan. You can't be late, Ja-uan."

Tuấn looked down the hall behind Donald. Everyone had disappeared. He took a step forward, and the bell rang.

"There it goes," Donald said and shoved Tuấn down to the floor. His head hit a locker.

"Go back to China, Chinaman," he heard Donald say.

He wanted to say "I came from *Vietnam. I am Vietnamese.*" But he didn't.

As Tuấn approached their apartment, he saw his brother standing outside. Bình swung a plastic bat in one hand and palmed a crumpled-up Coke can with the other. The bat they got from the Dollar General. The Coke can he probably found near the bayou because people were always throwing away stuff out there.

His brother threw the can up and swung the bat. He missed.

"You have to keep your eyes on the can-ball," Tuấn said.

Bình looked up. "I know."

Can-ball, they called this.

"But I have to blink, don't I?" his brother asked.

"Yeah, but you have to follow the can-ball still."

"Impossible."

Tuấn chuckled and they ran up the stairs and he let them inside.

He was making their afternoon snack—rice with Maggi sauce and lunch bologna—when Bình came to him with his notebook.

"They're giving you homework in second grade nowadays?" Tuấn asked.

His brother opened it up and showed him two words. On the left, his name, *Bình.* On the right, *Ben.*

"That's what I want people to call me from now on," his brother said, pointing to *Ben.*

"Why?" He pointed at *Bình*. He couldn't imagine his brother being called something else. Everything had a proper name.

His brother shrugged and gave a disappointed look. "I don't know. Easier, I guess." Then he added, "For everyone."

"But it's your name," Tuấn said.

"I can choose my own name. No one says I can't."

"Mẹ will be mad." He imagined their mother throwing up her hands like she did a lot of the time and saying, *You boys give me a headache—why can't you be good?* "And Dad . . ." Tuấn added but couldn't finish the sentence; he didn't know where it would go.

"I don't care what Mom thinks." His brother grabbed the note book back. "And Dad's dead." He walked away.

He didn't even look like a *Ben*.

Tuấn couldn't sleep that night. The dog—out there—was barking again. It was nearly three. Tuấn went to the window and tried to find it. No one in Versailles was allowed to have a pet. He squinted and looked out beyond the fence. It had to be somewhere out there. Something moved, and he took a step back.

A gecko. Just a gecko. They were always around. Them and palmetto bugs.

For a brief moment, he had the idea of leaving the gecko on his brother's bed and imagined him squirming and screaming. Bình (he would never call him Ben) didn't like any of the things Tuấn liked. Tuấn thought geckos were fascinating. He heard that if a bird grabbed a gecko, the tail would just fall off. In an instant, the gecko would escape, and later the tail would grow back. Bình didn't like any of that. It reminded Tuấn of their father. He didn't like him going outside to play and getting dirty. He remembered one time he was playing and it rained and he ran home muddy. His father looked up from his book and nearly screamed. His face screwed up in disgust. Tuấn could imagine Bình doing that; his face would be like their father's.

Tuấn reached up and held out his palm. "I'm not gonna hurt you, buddy," he coaxed. At first, the gecko avoided the hand, but eventually it stepped on. Tuấn cupped it in both hands—"What I tell you?"—and walked out of the room. In the distance, the dog began to howl, a long, whining howl that became almost like a cry.

"What could it be crying about?" Tuấn asked, looking at the gecko. "Let's take a look-see."

He opened the front door. Not knowing what else to do, Tuấn sat down and listened to the howling mix with the hum of air conditioners and the sound of frogs and crickets somewhere in the thickets of bushes and trees that surrounded the Versailles bayou.

When he was little, what he loved most was going to the bayou. In his mind, it was the best place to be because no one bothered him there. Being alone, he could do whatever he wanted.

One time he pretended he was a pirate, and Cô Lam, who lived in the apartment across the dirt road from them, called out from her window: "No respect!"

"I'm sorry!" he replied. "I'll be quieter."

"And I have to work tonight!" She threw a rolled-up newspaper at him, but it hit the water instead and sank.

People were always throwing things into the bayou. Heineken cans and cigarette butts littered the water along with whatever else was useless—broken lawn chairs, burned and scratched cookware, cardboard boxes. The trash of Versailles convened in the brackish brown waters of the neighborhood's back bayou. It convened and stayed and floated until it was too heavy and sank.

Nothing could survive here. But then there were the frogs and the crickets and that dog. He closed his eyes and listened.

———

In the morning, Tuấn woke up to his mother's shrieking.

"What are you holding?" his mother cried.

He felt something in his hands and remembered the gecko. To his amazement, it had stayed there all night. He felt its little claws. His mother shrieked again and Tuấn held his hand closer to his body. The lizard squirmed.

"Dirty! Dirty! Dirty! Let it go and come inside! Why are you outside? Do you know what time it is?"

Tuấn looked at the lizard, then at his mom. Hesitantly, he let the gecko go and went inside. At the doorway, his mother swept it down the steps and he swore he heard little pings as its body bounced.

After his mother pushed him out the door for school, he walked out of Versailles. As he passed Donald's house, he quickened his pace as the front door slammed shut and Donald came out. A brown-and-black dog with pointed ears was tied up to an old oak tree and began to run after him. It stopped as it reached the end of its rope. Disappointed, it howled the same howl that kept Tuấn awake at night. He knew then it must have been the same dog.

Donald stopped at the end of the driveway and was surprised to find Tuấn.

"You always had dog?" he asked.

"None of your business," Donald said.

A woman, the same large and bulbous shape as Donald, lumbered out. The fat woman carried a smoking cigarette in one hand and a bottle in the other.

Tuấn whistled to the dog and held out his hand.

"Quit it," Donald said. "He doesn't like you."

The dog whimpered.

"He likes," said Tuấn.

It didn't have a tag, it didn't have a collar. Just a rope around its neck. He looked at the dog's fur. Patches of it were missing like somebody had pulled them out.

Out of nowhere, Donald said, "Race you to the bus stop, Ja-uan," and pushed him aside.

As Donald disappeared, the woman got to the curb.

"That boy forgot his drink," she said and shook her head. She let the cigarette drop and stomped on it with her sandal. Her toenails were painted lime green. "Do you want a soda?" she asked.

That afternoon before lunch, Donald met Tuấn at his locker.

"See here, Ja-uan," he started. "I wanted to tell you I'm sorry." Tuấn didn't respond and Donald repeated himself as he wiped his face with the back of a hand. "Sit with us today." He reached an arm around and slammed the locker shut. "We'll start over. You and me and Tommy and Pete. We'll be friends."

Donald led Tuấn to his table, where Tommy and Pete, two other white boys, were already seated. Gripping his shoulder, Donald guided him to the bench.

"Doesn't Mrs. Trahan look like a horse?" Donald said as he sat down. "She has to be part horse, am I right?"

The boys laughed, though they weren't in Mrs. Trahan's class. One boy made neighing sounds while the other clapped his hands on the table to make a galloping noise. Donald eyed Tuấn.

"Maybe?" Tuấn answered.

"Maybe!" they echoed and took out their lunches.

"Oh, man!" Donald exclaimed. "Margaret forgot my soda. That's how stupid Margaret is. My dad's more stupider for marrying her." He opened his bag and took a bite of his sandwich. "Hey, Ja-uan. Old friend, old pal," Donald said, "do me a favor? Here's two dollars. Get me a Coke, why don't ya? And get something for yourself, too. Maybe milk, 'cause you're small stuff."

Tuấn looked at the crowded line. He looked back at Donald, who beamed.

"It's Tu-hung," Tuấn said. "My name is Tu-hung." He said it

slowly, enunciating the words the same way Mrs. Trahan did in class.

"Okay, okay," Donald said. "I get it. Now, a soda?"

When Tuấn came back, Donald was whispering to one of the boys. "Thanks, buddy!" he said when he noticed Tuấn. He grabbed the soda can and rubbed off the water.

Tuấn opened his lunch and stirred the leftover noodles with his chopsticks. His mother was angry that he and Bình hadn't eaten the leftover noodles she made two nights before for their after-school snack. "I don't make food to go to waste," she said. She went on about how money was tight as she threw in slivers of beef and packed it for his lunch. Tuấn lifted his chopsticks to his mouth and Donald screamed: "Bug-eater!"

In the Tupperware, a black lump moved. By reflex, Tuấn threw the container in the air. Tommy and Pete screamed but then laughed, an uncontrollable hoo-ing and hollering. The noodles landed on the table and in them a cockroach moved. More came out of hiding. Everyone in the cafeteria stood up, not knowing whether to run toward the mess or away from the roaches. Ms. Swanson came over.

"Who made this mess?" she demanded. "Whoever made this mess has to clean it up. Donald, was it you?"

"No! I swear! I hate those things! Yuck!" He screwed up his face and made it look like he was about to puke. "Ja-uan brought them in his lunch. I swear."

Tuấn stood up and started to gather the bugs into the container. It was not right to treat animals that way. They were living beings. How would Donald feel if he were treated that way?

"Look, he's saving them! He wants to eat them!" Donald yelled.

Tuấn put the container's top on. The bugs crawled around in their enclosed safety as he walked away. "Mẹ mầy," he mumbled.

"Y'all heard that?" Donald asked the cafeteria. "He said he's going to eat them anyway! He said it in his ching-chong!"

The kids laughed and their laughter echoed.

"Both of you! Detention! After school!"

In Ms. Swanson's room, Tuấn and Donald sat as far away from each other as possible until she told them to sit closer together toward the center of the room.

"I want to keep an eye on the both of you," she said.

Tuấn looked at the clock. They had an hour. Donald smirked as he drew in his notebook. Ms. Swanson came over and ripped it away from his desk.

"Eyes forward, Donald," Ms. Swanson said. "Straight ahead."

"He's not looking forward!" said Donald.

"Lie!" Tuấn said. "Your fault! Everything, your fault!"

"Settle down, both of you," said Ms. Swanson. "What both of you need is discipline. Haven't your parents ever spanked you?"

"I don't deserve to be here. It's all his fault!" Donald reached over and poked Tuấn, but Tuấn grabbed his finger and twisted it around. Donald whined in pain.

"Enough, you two. Do you want me to call your mothers?"

"I have no mother!" Donald yelled.

"You mother fat, too!" Tuấn added.

"Enough!" Ms. Swanson yelled, slamming her fists on the desk.

At three thirty, Ms. Swanson allowed the two to call their parents to pick them up.

The last time he got into a fight (in the first week of school when Donald called him a slant-eye and Tuấn slapped him on the cheek), his mother was brought in for a parent-teacher conference. He remembered her looking small in front of the teacher. "Yes, sir," she kept on saying. The teacher made her sign something and they left. On the bus ride home, she fumed. She was embarrassed, she said, with how he'd behaved. Tuấn said Donald started it; Donald called him a name and made fun of him.

"Then you look the other way," his mother replied. "You make yourself better than him by being a better student. You don't hit. You don't hit anybody. Not ever."

"That's stupid," Tuấn said. "He won't stop unless I hit him. He'll just keep on doing it."

"*Unless you hit him?*" his mom repeated, incredulous. "What would your father say? *Unless you hit him?* Ridiculous!"

She went on: Did he know it made her look like a bad parent? What would everyone say about their household? That she raised a savage? An ingrate? It didn't help that she was in this all alone—all alone. Those last words hurt him the most—"You don't have a father and your mother is in this all alone." If she was alone, what did that make him? It stung him. And he didn't know what to do with it; he didn't want to feel that way ever again.

Tuấn pretended to dial a phone number and spoke Vietnamese into the receiver. Afterwards, he went outside. He remembered an RTA bus stop near a grocery store. It must have been five or six blocks away. Not too far.

As he began to walk toward the main road, Donald's stepmother pulled up.

"Versailles, right?" she said, then looked over at Donald.

"Why don't we drive your friend home, too?" she said to Donald. Donald knitted his eyebrows, and his stepmother reached back to unlock the door. "Jump in," she said.

"Yes, ma'am," said Tuấn.

To Tuấn's surprise, the inside of the car was clean. Donald's stepmother turned on the radio. The music sounded like plastic bottles hitting each other, the notes rising with a woman's voice, singing who knew what. With each passing second, the song seemed to go faster. It reminded Tuấn of the car chase scenes on TV.

Donald's stepmother looked into her rearview mirror. "It's Donna Summer!" she said. "I wish I could get this goofball up here to listen to good music, but all he listens to is noise. All of it is noise."

Donald let out an angry sigh and rolled down his window. His mother took a right and then a left into Versailles.

"Donald, why don't you invite your friend over sometime?" she asked, slowing the car. "I can make tacos or something! He never invites his friends over. He's always playing with his toys. Two weeks ago, we got him a dog so he'd at least go outside. It's his only friend."

"His name's Walter!"

"His father says the problem is he's too much like his mother— too unfriendly. But look at you two! Golly!"

"Margaret!" Donald kicked the dashboard. "Will you just shut up? God! So embarrassing."

The car eased to a stop. Tuấn jumped out and watched as it pulled away.

The apartment door opened and his mom called his name. "Why are you home so late? And who was that?" She stood on the landing, her hands on her hips.

"Nothing, mẹ," Tuấn said.

She grabbed him by the shoulder and bent down to his eye level. "Look your mother in the eyes and tell her that," she said.

"Nothing," he said and ran in to his room. He slammed his door.

"You don't make things easy for your mother," he heard her say.

Walter barked into the night. Tuấn knew where the dog was. He went to the window. Stars dotted the sky. It reminded him of nights in Mỹ Tho. When he couldn't sleep, his dad told him to count the stars. Một, hai, ba . . . you could never get to one hundred without falling asleep. He remembered that. He held the memory in his mind like a breath.

In school, they made him count different numbers. He couldn't get his lips to say the words. "Won" was fine, "too" was easy, but it got harder. "Tree." "Far." "Fire." Donald would make fun of him and then Tuấn would count as fast as he could in Vietnamese— Một-hai-ba-bốn-năm-sáu-bảy-tám-chín-mười! *You can't count,* he'd tell Donald. *You know nothing.* Donald would call for Mrs. Trahan to tell her Tuấn was cussing at him, and she would believe him. She would make him sit in the corner for the rest of the period like he was in time-out in kindergarten.

Tuấn looked under the bed. The lunch container from that afternoon was still there. The bugs dotted the plastic, not moving except one on the lid near the hole he had made for them to breathe. Tuấn shook it gently, and the dots began crawling again. He counted all six.

He left the apartment barefoot and started down the road carrying the Tupperware of roaches. Dirt caked his feet and the rocks bit into his skin. For a second, he wanted to go back and get his shoes, but he was so far already. It was cooler than nights before. A cold front had come through, and the weatherman said it was perfect "sweater weather."

Under the stars, the apartment buildings became silhouettes. Walking, he heard birds singing. He didn't know birds sang at this hour. He felt delighted and surprised.

Tuấn passed the gates of Versailles and walked toward the bus stop. When he got to Donald's house, he stopped.

The lights were off. The dog stopped barking when it saw him. It began whimpering and pacing from one corner of the lawn to the other, stopping when its rope couldn't go any farther.

"Walter?" Tuấn whispered. He felt as if someone was spying on him, as if Donald was outside knowing he'd come this night, though he had only come up with this idea while brushing his teeth. He walked closer to the dog. A light came on and Tuấn froze.

When no one came out, he set the container down and went to the dog. It barked, then whimpered again. Its voice was weakening, vanishing from endless barking. Tuấn petted its head. It seemed more a phantom of a dog than a real dog, what a real dog should be—its size, its shape. It needed a bath. It needed food. The dog licked Tuấn's hand.

Tuấn moved to the tree to look at the rope knotted around it. When the dog began barking again, Tuấn whispered, "Shhh . . ." until it quieted down.

With all his strength, Tuấn pushed his fingers into the knot and tried to unravel it. The burning of the rope made him sweat and his palms became slick. It was tighter than he could have imagined.

After a couple of minutes, the knot was loosened and the dog began moving again, wagging its tail and panting with its tongue sticking out. Tuấn dropped the rope to the ground.

"Go," he said, too excited to whisper anymore. "Go!"

And, as if understanding, the dog ran out of the yard and into the street. Tuấn watched until it disappeared. He stood and waited to see if it would come back.

"Anh," a voice called out. *Brother.* Bình stood barefooted on the sidewalk under a streetlamp. "It's cold," Bình said, tiptoeing closer. "You got up. I followed you." He wiped his nose with his hand.

"It is cold," Tuấn agreed.

The two stood under Donald's tree in silence.

Then Bình spoke up. "Is the dog coming back?" he asked.

"No," Tuấn answered.

"Where do you think he's going?"

"Somewhere" was all he could answer. "But he's not tied up anymore. He's free." He liked the sound of those words—*He's free*—in English. They felt light and floated off his tongue: *He's free.*

Tuấn placed the Tupperware of cockroaches under the tree, next to the rope. "You won't tell anyone," he said.

"No one," said Bình.

"And nothing happened tonight."

"Nothing."

"Let's get back, then."

And they ran back to the apartment. For the first time in a long time, Tuấn felt happy, as if he were where he was supposed to be, out in the starlit night under such a full moon. He swore he felt a breeze run through his hair, though the air was still.

Ben

Most of Versailles was Catholic. There was one Buddhist family long ago, but they'd moved away. *Where do we belong?* Ben's mother would ask. It happened after every Mardi Gras. After the streets were cleaned of streamers, the king cake eaten, the tiny plastic baby tossed out with the trash (though Ben always wanted to keep them), and the beads packed away for the next year (a tangled mess no one would use again), Versailles became quieter, calmer, more severe.

On Sundays, the neighbors—the Phạms, the Ngôs, the Nguyễns—dressed up for church, the women in plain áo dàis and the men in button-ups tucked into their pants. *Are you going to Ash Wednesday service?* they asked Ben's mother. *What about Palm Sunday? What about fish dinners? Do you have any new and exciting ways to cook fish? Fish on Fridays?* His mother was offended.

Leave me and my children alone, she seemed to say with her eyes, though it would have been too rude to say it aloud. She learned a new phrase from one of her customers at the nail salon: "Bless your heart," which meant, secretly, that they were dumb or lacking mental faculties or were otherwise impaired, but there was not a thing to be done about it—how pitiful they were, how one could pity them all day long until the cows came home. She said it to them all the time: *Bless your heart! Bless your heart! Bless, your, heart!*

From February to April, Ben's mother tried not to talk to anyone in Versailles if she could help it. After work she would walk to their apartment, her breath held in, her posture rigid, her eyes down. A year without talking about Easter or Lent was a successful year, she would say to the both of them, Ben and his brother. Their family was never one for ideologies, she would say, and their father would have been against it all; Catholicism or communism, it would have been all the same to him.

Ben never knew his father. He was killed, according to his mother, after the war. The war, from what he had gleaned from books and TV, had been between communism and non-Communists. The Americans came to help the fight against the Communists. His own father was not a Communist. He was a teacher and a free-thinker who despised Communists, and because of this they killed him. He died a hero. That's the word his mother used, *hero,* whenever Ben asked about him. Whatever else he knew of the man were echoes of would haves, could haves. *He would have thought this . . . he could have done this, your father. . . .* Not a real-life father but a ghost of a father, an afterimage of a father.

"That's why we don't live in Vietnam. We live in America," she would continue, "where we can think what we want and not get arrested." Last year, they became citizens—one of two families in the neighborhood so far—and it was something she took pride in. Ben didn't know what it meant, how their lives would be different than before, but he knew it was something important, momentous: that night they ate cake at Gambino's.

The summer between third and fourth grade, as the sun was

setting one evening, a priest arrived in Versailles. He had a dark blue car with wood-grain panels. No one recognized it, and at first everyone stuck their heads out their windows to have a look. When the priest stepped out, he carried a large stack of door hangers. He began his journey door-to-door. Ben could hear his fist on wood every few minutes, at first hard and vivacious, but as the night continued it became softer, quieter. By the time he arrived at the last apartment, their apartment, they didn't hear his knock and knew he was there only because they were expecting him.

He introduced himself as a priest who had come from Houston by way of Saigon to set up a brand-new church in New Orleans. A very special church. A Vietnamese church. It would also be a community center and safe place for everyone. Imagine ping-pong tables, he was saying, and basketball courts. And classrooms for catechism classes, English lessons for adults, and Vietnamese lessons for the kids. The priest looked at Ben, who stood behind his mother at the door. Ben smiled and he held his hands behind his back. His mother didn't look like she was paying attention.

"That's the dream, anyway," explained the priest, "the Almighty willing. Right now, we rent a storefront off Chef Menteur. Next to a Winn-Dixie."

"Ah, Winn-Dixie," his mother said, as if, out of everything she was told, this was the one thing she understood. She looked at one side of the door hanger and flipped it to the other. But in the motion of it, the paper—thick like cardboard, so it would stay put on all the doorknobs—sliced her finger. In the next instant, the hanger flew out of her hands and dropped down off their landing.

"Trời ơi," she whispered as if she didn't want anyone to hear. She turned around and walked to the kitchen sink. Ben moved out of the way, so intent she seemed to get there.

The priest came running after her. "I am so sorry, cô. So very sorry."

Ben closed the door because he wanted to be helpful.

The priest was younger than Ben expected. On TV, when you saw a priest, they were always chubby, old, pale men who mumbled when they spoke. But this priest was skinny with golden brown skin and a thick head of black hair. And, of course, he was Vietnamese. You never saw Vietnamese priests on TV. You never saw Vietnamese anything. A Vietnamese priest in real life—that was amazing!

His mother ran the water over her finger as the priest stood by. He kept on apologizing, and his mother was obliged to keep on telling him, annoyed, it was no one's fault. She rummaged around the drawers for a bandage. They kept their first aid in the last drawer, but she kept looking elsewhere in her frenzied state.

"Let me help," the priest said.

"No. Thank you," his mother said when she found the box of bandages. She emptied it onto the counter. They were all different sizes, so she had to look through them before finding the right one.

The priest left after that, telling her she should consider joining their congregation: Our Lady of Saigon. They could come to mass tomorrow or Sunday. "Or anytime, really," he said. "Our doors are always open. We're here to serve the community."

His mother didn't answer.

"We hope to see you," the priest repeated, and she closed the door.

"Catholics," she proclaimed after watching his car pull away, "they can believe whatever they want, but that doesn't mean they can go around telling you what to think or do or believe!" She opened her eyes wide at him as if she were about to say something important, a lesson he should learn and take note of. "That's why we left Vietnam, you see?"

"But you left Vietnam because of the Communists," said Ben.

"We left," she said, as if he should've remembered, "because people like that are dangerous." She peeked through the blinds. Ben wanted to know what she meant by "dangerous." "I can't believe everyone is falling for it. Bless their hearts. Bless all their hearts!" Suddenly she gasped and pulled away from the blinds. She walked toward her bedroom, and Ben wondered if the priest saw her spying.

"We're Americans," she said. "This is ridiculous!"

The next day, it was all he could talk about with Addy: the priest, his wood-paneled car, the door hanger that cut his mother. He showed it to Addy.

Addy lived out on Bullard Avenue, where all the families were from Haiti, the same way all the families in Versailles were from Vietnam. But instead of apartments, they were all in houses, small one-story buildings of whitewashed wood that made them look old and fragile. Ben thought they looked like they were made of paper.

In third grade, Addy had been the new girl in school. Ben's previous best friend, Shirley Daigle, had just moved away last summer (they promised to keep in touch through letters, though they both knew it wouldn't happen, Shirley being an overall bad writer and Ben not knowing what to say in these letters), and Ben's ears had perked up when Mrs. Brownworth said they had a new student.

A counselor brought her in. She was a small black girl who wore her hair in an afro. She wore jeans and a pink Minnie Mouse shirt, and her backpack was a bright cherry red. The frames of her glasses were red, too, and so was the plastic ring she wore on her pinkie, Ben would later notice. Mrs. Brownworth introduced the new girl as Adelaide Toussaint and said that she just moved to New Orleans from Miami.

The girl corrected her then—interrupting the bulky, scratchy-voiced Mrs. Brownworth!—saying that she was actually called Addy and that they, her family, were in Miami for a while, but they, her dad and her, were really from Port-au-Prince in Haiti— did Mrs. Brownworth know where Haiti was?—which is very far away from New Orleans, and the weather was nicer there than it is in New Orleans, though she didn't have much room to complain because her daddy, she said, said complaining was the devil.

Mrs. Brownworth didn't know what to say after the lengthy speech and no one else did, either. Addy stood at the front of the class beside Mrs. Brownworth. It was silent until two blond girls in the back, Shannon and Ashley, started giggling, and soon the entire class was giggling, too, except Ben, who didn't see anything funny about anything. Addy stared at them all and shook her head. "Timoun dyab," she said, like an adult reprimanding a school of children. No one knew what it meant and they kept laughing. Ben knew, for reasons he did not understand, he wanted to be her friend.

At recess, as she sat alone under an oak tree watching other girls play hopscotch, Ben approached her and sat by her side. They both watched the girls skip across the chalk-drawn squares. There were five girls in all, including Shannon and Ashley. The entire group had been through the hopscotch once and were starting all over again when Ben said, "I have marbles."

Addy didn't say anything back. He wasn't even sure she'd heard him, so he said it again: "I have marbles." For good grades, Bà Giang had gifted him a set of marbles, and Tuấn became infuriated because he said (in his broken English that always made Ben cringe, though he would never admit that to anyone) first grade was for babies and easy and it was all unfair. (He stomped off to their shared room and their mother yelled back, "Well, life is unfair!") The marbles came in a mesh bag, but that didn't keep up for too long so he stored them in a Ziploc bag instead. He opened it and showed her. Each marble was different. Ben often thought there were as many marbles as there were people. This one, the first one he showed Addy, was white with different-colored polka dots. It was the size of a grape, larger than all the others. He held it in his palm and showed her another one, a clear one this time with a brown swirl in it that reminded him of the Cinnamon Toast

Crunch they served for breakfast at school. He reached in again and took out a handful. He jiggled them and they clattered against one another. (*This is what teeth sound like,* he always told himself.)

Out on the hopscotch squares, it was Shannon's turn. She wrapped her hair in a scrunchie and was telling her friends, "I can do it backwards," and they were all saying, "No way. No way, Shan. You can't do it! No way!"

"I bet," she insisted, "with my eyes closed even." Her hands were in the air, already triumphant, celebrating. "Here I go," she exclaimed, jumping into the first square with one leg. She landed perfectly. She jumped again and landed safely.

"Look," Ben whispered when Shannon landed on the next jump, a pair of squares side by side. He slid his fistful of marbles across the blacktop, aiming for the chalk-drawn squares. Addy squinted her eyes. At this distance they were so small he couldn't even see them. Addy smiled.

Shannon stepped on a marble, then suddenly began losing her balance. She let out a moan as she flapped her hands—her hands like birds trying to grab on to something (a crumb of air, maybe) to keep from falling, but it was too late. Within the next second, she flew across the hopscotch squares and landed on her back on the ground at the edge of the blacktop, half her body in the dirt. The boys playing basketball stopped and watched. A few laughed. Shannon let out a long, wailing cry, not of pain, but of embarrassment, Ben was sure. The other girls ran away.

Ben and Addy held in their own laughter, covering their mouths, under the shade of the old oak tree.

"That was good for sure!" Addy said.

They became quick friends after that.

Addy studied the door hanger.

"Sai-gon," she read.

Ben told her about the priest and the new church and how his mother slammed the door on him. (This last part Ben made up to make the story more exciting.) He said his mother didn't like Catholics because they were like the Communists.

Addy was not offended because she didn't know anything about Communists. She was Catholic; her father, too. What Catholic meant, Addy didn't really know, but she said this: "It's like a club. A secret club. We have to wake up early on Sundays and we go to this small, little building out in Little Woods. They chant and we stand up and sit down. Sometimes we stand on our knees."

Ben pictured exercise videos on TV with women and men in neon pink and green leotards jumping up and down to music. "And the adults eat bread," Addy added, "and sip wine. And the kids, we go have playtime in the back, where there's juice and animal crackers and music on a tape player." She thought for a moment. Addy's father, inside the house, was cooking joumou, and the smell of cooking beef wafted out into the sticky summer air. It made Ben hungry. "It's like a party," Addy said. "Every week, a party."

"Like Mardi Gras?" Ben asked.

"Exactly like Mardi Gras," she said.

The priest returned to Versailles the next week. On Saturday morning, Ben heard laughter outside by the bayou. He heard the sound of a rubber ball bouncing against skin. He got dressed and ran out. And there they were: the priest and the teenagers of Versailles. Ben ran down barefooted.

Two metal poles with a net in the middle were staked into the ground. Five teenagers stood on one side of the net, four on the other. A volleyball rallied back and forth, the teenagers jumping into the air to hit it with both hands. The priest stood to the side watching. He was wearing the same clothes he wore last time he visited, but this time a whistle, like the ones gym teachers wore, hung from his neck. His forehead was slick with sweat and glistened in the sun. Every few seconds, he wiped a paper towel across his entire face. Other times, his head went back and forth, following the ball's trajectory in the sky. Ben did the same. Then a boy, one of the Nguyễns' sons (Ben remembered his name being Huy but everyone called him Joseph), jumped right up close to the net and slammed the ball down. It bounced on the dirt hard and ricocheted into the bayou. Water splashed the players but didn't reach Ben or the priest.

"Holy hell!" someone said.

"Why you gotta do that?" said someone else.

The priest blew into the whistle and held his hands in the air to signal a time-out.

"Maybe we should break," the priest said. "And Joe, get that ball, will you?" Joseph shook his head with a grin and the teenagers dispersed, some heading to a blue cooler off to the side and popping open cans of Coke.

"Is this what Catholics do?" Ben asked.

The priest took a quick breath as if he'd just noticed Ben was there. He patted his head.

"Hương's boy," said the priest. "You scared Cha Hiệu."

Cha meant *father*, Ben knew that much, so he asked, "Who's Father Hiệu?"

The priest laughed, a good belly laugh. "*I'm* Father Hiệu!" he said.

"Oh," Ben replied, not able to think of anything else to say. Then "Whose dad are you?" He scanned the teenagers.

"I'm not anyone's dad," the priest said. "They just call me that. It's . . . we take care of everyone. Like they're our children. I'm a priest."

Ben noted that he said "we," and he imagined a whole sea of fathers, wearing the same black jeans and black shirts with white squares on their collars. They moved with synchronized movements like marines in a parade.

"My father died," Ben said. It felt appropriate, while they were on the subject of fathers.

"I'm so sorry!" The priest looked worried now.

"No. It was a long time ago. Before I was born. He died like a hero in Vietnam. That's what my mom says."

"Still. No child should go through that. We've been through a lot, all of us. But on top of that! No child should grow up without a father." He looked like he was about to tear up, and Ben felt bad he'd even brought it up.

"Don't worry," he said. "You're here now."

"Ah!" the priest exclaimed, as if suddenly everything made sense. "Yes, of course."

Just then, Joseph came up to Father Hiệu with a Polaroid camera. He'd taken off his shirt and wore only his shorts. His body was wet. Ben thought he should look away.

"Take a picture with us!" Joseph said.

"But who?" Father Hiệu said. "Someone needs to take the photo."

"Hey, you, kid! Hey!" Ben realized Joseph was talking to him. "You know how to use one of these?"

Ben's mother found the picture later that evening.

"What's this?" she asked, holding it up.

They were having dinner. Tuấn was in the living room watching a kung fu movie. From the kitchen, Ben could see Bruce Lee's body flying into the air.

"Where you find that?"

"Outside, by the steps."

"So *that's* where it was." He'd forgotten all about it. After he took the picture, Joseph had switched places with him. In the picture, he stood next to Father Hiệu, a full-teeth smile glowing on his face. After the picture, they let him play volleyball, though he wasn't any help (too short!). He got in the way more than anything else, but the teenagers didn't seem to mind. He held out his hand to his mother.

"Didn't I tell you not to play with these kids? With ông cha Hiệu?"

"But they were playing volleyball. I haven't played volleyball before. And they let me. They let me play with them. I didn't even have to ask. They asked me. What was I supposed to do?" He held out his hand again. He should keep it in his journal. Last year in school, they had to write in a journal once a week for thirty minutes. Ben liked it so much he'd made it a habit all through summer. He would write the day's date in the top corner and glue the picture inside.

But his mother didn't look at him. She went to the drawer and took out a pair of shears, the kind she used to cut through meat. She headed for the trash and began cutting up the Polaroid. Each piece fell heavily. "In Vietnam . . ." she muttered. "Your father . . . In Vietnam . . . Embarrassing . . . Your poor mother . . ."

"Tuấn!" she shouted when there was nothing else left to cut.

"What? Why bring me into this?"

"You're supposed to take care of your brother."

"I do. Who says I don't?" He was in the kitchen now.

"Make sure he doesn't hang out with Cha Hiệu and those other kids," she said. "If only your father was here; he'd be ashamed of all of us."

"It's not like he matters anymore!"

"How can you say that? We sacrificed everything—so you can have a roof over your head in a free country. Have some respect!" She was shaking now. She looked like she was about to say something else but stopped herself. "Eat your dinner," she said and left for her room.

———

For the next several weeks, Ben stayed inside with his brother. They watched TV in the morning, and around lunch Ben would go to his room and read. By the window, he could hear the teenagers and Father Hiệu. Sometimes, they played volleyball. Other times, they played in the bayou.

One day, Tuấn asked if he wanted to play can-ball. Summers past, when they played can-ball, Tuấn would tell Ben about their father. He had black hair like they did, and he had their same long nose. He had big hands—big at least to a five-year-old, which was the last time Tuấn saw their father—and he had a hard spot on this left thumb from writing too much. Yes, he was left-handed— like you, Bình. Sometimes he wore glasses when reading. He was what you would call "bookish" or book smart. He was also kind. Often he came home with candy but only if you answered a question. Sometimes the questions were easy: What is the capital of South Vietnam? (Sài Gòn.) Or: What is the name of the river that passes through the city? (Sông Sài Gòn.) But sometimes you had to think really hard: If a tree falls in the woods but no one is around to hear it, does it make a sound? Is this cup half full or half empty? He was a man who thought a great lot, Tuấn would conclude, and after running out of ways to describe him—or maybe he forgot everything else about him—their can-ball sessions stopped.

Tuấn stood at their doorway with a bat and the plastic bag they used for recycling. They now had not only soda cans but soup cans, too. For quick meals, their mother diluted Campbell's Cream of Mushroom and stirred in rice and peas. None of them liked it, but they ate it anyway.

Ben stood in one end of the small front yard of their apartment (where the adults parked their cars) and Tuấn stood on the other. Ben was the first to bat. They would each have five swings. Like baseball, they had nine rounds. Whoever hit the most cans at the end won. Tuấn wound up his arm. A Coke can was first.

"I haven't done this in a long while," he yelled across the yard, "but I'm not gonna go easy on you, you hear?"

"Show me your best," said Ben. He scuffed up the dirt in front of him with his shoes, the way baseball players did on TV. He spat on the ground.

"Here I go," Tuấn said, spinning his arm. "And here it comes!" He let go and Ben swung and missed. The can flew past him.

"What I tell you?" Tuấn said.

"I was just warming up. Throw me another," Ben said.

Tuấn reached into the bag. A volleyball flew between them and rolled toward Ben. It stopped a few feet short of him as one of the teenagers ran to retrieve it.

"My bad," he said. He kicked the ball up like it was soccer and caught it with both hands. "You can join us if you want, both of you. We're just playing volleyball over there." He pointed to his friends, who waited with their hands on their knees.

Ben looked at Tuấn, and Tuấn hesitated for a second before telling him no. The boy left, running toward his friends.

Tuấn, meanwhile, returned to the bag and dug out a Campbell's can. "They're not having fun anyway," he said, throwing the can up and down. Ben followed its movement. "They're not better," his brother continued, "I'll tell you that much." In a quick motion, Tuấn turned around and threw the can as hard as he could toward the teenagers and the volleyball net. The both of them watched as it sailed through the air and fell soundlessly onto the dirt. It didn't look like anyone noticed at all.

Ben's mother didn't care that Addy and her father were Catholic, the same way she didn't seem to care that Bà Giang was Catholic.

She had met them once during parent-teacher conferences. Ben had introduced them as "my friend" and "my friend's dad." They sat in the hallway waiting for their turn with Mrs. Brownworth. As

Ben and Addy talked about last night's episode of *Punky Brewster*, Ben's mother and Addy's father bonded over the fact that they were both immigrants—how hard it was to get the foods they grew up with, how their kids would never know what it's like to live a difficult life, how easy their kids had it.

But, Addy's father added, what a gift that is—to give your child opportunities you never had, a life you couldn't even dream of.

"But they don't even know how lucky they are!" Ben's mother replied.

Addy's father laughed. "Yes! How true!"

On the bus ride home, Ben's mother told him how she thought Addy and her father were good people.

She allowed him to go over on weekends, and on Saturdays Ben would ride his bike over to Bullard Avenue. Most of the time they played in Addy's tree house. For lunch, they ate ham sandwiches with extra mayonnaise. (They didn't eat mayonnaise at home, so Ben ate as much as he could when he was with Addy.)

Some nights he stayed over, and early the next morning Addy would tell him to stay asleep; they'd be back in an hour. He would look up from the couch where he slept and she would be dressed up in a clean and simple black dress. She wore white stockings and black shoes with buckles. Proud of herself, she would curtsy and spin around to show off. Behind her, her dad would be dressed in tan slacks with a button-up shirt, a tie, and a jacket. Addy's dad painted houses for a living. To see him dressed up for church was a surprise to Ben. When he saw him like that for the first time, Ben wondered if his dad ever dressed up. He tried to picture an Asian man—he had no idea what his own dad looked like since they had no photos of him—in a suit with his hair combed back nicely. He could picture only Father Hiệu.

Addy and her dad went to church at seven in the morning. They would come back by nine, and the three of them would have breakfast together, with Ben staying through lunch.

He saw this happen enough that he got an idea. One Saturday before his sleepover, he packed an extra-large bag, the one Tuấn used for gym class. He packed his regular stuff: clothes, pajamas, toothbrush and toothpaste, a book of ghost stories (because they read them at night with the lights off and a flashlight on), and, without anyone noticing, his special clothes—black pants, a white button-up shirt, and a black jacket, which he'd worn when they became citizens. He didn't have any fancy shoes with buckles the way Addy did, so he just cleaned his sneakers with dish soap in the bathroom. He'd never been to a church before, but he knew it was a serious place. He couldn't wear muddy shoes there. He imagined people sitting in rows and rows of wooden seats, bowing their heads in prayer, all of them with clean shoes.

When his mom asked him why he was bringing a bigger bag, he said they were going to play Sorry!. He even opened it to show her; the Sorry! box lay over his clothes. She inspected it for a long second before telling him to be safe. He hopped on his bike, smiling all the way to Bullard Avenue.

When he saw Addy's dad, he asked if they could go to Our Lady of Saigon. "It's a Catholic church," he told him. He gave him the door hanger and he flipped it over. If he noticed the small bloodstain, now brown, where his mother cut herself, he didn't say anything about it. Addy's dad said, "I've never been to this church before," and took out his map to scan the network of roads.

"It's near Winn-Dixie," Ben offered.

Addy didn't understand what was happening or why he was asking this, but her father smiled then. "We get up at six thirty sharp," he declared. They would all go to Our Lady of Saigon together. For Ben's sake, Addy's father added.

They didn't stay up that night reading scary stories, though it took a long time for Ben to fall asleep. He dreamed of going to church and Father Hiệu standing at a lectern—like the priests did on TV. In the dream, the church was a tall building with stained-glass windows, and the pews were made of dark brown wood. In the front seats, nuns kept their hands together, and Father Hiệu, seeing him enter, nodded his head. After church was over, they were all back in Versailles and had a picnic and played volleyball.

When six thirty came, Ben was already awake. They got dressed and were out of the house at seven.

"Now you see what we do every Sunday," Addy said.

"But different," said her dad.

"But different," she echoed.

All the way, her father kept looking at his map, spread out in the passenger seat. He got lost twice before they found it.

As Father Hiệu had said, it was just a storefront. Still, Ben was disappointed. It wasn't like the church from his dream, and it wasn't like the only other real church he had ever seen, St. Louis Cathedral in Jackson Square. They had always passed it without a second glance, but now he tried to remember what it looked like and how this storefront, with shopping carts left stranded on the sidewalk, disappointed him. Addy's dad parked the car and rushed them out.

"Late," he said. "We're very late. Go, go!"

They ran toward the storefront church and Addy's dad ran ahead to reach the door first. The door creaked as it opened, but no one seemed to notice. They shuffled inside and rushed toward a row of empty metal chairs in the back.

A boom box played organ music as everyone stood. From where he was, at the end of the row, Ben couldn't see anything except that everyone was Vietnamese. He looked across the aisle and saw Joseph. The sun was beaming on him like a spotlight. He wore a blue button-up shirt and a pair of dark blue pants. He had a red tie. His shoes were brown leather, and he bounced back and forth on his heels while mouthing the prayers. Ben couldn't imagine him saying these words; he'd never heard Joseph talk in Vietnamese.

Ben stuck his head out into the aisle and saw Father Hiệu standing in the front next to an older man with white hair wearing an elaborate green robe with gold thread markings that looked almost like a dress but bulkier. Father Hiệu wore a robe, too, but his was white and had no markings. There was no lectern, only a small table that reminded him of the desks at school. A woman walked toward the stage then, holding a book in the air. When she stood behind the table, everyone knew to sit down. She opened the book and read from it. It was all in Vietnamese, of course, and when Addy looked over at him in confusion, he just shrugged. Her dad, meanwhile, stared ahead as if he understood all the words, and when the woman was done he nodded as if in agreement just like everyone else. The woman walked off the stage, the organ music started again, and everyone stood up. Another prayer commenced. Everyone bowed their head and lifted their hands in the air and chanted in a singsong voice. Ben bowed his head and did the same, minus the chanting.

Suddenly, something pulled him out and everything became a blur. He felt nails on his shoulder. He looked behind; his mother's angry face looked back.

"No son of mine," she told him, dragging him out. The prayers stopped abruptly, Ben noticed, and everyone watched. He felt their eyes on him and he felt his face turn red. Joseph was looking at him and so was Father Hiệu from all the way up front, standing on his toes to see over the crowd.

How did she know? Ben was thinking. *How could she possibly know?* He closed his eyes tight. *Maybe,* he was thinking, in the back of his mind, *they can't see me if I don't see them.* It was so quiet, almost silent, except for the dragging of his sneakers across the linoleum floor, that he couldn't believe what was happening until his mother spoke up again.

"You embarrass me," she said. "You embarrass your poor mother. And your father. Your father would not approve."

He shut his eyes even tighter. He would like to know this father.

This father who would not have approved of anything he'd ever done. He would like to meet him and give him a piece of his mind.

Feeling like it was taking an awfully long time to get to the door, Ben opened his eyes. A long black scuff mark followed him on the floor. A trail of guilt. He heard their whispering now. Everyone from Versailles. All of them. He looked up at his mother, who was wearing jeans and a T-shirt. *Jeans* and a *T-shirt,* in a *church*! And her shoes were dirty!

He closed his eyes again and started pinching himself, hoping it was all a dream, that he'd wake up any second and he'd be somewhere he'd never been to before, with a different mother, a different brother, and maybe even a father. He would be sweaty in bed and near tears and they would all surround him lovingly and ask worriedly, "What's going on? What's wrong?" chanting that until they realize he's only had a bad dream. "You're fine now," they'd say. "It was a bad dream. You're fine now, Ben. You're fine!"

He opened his eyes when they were outside and had half a mind to run away. But the look on his mother's face was serious and tired. She didn't bother talking to him or looking his way. She took up her Winn-Dixie bags and he followed her to the bus stop.

Hương

The car purred like a tiger. A vague, blue, metal tiger. The salesman, a người Việt—though Hương didn't ask where he was from—named Vinh, said it was a 1975 Oldsmobile Omega with a 4.3-liter V8 engine, a three-speed automatic, 170 horsepower—old but runs like a dream. A classic!

What this meant, Hương couldn't tell. What she needed, she told Vinh, was something to help her get around. She lived all the way out in New Orleans East; everything else was over the bridge: the grocery stores, the nice restaurants, work. She couldn't keep on borrowing Bà Giang's car.

When Vinh asked her where New Orleans East was, she said it was away from the city—part of it yet not.

"An interesting place," she said. "I live in Versailles. All of us are người Việt; we all came after the war." She guessed the man must be new in town. She'd been seeing new người Việt coming to New Orleans, replacing those who left for Houston or California.

"I don't want anything fancy," she added. "Something that is enough."

"Chị," he said, "you need something pretty and something that lasts long. Something that can take you out of the city, out of the state, but also to work. All in style." He patted the car, then wiped his handprint.

"Bà Giang told me to come here and I won't be cheated," Hương said, "but I'm seeing that I should take my business elsewhere."

"Don't say that, chị . . ." He took a step forward, so she took a step back.

"Hương. Tên tôi là Hương."

"You can trust me, chị Hương. This runs like a dream. Would a fellow người Việt deceive you?"

Yes, she thought, *a fellow người Việt would deceive me.*

"Let me take you for a ride," the salesman added.

"It's too fancy," she said. "What's a V8 engine? What's that? Who needs that? I just need a car. How about another one?" She couldn't understand why car shopping had to take so long, why someone couldn't buy a car like they would buy an apple or a bag of rice. All this chitchat. "What else have you got?"

She took a tissue from her purse and wiped the sweat from her forehead. After all this time working inside an air-conditioned nail salon, she was now unaccustomed to the early July heat.

"This car is the perfect car for you, chị Hương. Why don't you take it for a ride? A ride around the block?"

"Does it have air-conditioning?" Hương asked.

"It does. The best cool air in America." He waved the keys. A small smile lit up his face.

First, Hương drove down small neighborhood roads, then onto Claiborne.

Vinh turned on the radio. "See, chị, this is the radio."

He turned on the air-conditioning. "See, chị, this is the air-conditioning." He pressed down on the horn to show her its vitality, its strength and loudness. "For when you're stuck in traffic," he said.

At one point, while he showed her the space in the glove compartment and flipped through the car manual, she veered off onto a ramp and before she knew it, most of the traffic disappeared. Hương saw a speed limit sign: sixty-five miles an hour.

As Vinh rattled off more car specifications, the city faded from her rearview mirror. Gone were the high buildings, the glass-windowed towers, the concrete. Ten minutes more of driving, and it all disappeared.

A sense of happiness came over Hương as she realized this was the first time in a long time she had left the city by herself. She reminded herself there was more to the world than New Orleans, more than that city. She felt she needed to celebrate as she crossed the city limits. She imagined leaving. Her boys were off at school and they would come home and wait and she would not be there! The next day they wouldn't go to school. They would stay home all week. They would fail their classes. The schools would visit. Not finding her there, they would call. *Ms. Trần,* they'd say, *how could you abandon your sons?* Yes, *abandon,* and all at once she felt guilty for thinking it. How could she abandon her sons? How could she even think of doing that to them? They were all alone in the world. She was just weary; that's what it was—tired, old, and weary.

"Anh Vinh," Hương said, "which way back?"

"You're doing just fine. Do you like the car? That sound you hear means the engine is working great—just great!"

"Anh Vinh," she repeated, "which way back?"

Vinh leaned over the center console and peered into Hương's face and saw the fear in her eyes of driving too far, too fast.

"Chị Hương," he said. "Would you like some longans? They don't sell fresh longans here in the States very much, but there's this woman . . ." He paused and looked out the window, watching the signs pass by. "There's this woman in Buras. She owns an entire orchard of them, an entire orchard of longan trees."

Hương remembered the longan trees of her childhood. She remembered the leaves blowing in a soft breeze, the inescapable fragrance hanging in the air, the sound of rough fruit as it fell to the dirt with a muted thud. She hadn't thought about longans in years.

"Yes," she said, at last. "Longans. Take me to the longan trees."

The drive took over an hour. As she drove, her body sat stiff; she was afraid she would be caught any minute. But the farther away they got, the more relaxed she became. She drove with one hand and leaned back. After a half hour of driving, the radio became static and the two started talking.

Hương told Vinh she was a professor's wife. They, the Communists, called for her husband. After his time in a reeducation camp, they migrated to the countryside. Then they migrated out of the country, or at least that was the plan.

Things got complicated after that. He got left behind as she sailed on. She tried to contact him—she still kept her letters and cassette tapes in a shoebox in her closet—but to no avail. One day, out of the blue, he did write back, telling her to give up her search. At first, she was devastated. But Bà Giang had a different perspective. She said the Communists were monitoring the letters. Yes, Hương could agree on that—but what of it? Most likely, the old woman said, they confiscated the letters and he never saw them, except for the ones he did answer. Maybe, she went on, he stopped writing because he was trying to protect himself; who knew what was going on over there across the ocean, what happened after he sent Hương his final, brief postcard? In the end, perhaps it was fate that they should never meet again. That didn't explain, however,

Công's long silence. If he was truly trying to get to her, get to them, he would have written earlier, wouldn't he? And then there was the night they left. He had paused, she remembered. But perhaps Bà Giang was right: the fates—or whatever force was behind the universe—must have had something else in mind for their destinies. It didn't make it hurt any less, any of it. In fact, it made it hurt more: in the grand scheme of things they'd never stood a chance.

Still, sometimes she wrote to him in the way a schoolgirl might write in a diary; it calmed her, imagining talking to him, giving him her innermost thoughts. *Dear Công, Another day in New Orleans,* she would scribble down. *Your sons are growing up so fast, fast as light, fast as seconds, you wouldn't recognize them because I don't. They are not like you and I don't know what to do.*

She didn't say any of this to Vinh (he was a stranger, after all) and simply said things got complicated. Life is already complicated, she said, and when you add war to that, no one gets what they want.

Vinh agreed. He told Hương he'd been in the South Vietnamese Army.

"The South Vietnamese Amy," he said, "was the best army there ever was in the world." After the war, they sent him to a reeducation camp. "When I left Vietnam for good, I first went to Malaysia, then to Alaska, then Oregon, then Texas, and now here!" He sounded like he wanted to say more, but Hương didn't urge him on. Besides, he told her they were almost there; just take the next exit and get on Highway 11.

The trees on the highway gave way to flat wetlands, empty of everything except water and mud. Hương felt the need to slow down—the land was bereft, holy even—but Vinh said to keep up the speed.

When they came to an old trailer house, Vinh motioned her to stop, so Hương parked the car and they got out.

Vinh walked leisurely as they passed the house and into the backyard. He knew this place; he walked confidently and knew where he was going. Hương tried not to slip in the mud as Vinh told her the woman who owned the orchard was from the Philippines. She wondered how Vinh and the woman knew each other.

In the backyard, to Hương's surprise, trees stood in rows and rows, everywhere. Her mouth opened in astonishment. There must have been hundreds of them, and each stood heavy with leaves—and longans, bunches of longans, hanging there among the leaves. She wanted to grab them all, carry them in her arms, bring them home.

Vinh led her to a table and tent to the side of the orchard. The blue of the tent made everything inside seem underwater. There, a small, elderly, brown woman sat alone peeling longans. A radio played old jazz as she worked. The woman looked up when they approached.

"Longans!" she said. "We have longans! So many!" Suntanned skin, wrinkle lines, and small smiling eyes—she could have been someone's grandmother, someone's great-grandmother, even.

"You back again!" the woman said to Vinh. The woman clapped and let out a laugh. "I told you—longans really good! Good for health! Longevity!" She looked at Hương and nodded her head. "You try longans?" she asked. "Good for health! Longevity! Beauty! Here, here, here!" The old woman picked up a longan and pushed her thumb into the fruit. Once the rough exterior gave way, she began shucking the shell-like skin.

"See?" she said when all that was left was a thick white ball. She held it up and turned it around like she was a showgirl on a game show—*What a wonderful fruit! A most gorgeous fruit! This fruit could be yours!* She reminded Hương of Vinh in the car lot.

"They called 'dragon eyes' because the seed—the seed big, black, shiny—look like eye of dragon," she said. She handed Hương the fruit.

From her hand, Hương could already smell the sweetness. She remembered the subtle crunch it made when you bit into it, the feel of the seed in the mouth, rolling like a marble on the tongue when all the flesh was swallowed. Hương held it gently and bit into it slowly, wanting the flavor to last, wanting to picture herself in an orchard, so very much like this one, on the outskirts of Mỹ Tho, the hot, aching sun warming her neck, the juices of the fruit cooling and giving her relief from the heat, a time that was simpler, before war, before marriage, before the fall of a country. . . .

She put the rest of the longan in her mouth and chewed.

What refreshment, she thought. *What pleasure. What memory.*

Vinh handed her a cluster of longans still hanging on their branch. She felt their roughness, then his warm skin as it touched hers. She wanted to bring a whole bag home, for Tuấn, who hadn't had these in so long, and for Bình, who never had.

"Thank you," she said. "Thank you, anh Vinh."

Hương did not buy Vinh's car. She decided on a cheaper one from the dealership that sat across from his, but it wasn't the last she saw of him.

One Saturday, she drove by to see if he was in. Coincidentally, he told her, it was his lunch break, and she said she knew a sandwich place down on Magazine Street, if that wasn't too far. She said she could drive them there in her new car.

At Casamento's they both ordered oyster loafs and cans of Barq's.

"This was the first American sandwich place I went to when I got here," she told Vinh. "We went out on a group lunch and I didn't know what I was getting. So imagine how surprised I was when they bring out this behemoth." She pointed to her own sandwich, two thick cuts of white bread trying to contain a mountain of fried oysters. "It's not the best sandwich I've ever had, but it brings back memories. But don't tell anyone here that."

Vinh said he'd never been to any place that took food more seriously than New Orleans. He said he once made the mistake of calling a muffuletta just a sandwich, and the cashier—a petite-looking woman with a scratchy voice—refused to give him his food.

Hương laughed. "Yes, that sounds about right."

"Why here? Why New Orleans? Why stay?" Vinh asked.

"I could ask you the same question, anh Vinh," Hương replied, and then, "We just ended up here and we never left. But you, you're a traveler, anh Vinh. Why New Orleans?"

"I go where the jobs are," he said. "Simple as that."

There was more to that. Hương saw it in his eyes, as if he were waiting for her to ask him to tell more. But she didn't press him. She knew everyone had their own pasts they wanted to leave behind. Not secrets, exactly, but something to be guarded just the same, with some guarding it more urgently than others. It gave her a vague feeling that they were the same type of people.

After lunch, she drove him back.

Every weekend, somehow, she found herself on that side of town and he was always working then, too. She drove them to her favorite places in New Orleans—"Think of it as a welcome gift," she said—and they alternated who paid.

It was when they were strolling along the river walk, eating ice cream cones, that she realized this had become her city, the place she lived but also a place that lived in her. She'd picked up its vocabulary, developed a taste for its foods, grown accustomed to its weather—the heat, the humidity, even the minor hurricane here and there. She remembered how scared she was when she first arrived, how she clutched her belongings (and her sons) close to her, afraid that something might happen. Nowadays, she walked freely, unafraid.

Vinh pointed to the St. Louis Cathedral looming across the street. "It's been forever since I've been to a church," he said.

"I wasn't raised with religion" was all Hương said. "Though everyone in Versailles seems pretty religious. They even built their own church with everything in Vietnamese—services, Bibles, pamphlets. But I don't understand." If war had taught her one thing, it was that ideology—how you believed the world should be, what you would die to uphold—was always flawed, and though innocent on its own, it could lead to tragedy.

"For me it's always been a private matter," Vinh said as if feeling Hương's uneasiness.

"That's all I ask," she said. They had been quiet for a while when she said, "They give tours. We can go."

"No, that's fine," Vinh replied.

"If you want."

"No, truly," he said and took her hand.

Together they walked back to the car.

What kind of man are you, anh Vinh? Hương thought along the way but didn't ask.

Ben

en grew suspicious when his mother told him to call the man Uncle Vinh and said he was going stay with them for a week. He was going through bad times because he'd lost his job, she said. Uncle Vinh wasn't family, but they should treat him as if he were.

Vinh came in during the first heat wave in years, and the temperatures were over one hundred degrees. A fan blew in the living room because the AC was out. Vinh told them, Ben and Tuấn, he came from Galveston and Coos Bay and Homer—Texas, Oregon, Alaska.

Ben questioned his story like Ben questioned everything else. "How can you *be* from so many places?" he asked. "You can't be from two places, let alone three." Vinh looked at him as if he didn't understand his words, so Ben said instead, "You're lying."

"I never lie," Vinh said. To prove it, he showed them his tattoos, his travel marks: the head of a longhorn with smoke puffing out its nostrils on his right arm; a majestic red salmon flying

above the water on his left; on his chest, a bear, huffing and puffing, its eyes red, its teeth showing like it was hungry and ready
to gorge. Watching Vinh, Ben saw how different they were. There
were bumps and grooves of muscle instead of flatland flesh and
xylophone rib bones, and most of his skin, exposed to the sun, was
tanned to a darkness. But underneath his shirt, Vinh's color was
the same as Ben's, a pale caramel, like they, the both of them, were
made of the same clay. He wanted to stand closer to Vinh, but Tuấn
took a step forward and poked a finger at the bear.

"That's the funniest thing I've ever seen," he said. "What you
gonna get while you're here, a stork? A Louisiana stork?"

"It's a pelican," Ben interrupted. "The state bird is a pelican,
stupid."

Tuấn continued, "That's not a tattoo. It's a teddy bear." He
stopped laughing when Vinh grabbed him by the shoulder. Ben
saw his fingers making craters on his brother's skin.

"Respect your elders, child," Vinh said.

For a second it looked like Tuấn was in pain. Then it looked
like he was annoyed. With a push, Vinh let go and pulled his shirt
back on.

"What do you kids know, anyway?" Vinh mumbled.

Their mom walked in from the kitchen, chopsticks in hand. It
was one of her days off. She pointed the sticks at her sons.

"There won't be any fighting in my house," she said. The scent
of sizzling fish and chili peppers wafted into the living room. "Pretend Uncle Vinh is family. Pretend this for your poor old mother.
Tuấn, don't push Uncle Vinh."

"I didn't push him. He pushed me."

"Just do this one thing for your mother. Làm ơn!"

Ben carried Vinh's suitcase down the hall and showed him the
room he and his brother shared. With one foot, he slid over a pile
of books from the library. Unlike elementary school, the middle

school let you check out as many books as you wanted; he'd stuff his backpack with mystery novels, sci-fi stories, and Choose Your Own Adventures until he couldn't fit any more in.

Ben set the suitcase down. It wasn't heavy, at least not in the way he expected for someone who'd packed up his life and moved across the country. He must have left in a hurry or he didn't have many things. Ben let go of the handle, hoping the suitcase would drop and fall over, the flimsy locks opening to reveal the contents; but it didn't.

"This is our room," he told Vinh. He pointed to a bed against one wall. "That's my bed, but that's where you'll sleep." He pointed to Tuấn's bed. "I'll share with Tuấn." They were both twin beds. In earlier years, Tuấn and Ben shared one bed. Tuấn said Ben took up too much space, and in the middle of the night Tuấn would hold him in headlocks, squeeze him at the throat with his knees, or push him against the wall. One time, frustrated with it all, Ben bit his brother on the arm and left a mark that didn't disappear for months. It wasn't until Ben was five that they got the second bed.

"Nice view," Vinh said, opening the window. He leaned against the bars that covered half of the window.

"You gotta be kidding me, right?" Ben said. "It's ugly here. I don't know why anyone would ever want to come here." He joined Vinh and looked out at the dead grass and the mud. And beyond that, the bayou, where a plastic trash can floated in aimless circles. It was time someone went out and got that, but no one ever did anything. "I mean on purpose," he added.

Vinh tapped his hands on the bars and laughed. "I won't be here long," he said. "I'm just a guest." He went to his suitcase and opened it. In the next instant, Ben was disappointed to see only clothes and not many of those, either. Vinh pulled off his T-shirt to change into another one. And again, that same skin flashed before Ben's eyes before it was replaced by two large owl eyes and the word HOOTERS.

"Just call me Vinh, no 'Uncle,'" Vinh said.

———

That first night, Ben couldn't sleep. He felt eyes on him, though his nose was pressed against the wall. Tuấn's sweaty back, slick and pungent, pressed against him. For the first few minutes, he tried to push back, but his brother didn't budge.

He must have lain awake for hours before he heard the springs on the other bed move. When the padding of feet faded, Ben climbed over his brother, bounced on the hardwood, and stood for a minute looking into the dark.

Vinh was gone. The sheets lay disheveled, the door open.

Walking into the hallway, Ben saw light under his mother's door. At first he hesitated. But when he heard his mother and Vinh talking, he walked closer, trying to make out what they were saying. At the door, he squatted and aligned his eye with the keyhole.

Nothing—he could see nothing.

"Vinh," he heard his mother say. They both laughed. His mother was happy. As far as he knew, she was never happy. She went to work and came home and cooked dinner and went to her room, where she sometimes watched *Paris by Night* and listened to Vietnamese folk music on cassette tapes. Unlike other parents, even Addy's dad, she didn't go to PTA meetings or parent-teacher conferences, at least not any longer. And you could forget about parties like Versailles Day or Mardi Gras. She didn't even buy king cakes anymore. (Too expensive, she would say when he asked.)

Her present happiness made the air feel electric, made it hum and vibrate. It made him realize that perhaps she was lonely all this time. She needed a friend. He almost smiled, but when the sound of bare feet hit the floor, he made to run back to the room. The door opened and Vinh came out. Hoping he wasn't found, Ben detoured into the bathroom and slammed the door. He let the water run for a good minute before coming back out.

At school, Ben talked to Addy about Vinh. He told her about the tattoos, about Alaska, about the whispering in the middle of the night.

"He sounds interesting," Addy said.

It was after school and they were waiting for Thảo, Tuấn's girlfriend. Thảo was a year older than Tuấn and gave Tuấn rides because he didn't have a car. Since Ben's school was on the way home, they picked him up, too.

"Is he good or is he bad?" Addy asked.

"I don't know," Ben said. "He's supposed to be gone by the end of the week."

"Then what?"

A white van pulled in to the parking lot.

"He's on his own. He's new to New Orleans, he said. He hasn't got a tattoo from here yet."

"Is he staying?" Addy asked. "I mean, is he staying in the city?"

"Don't know."

"Maybe," Addy began, "he might be your new dad?"

"Gross! Don't say that, Addy!" Ben stuck out his tongue. He couldn't imagine his mother falling in love. She was not the type to believe in love. Love didn't pay the bills. It didn't cook dinner. It didn't provide for a family. For all intents and purposes, love was too impractical.

The van pulled up and its front passenger window rolled down.

"In," Thảo said. She played with the rearview mirror and readjusted her bandanna around her hair. The speakers blasted a song with flamenco guitars and heavy maracas and bongos. The lyrics were in Chinese. " 'In,' I said," Thảo said, this time in Vietnamese.

"What happened to your other car?" Ben asked.

"Fire."

"Fire?" Since he'd met her, Ben had the feeling Thảo was a liar.

She was quick and invariably had an explanation for everything. They always sounded unlikely. "What kind of fire?" Ben asked.

Thảo rolled her eyes. "A big fire," she said. "Now, the both of you, get in."

Ben opened the side door and found Tuấn sprawled across the middle row. "Move over," he said.

"Sit in the back," said Tuấn. He lifted his head, then dropped it back. He laid a Saints cap, which he got last Mardi Gras, on top of his face. As Tuấn had been walking in the Quarter, it fell off a balcony and landed right on his head, at least according to Thảo.

"How's your father, Adelaide?" Tuấn asked, his voice muffled.

"Fine, Tuấn."

"How's his painting business coming along?"

"He's fine, just fine."

"What's with the attitude? Can't a brother ask? All I'm saying is that I haven't seen him in a while. That's all I'm saying."

"He's fine," she repeated.

"Walgreens run!" Thảo said, making a sharp left turn. A car honked its horn and Thảo cussed at it in Vietnamese. She parked the car in a handicap spot and unlocked the door. "Bình," Thảo said (she called Ben only by his Vietnamese name), "why don't you get whatever you want? I'll pay for both you and Addy."

"Why don't you two go in, too?" Ben asked.

Thảo reached into her purse and pulled out a crumpled ten. "You can keep the change," she said. "Get a Coke for me," Thảo added. "Tuấn, what do you want?" She slapped his knee. "Get him nothing."

Inside, a white man stood by the cash register reading a magazine. When he saw them come in, he laid it down.

"We're not no hangout for kids, you know," the man said.

"We're just getting sodas," Ben said, projecting his voice. "Just keep walking," he whispered to Addy.

The man raised his voice. "We're not no hangout. If you come in here, you have to buy something. Are you buying something?"

"Yes, sir. We're buying, sir." Ben shook his head.

Someone else came in. The man went back to his magazine.

Through the glass door, Ben couldn't see Thảo's van anymore. He didn't like Thảo. He'd first met her when she came over to Versailles to pick up Tuấn. Their mother wasn't home and Tuấn invited her in for Café Du Monde coffee. As they let it brew, Thảo said chicory coffee was good for hangovers. They talked about the party they both went to the night before and how late she had stayed and how much Tuấn missed out for not staying. Ben was struck by her beauty—her highlighted hair, her pink fingernails, and her sense of fashion: she wore a plaid skirt and white blouse and leather cowboy boots that went up to her knees. Despite this, there was an unexpected roughness about her. She was loud and wore a suspicious smirk. Worst of all, she made Tuấn act weird. He became meaner to everyone when she was around, as if he was competing with her. Their mom didn't like Thảo, either. "If you ever bring home a girl like that," she would say, "I'll chop off your hands," though Ben didn't know what hands had to do with anything.

After Ben paid for their sodas, they walked outside but couldn't find the van.

"They could've parked somewhere else," Addy reassured him.

There were two sedans, a blue private-school bus, a bike tied to a lamppost, but no van.

They walked behind the store, where the dumpster sat, and there they found the van alongside a yellow sports car. Tuấn and Thảo were standing and talking to a group of older Asian boys. When they saw Ben and Addy, they hushed and looked at Tuấn.

One of them said something in Vietnamese and slapped Tuấn on the chest. "Em bé mày"—your baby brother—was the only thing Ben could understand. The older boys cackled. All of them wore matching black tank tops. Most of them had tattoos on their arms. When he took another step, Ben noticed one of them had a gun strapped to his belt. Another had a gun hanging out of his back pocket. Another held one by his side. All of them had guns except Tuấn and Thảo.

"Tuấn, watch out!" Ben began, but his brother stampeded over and grabbed him by the arm.

"What's wrong?" Ben asked. "Who are those boys?"

Tuấn pulled Ben and squeezed his arm tighter. When they were out of sight of the boys, Tuấn released his grip.

"Don't you ever do that again!" Tuấn said.

"Do what? What do you mean? What did I do?" Ben dropped the bag and the soda bottles began rolling. He started to go after them, but Tuấn pushed him down.

"Don't you ever do that again," he said, yelling so loud this time his spit sprayed the air.

Vinh stayed with them past the end of the first week. He stayed another week. Then another.

He was always there when they got home; they'd find him sitting in their kitchen and drinking coffee, Vietnamese style, or he'd be sleeping in their room. When Vinh came to, he would look startled, then a smile would grow across his face and he'd ask them if they were hungry or if they wanted anything to drink. He played host in their own house.

He'd fix them something—noodles or rice, chrysanthemum tea or Tang—make small talk, and then return to sleep shirtless as his chest inflated and deflated and the bear tattoo grew and shrank.

Ben was fascinated. He learned Vinh used to be a fisherman, a farmhand, and a used-car salesman. He was fired from all of them, he said. Vinh liked to watch boxing on TV and didn't like spicy food. That he was Catholic surprised Ben the most. His mother did not seem to like Catholics as a whole, though she made exceptions for those she liked. She tolerated his praying voice each night before bed, a singsong voice that was melodic and sad. Vinh went to church on Sundays, too, walking to Our Lady of Saigon late in the morning instead of borrowing Ben's mother's car or taking the bus because, Vinh said, walking gave him fresh air and time for reflection.

Ben wrote a story for school about a man who went from town to town, marrying widows and stealing their most precious items—a metal urn of a husband's ashes, a wedding band that was no longer worn but still cherished, a wedding day photo with a bride and groom smiling. In the story, Ben made a twist: the man was misunderstood. He stole these pieces of personal history because he had lost his own; he had amnesia and wanted to make a new life.

As Vinh slept one afternoon, Ben went through his suitcase. The only thing of interest was his wallet. Vinh still had an Alaska driver's license. There was also a credit card, a stick of cinnamon gum, ten dollars in ones, and a card with what Ben concluded was the Virgin Mary on one side and a prayer in Vietnamese on the other. Disappointed, Ben put the wallet back where he'd found it.

How could a man, unbound by life and responsibilities, be so boring? If Ben were to leave, he would collect everything he could find, keepsakes of a life lived and lived well. It dawned on him that Vinh was a silly old man. He would never be like him, didn't want anything to do with him. It made him sad for his mother.

Was his own father anything like Vinh? Did she go out of her way to get his favorite beer? Did she make his favorite desserts on her days off? Did he make her smile the same way? And did they take long walks in the evening, strolling into the sunset, two figures hand in hand? He would never know.

For a brief time he thought Vinh might be his actual father—not dead after all these years but miraculously alive—and his mom was just waiting for the right moment to reveal the truth: she was wrong and he hadn't been killed. They had the same skin color, after all. A part of him waited for the revelation. He imagined himself acting surprised, then blushing bashfully because he'd confess he knew all along. *Smart boy,* they'd call him, and afterward they would all go to Gambino's to celebrate.

But everything was wrong—the nose was fat, not thin and long; he didn't wear glasses; his hands were big, but where was that hard callus from writing on the left? The theory would not hold up. He threw it away.

The next afternoon, Tuấn and Thảo were late. The buses came and left. Soon the parking lot was empty, too. Mrs. Easton, the music teacher, asked if they needed a ride home. Addy said yes, but Ben said they were waiting for his mother to pick them up. Mrs. Easton said, "Great," and left.

Thảo always came on time. She was punctual if nothing else. When the sun was setting and the shadows of birds flew into the distance, Ben became anxious. Addy made him more anxious.

"What if there was a car crash? What if your brother did something wrong? What if *she* did something wrong?"

"Like what?" Ben asked.

"I don't know," Addy said. "Rob a bank? She's the type who would rob a bank."

"Yes," Ben agreed. "Yes, she is." He smirked, imagining Thảo and his brother robbing a bank, Thảo with her southern twang and Tuấn with his mangled accent like their mother's. "Maybe there's an accident and they're stuck in traffic," he said.

"That girl is an accident," Addy said. Ben laughed and they high-fived each other.

As it got later, Ben imagined Tuấn dumping Thảo—that was why he was late. He didn't have a ride but he was walking. Hours later, into the night, even, his brother would arrive at the school. "Let's walk home," he'd say. And they'd walk and talk. They hadn't talked in a long time. It was like he didn't know who his brother was anymore. *God,* he thought, *Thảo is terrible; girls are terrible!*

An hour later, Thảo's van pulled up. She unlocked the door and waited for Ben and Addy to hop in. Inside, Tuấn was lying in his seat, a T-shirt covering his face. He didn't say anything. Ben closed the door.

"How you feeling?" Thảo asked Tuấn when they got back on the road. He let out a groan and Thảo snickered. She turned up the music and made a right-hand turn.

After Thảo dropped them off, Ben saw the bruised eye, the right one circled in purple and black.

Ben gasped. "What happened?"

"Shut up, will you?"

"Was it a fight or something?"

"Open the door," his brother said.

"Was it Thảo? Did Thảo do this?" After Ben said it, he realized how stupid it sounded, a girl beating up a boy. "Thảo did something," he said after a pause. "Thảo's fault. It's all Thảo's fault, isn't—"

"Open the door, will you? Stop being gay already!"

Ben unlocked the door. Vinh was doing push-ups in the living room when they walked in. He looked up, stopped his routine, and walked over. When he got to them, he placed his hand on Tuấn's face.

"Trời ổi. Your mother won't be pleased." He touched the bruise, and Tuấn turned his head away.

"It wasn't my fault. It wasn't," Tuấn said.

"You shouldn't be fighting. Especially if you can't."

"Shut up," Tuấn said. "You're not my father!"

Not my father, Ben repeated in his head. *Not my father,* as if it was a useful phrase.

Vinh ruminated over the words, and, amused, he went to the freezer and filled a plastic grocery bag with ice. When he came back, he guided Tuấn to the couch and eased the cold bag over the eye.

"Rest," Vinh said, "but don't let this happen again."

After several minutes, Tuấn left for his room and Vinh followed after. The last thing Ben heard was Vinh telling Tuấn, "Let me tell you something, son," before they both disappeared into the bedroom.

Later his mom told Vinh Tuấn should've known better than getting into a fight. She had told him before—don't engage, look the other way, move on.

"I try so hard," his mother said, "to raise them right. You've no idea. If something were to ever happen . . . I don't know. It's my job to keep them out of trouble, to make sure they become good people." She paused. "Their father . . ." she said, and trailed off. She stood up and her voice became muffled as she walked across the room. "These letters . . . They would be devastated if they knew. That's why . . ."

Ben strained to hear more and waited a few more seconds before giving up and walking back to his room. He climbed in beside Tuấn, who lay belly-up with a cool, wet paper towel on his bruised eye. Ben couldn't sleep that night, and Vinh didn't come back to his bed.

Tuấn

The Southern Boyz said Tuấn was a good recruit. He did what he was told. He knew where to be and when. Tuấn was a good man, and they trusted him. And Quang, smoking a cigarette, said his new nickname should be "Handy" because he was useful.

"Hey, *Handy!*" said Sáng, testing out the name in his thick accent, which made it sound like "Hon-dee." He twirled his Heineken bottle to see how much beer he had left. "*Hon-dee,* come over here. *Hon-dee,* go run this over to Quang." Everybody giggled.

Tuấn lifted his bottle to his lips. Already, he could feel his cheeks heat up and redden. He rubbed at the scruff on his face—an attempt to look older—to hide his blushing, though he was sure the beer made him glow.

They were in Quang's laundry shed behind his house. The three of them gathered around a roughed-up coffee table with ring marks from sweaty bottles and cans and cups while Thảo was out getting more beers. They were all under twenty-one, but Thảo could sweet-talk the toughest of them; Thảo always got what she wanted. The washing machine was going, banging itself against the concrete floor, so Tuấn got up and kicked it a couple of times, which did the trick.

When he sat back down, Quang, the King of the Southern Boyz, placed his empty bottle on the table and leaned back into his chair.

"But, Tuấn," he said, his voice becoming serious, "you still have to prove yourself. Do *something* for the team." The way he said "something" made the word sound heavy and foreign. Quang took a drag of his cigarette. He held it like a Vietnamese man, or so he claimed, with three fingers instead of two the way they did back in the Motherland, though none of them had seen Vietnam in a very long time. "Then," he went on, "you can be part of the *gia đình*."

That word. Tuấn noticed it every time. Quang never called them a gang, though they were that and a notorious one, too. (They even made it to the front page of the *Times-Picayune*—twice. Once for arson and another for a home robbery down in Uptown, both before Tuấn's time with them.) Quang never called them a gang; it was always *family*. And soon, Tuấn saw it was true. They took care of one another. They were there for one another. If someone messed with you, you just tell the Boyz and they'd nod and they'd grin and you know you could consider it taken care of. Sure, they fought and argued sometimes, but what family didn't? He felt at home in Quang's laundry shed more than in his own apartment, where his mother was always tired, annoyed, or dissatisfied (something was always wrong: his behavior; the obnoxious tourists in the Quarter, who she felt invaded an otherwise decent city; the other people who lived in Versailles—including those who moved away, abandoning their apartments and letting vines grow on the walls and bricks turn green, making a place where hooligans from all of New Orleans East trespassed to get high), and his brother lazed around, reading books while sprawled out on the bed with a blank, bored look on his face—a type of dissatisfaction of life in itself. And then there was Vinh, his mom's boyfriend. Tuấn didn't know what to do with Vinh. He was supposed to stay with them for a week but then ended up just staying. He felt like an extra organ on a body, like a third arm or an additional leg. The man—his habits, his ideas, his being—didn't mesh with the rest of their family. To add to that, Vinh stayed home day and night, becoming a persistent presence that made home feel less like home.

Tuấn was through with all of that. The Southern Boyz offered the opposite of that—meaning camaraderie, family.

"Do something," Quang repeated and picked up a bottle cap from the table. He began flipping it in the air. Three throws and he let it fall to the floor, where it bounced off the concrete and went rolling in a circle before settling.

"What?" Tuấn sat up in his chair. His pulse raced. To be part of this family, to get that tattoo—the crescent moon–shaped outline of Vietnam with SBZ written vertically—Tuấn knew he would do anything. "Anything. Nói đi," he said.

"Wei Huang Market," said Quang, "on Bourbon." Just then the door opened.

"Trời ơi," said Thảo. "Hôi quá. Smoke outside, y'all. How many times have I told you?"

"It's my place," Quang said. "I do what I want."

Thảo coughed. With a case of Heineken in her arms, she walked over to Quang and grabbed his cigarette. She took a quick drag before throwing it on the floor and crushing it beneath her cowboy boots. The leather was as thick as Tuấn imagined it would have been if it was freshly cut from a cow; its deep brown color reminded him of dry blood. "Help me with this, will you?" she said, tapping the box with her fingers.

"Good haul," said Sáng, reaching for the case.

"I got a discount," she replied.

The story from Quang is, the Southern Boyz, as it is now, started in 1975, when the first Vietnamese refugees were just settling in the States, to protect them from being taken advantage of in their new home. But if you wanted to really understand the Southern Boyz, Quang said, you had to know its full story, and it starts during the American War. "Which is what we call the war over there," said Quang, who liked to tell this story around a bonfire when the whole family was over on summer nights.

"The Americans were leaving our Motherland behind. And the Communists, they were coming, you see? So these men, they set up a militia of their own to protect the women and the children, because it is always the women and the children. These men, they called themselves Lực Lượng Miền Nam. The Southern Force. They watched over Saigon and all the other Southern towns. But the thing was, they pretended they were like other people. No special uniforms or anything. That way, the Communists didn't know who they were, and when they least expected it, they attacked.

"But, of course, they had to leave like the rest of us. Still, they promised no one would ever hurt their people again. This I heard from a man on the boat, Chú Long. He came to New Orleans with us, too, where he continued the Southern Force, but with a new name.

"Remember a couple of years ago," Quang continued, "when Ông Nguyễn the fisherman and his men were vandalized: CHING CHONG GO HOME? Remember what happened to those three white fishermen?"

Everyone nodded. Everyone knew. One night, after a successful haul from the Gulf, the fishermen went to a bar in Bayou St. John. They were so drunk by the time two o'clock in the morning came, they were stumbling out onto St. Philip Street. It was when they turned the corner, down a street without light, that they were attacked. The fishermen were found lying out on North Lopez Street the next morning, bruised and bloodied; one was missing a front tooth.

"It was a sign to these men," said Quang. "Don't fuck with us!"

Here, you can imagine Quang squeezing the rest of the lighter fluid into the fire and the flames jumping wildly and the bottle itself dropping into the heat, where the white plastic melted. He lit up a cigarette. "Can you imagine how life would be if we weren't here? If men like Chú Long never came to New Orleans with us? What kind of world would this be? That kind of world is the kind of world I don't want to live in."

Tuấn nodded. Yes, it was something to believe in. Yes.

When Vinh told him the Southern Boyz were bad news, Tuấn told him this history with pride as if it were his own. Vinh laughed in his face and called him gullible. "Those boys don't know anything," Vinh said. "Just a bunch of kids playing. You want to know the real story about Vietnam."

"I know the story," Tuấn said.

"But you don't," Vinh said.

Wei Huang Market was one of the last Asian grocery stores left on the 500-block of Bourbon Street. It was where Tuấn's mother went because it carried the rare Asian foods she couldn't find anywhere else: fish sauce, lemongrass, sticky rice. In its small space, it seemed to have everything.

Madame Wei, a seventy-something-year-old woman who wore her gray hair in a bun, ran Wei Huang by herself even after all the Chinese shops on Bourbon Street left. The business was her father's. Her brother had inherited it, but he left. So did everyone else. Everyone except Madame Wei. If it had not been for the Vietnamese coming, Tuấn had heard her say, years ago when they started shopping there, Wei Huang would be out of business.

But Wei Huang was bad for the Vietnamese of New Orleans, said Quang. Though it was in the Quarter and they were out east, people are creatures of habit and would continue to buy from her despite the Vietnamese-run groceries right in their backyard. This was why Tuấn was sent. To give her a message so violent that she would pack up and go away. *Sayonara, China Lady*—or whatever it was they said.

"Người Trung Quốc don't like us anyway," Quang added. "Know our history," he said. "Know *your* history." The Chinese, Tuấn learned, occupied Vietnam for a thousand years. Then came the French.

The next week, in the afternoon, Tuấn walked down Bourbon. Wei Huang sat between a liquor store and a shop selling souvenirs. As he came up on it, Tuấn slowed his pace. With his head down, he moved his eyes toward the window. The shop was empty, except for Madame Wei, who stood reading behind the counter at the front. The loud teenagers in the souvenir store next door made Wei Huang look and feel emptier. He walked into the souvenir store—the Fleur de Lis Gift Shoppe, one of maybe four in the Quarter—and pretended he was interested in the spinning rack of bike license plates. All of them had names not like his: Ted, Tom, Tommy, Tony. The teenagers giggled some more.

Quang told him to first scan out the place during the daytime. Then, later, at night, when she was about to close, come in with a weapon. Threaten the old hag. Knock stuff to the ground. Smash her window. Tell her to give you money. And when you're done, tell her who you are and where you're from and what you're about. Tell her all of this so she knows, that old woman, that this isn't her territory. Not any longer. Tuấn pictured himself yelling at Madame Wei, who was shorter than he was and who wore wire-frame glasses.

"Not anymore," he would say. "This is not your place anymore. Out!" he'd screech. "Out!"

It would be easy, wouldn't it? He'd fought younger, stronger guys before. Big Black boys with bulging muscles. Sweaty Mexicans who thought they were big shots and sprayed over the SBZ signs across town. An old lady? He would only have to scream and she'd run.

A white man with a neat haircut came up to him then. "Having trouble finding your name?" he asked. The man wore a name tag. Tuấn didn't see his name, but he saw CO-MANAGER. "What's the name?" the man said. "We can see if we have it." The man bent over to inspect the license plates. "Is it Tommy? You might be a Tommy. You know, we have other names in the back, too. I can check. You can't leave New Orleans without a souvenir!" The man smiled.

"No," Tuấn said. He shook his head. "Never mind."

He walked out of the store and past Wei Huang again. The neon sign on her window didn't light up anymore and there were oily handprints on the glass. Inside, Madame Wei was now eating lunch next to the cash register. Then, out of the corner, a familiar figure came toward the counter with a two-liter bottle of Coco Rico soda, the kind his mother used for cooking. Vinh. He stopped at a case and grabbed a bag of bean sprouts. He said something and Madame Wei laughed. As she began ringing him up, Vinh took out a pen and a small pad and wrote something down or crossed something out. His eyes scanned the store and stopped at the window.

Tuấn began running as Vinh came to the door.

"Tuấn," Vinh called.

Tuấn looked back and saw Vinh standing on the sidewalk. When he turned back straight ahead, he bumped into a tourist and they both fell.

"Sorry," Tuấn said. "Sorry, sorry." He helped the woman up. He was about to start running again, but a hand gripped his shoulder. He tried to shake it off, but it was too strong.

"Tuấn," Vinh said. "What you doing here? Don't you have school?"

"Let go!" He tried to pull away.

"What you doing here?" Vinh repeated.

"I could ask you the same. What you doing here?"

"I'm a free man," Vinh said, and laughed.

"I'm eighteen. That makes me an adult. Let go!" It made him feel like a child again, begging to be let go. He pulled harder. Vinh tightened his grip. "Let go. I'm an adult! You can't do this to me."

"Eighteen, but you're still a boy. Still a kid."

"You can't tell me what to do. You're not my father!" Tuấn said. Did he scream it? Was everyone looking now? Where was the tourist he ran into? A sense of embarrassment came over him. His face was red, he knew. He closed his eyes. "You're no one, Vinh. God, you're nothing."

Vinh let go, and, suddenly released, Tuấn fell down heavily.

"Kid" was all Vinh said in a shaky voice, as if a nerve had been hit, and walked away.

Two nights later, everything was planned.

Quang gave Tuấn a steel bat. Wei Huang closed at ten. At 9:55, Tuấn would arrive at the store. Madame Wei would be standing behind her counter. She might be reading her book or she might be closing up, counting her money. Tuấn would push the door, and as it opened there would be the sound of the bell tied to the door. *Ting-ding!* Madame would look up from whatever she was doing. "Oh, allo!" she would say. "We about to close. Can I help?" And Tuấn would say, "No. I'm just getting back from baseball practice and was hungry. Can I look around?" To this, Madame would answer, "Yes," because she never says no and she is not one to be rude. And anyway, extra money—like a dollar for a snack—is a dollar she wouldn't otherwise have, and because the Chinese are greedy, greedy people, she would wait. If she was counting money, maybe she tries to hide it. Meanwhile, Tuấn would walk around. It is a small shop. Just four walls and a long shelf in the middle. After one loop around, he would come back to the counter, empty-handed except the bat, which by now he is swinging threateningly.

"Are you looking for something?" she would ask, pushing up her glasses, which would be greasy, too, because the Chinese are not a clean people. "Oh, me?" Tuấn would say. Then he would raise the bat and bring it down on the glass counter. *Crash!* Next, he would bring it down on her display case, shattering the glass in one swift movement. *Slam!* Finally, he would smash down that annoying waving cat on the counter. She would be screaming now and asking you what is it you want. Is it money? And it is now that you explain. You explain everything to her: you tell her who you are and where you're from and what you're about. And she would understand. She would run out of the store, arms waving in the air. Wei Huang would be closed the next day. It would disappear in the next week. It would be replaced by another souvenir shop with tacky trinkets in a month. Tuấn would be part of this strange, violent family with a strange, violent history. He would create a new New Orleans.

When Tuấn came home, his mother, brother, and Vinh were already there. She walked between the stove and the kitchen table. In recent months, she'd taken on bookkeeping for the nail salon. She'd look at the numbers in the ledger open on the table and return to the frying pan on the stove.

Tuấn headed for his room but stopped when his mother called him.

"Are you staying for dinner?" she asked him.

"I'm not grounded." He looked over at his brother, who was reading a weathered paperback book.

"That wasn't the question," she said. "Are you staying for dinner? You should stay for dinner. I work all day so you have food on the table. And you don't even eat at home most days."

"I'm busy, mẹ."

"Are you still hanging with that girl, Thảo?"

"He is," Bình chimed in.

"No one asked you, retard."

"No need for name calling," said Vinh. "In this house, we respect one another."

Bình rolled his eyes.

"No, mẹ," Tuấn told his mother.

"Don't nói láo."

"I'm not lying, mẹ."

"That girl bad trouble," she said in English. "Those other boys she hangs out with. If your father were here, you know he wouldn't approve." She shook her head. Then, as if remembering what she'd asked in the first place, she repeated, "Are you staying for dinner?"

"No, mẹ."

"I'm just trying to take care of you," she said.

"I know, mẹ."

She held him by the shoulder and looked into his eyes for a long time. He wondered what she was trying to find. "Okay," she said.

Bà Giang let herself in and Tuấn's mom began setting the table.

He went to his room and packed the bat and the black clothes he needed. By the time he got out, Vinh was sitting on the steps, reading a Bible and drinking a Coke.

"It'll be a while until dinner," Vinh said. "You know how talkative Bà Giang is."

Tuấn wasn't going to answer but decided to, feeling the way they left things on Bourbon Street hanging in the air. They hadn't talked about it since, and it didn't seem like Vinh had told his mother. "Yeah," Tuấn said.

"Where you going?"

"Friend's house."

"It is the Southern Kids?"

"Southern Boyz," he corrected, trying not to raise his voice.

"You want to know the real story of Vietnam, kid?"

"I don't have time right now. I have to go."

"Well, I tell you this. Look at me. Look."

Tuấn sighed and looked Vinh in the eyes.

"Everything was a mess," Vinh began. "War makes everything a mess. And everyone is guilty of doing something bad. No one came out of it not doing anything bad, even all the good guys. It was a mess. That's why I became Catholic." He grabbed on to the small gold cross necklace he always wore. "A nun at the refugee camp, she said our past—we can make up for it. We just have to *choose* to do it."

"What's that supposed to mean? Why are you telling me this?"

"I'm saying we can always choose to do good, even if we've done bad," Vinh said. "It's why I look after you all. It's maybe the one good thing I can do in the world. I'm here to stay, kid. I'm here to look after you and your brother and your mother. That's what families do, you know?"

"What does this have to do with anything? I'm gonna be late."

"You have a choice," Vinh said as Tuấn walked away, not yelling but keeping his voice steady. "You always have a choice."

"I don't need a guardian angel," Tuấn yelled at the bottom of the steps and ran off.

When he got to Quang's laundry shed, Thảo was flipping through a magazine on the couch. The radio played "Motownphilly." Outside, the sun was setting, marking the sky purple and blue and orange.

Thảo pulled the blinds closed and they sat down on the couch. He spread out lengthwise, laying his body down, and Thảo spread herself on top of him. She placed her head on his chest and held his hands. Her own hands, somehow, were always cold.

"What you're doing," she said. "It's very brave."

"Really?"

"Yeah. Really. None of the other guys would do it. But you, you stepped right up. That's why I like you, Tuấn. You're a doer. You do things. The other guys just like to talk. They're talkers. They're more like . . . I don't know, managers!" She laughed and massaged his hands. Her hands were freezing, and he wanted to pull his away. Tuấn moved his eyes to the door, then the blinds. Thảo tugged his chin and her lips met his. When she let go, she massaged his chest and moved down his torso.

The first time they had sex, all he remembered were hands. Her hands were everywhere. Freezing. He imagined it was what snow felt like. Not knowing what to do, he moved his hands, too, but they fumbled and shook because he was so nervous. She wasn't. Thảo was experienced, and she did not approve of his slowness and clumsiness. After he came, she got off him and he closed his eyes. When he opened them she was gone. He called her at home. She said he looked so peaceful she didn't want to disturb him, so she left. He didn't tell her, but he felt used. Though he enjoyed it, the feeling of her body against his, the speed of it all, he couldn't shake that feeling. He wanted more of her.

When he first met her, he had never met a Vietnamese girl so proud of being Vietnamese. All the other girls acted, somehow, more American. They had their Vietnamese names—beautiful names, he thought—but they told everyone to call them by their American names—Samantha, Becky, or some other bland name. But Thảo was Thảo. She spoke Vietnamese fluently and, though he had forgotten most of it, it still sounded beautiful to him. It gave him butterflies, still, when she said người yêu or cưng ơi, less because they were terms of love but because they were Vietnamese. That she hung out with the Southern Boyz made sense.

"The Việt girls here with their white names and straight As think if they do everything right they'll be fine, they'll have a happy life," she once told him. "But they forget they're người Việt. We'll never be American enough for the people here. People look at us a certain way and they always will."

There's truth in that, Tuấn thought. He'd lived most of his life in New Orleans, yet there was always a feeling that he didn't belong.

"That's why I like SBZ," she went on. "They have Việt pride."

When they finished this time, he didn't fall asleep. He looked at his watch. Nearly seven. He had time to kill.

"Do you want to grab a burger or something?" he asked as she got dressed. She looked up as if surprised he was there.

"I'm not hungry," she said after a long silence.

"Okay."

"I'll see you later, Tuấn."

"When?"

"Later," she said.

"Okay," he said.

She picked up her purse and left.

At 9:50, Tuấn sat beside a trash can on the corner of Bourbon and St. Louis. The sidewalk was moist because it had rained on and off during the day. Clouds hung in the sky under the moonlight. Tuan took in a breath of air and held it there until he couldn't take it anymore, letting it out furiously. His hands shook and the bat shook, too, making a soft, tinny, irregular rhythm on the concrete.

At the laundry shed, Quang had told Tuấn he was proud of him. He had patted Tuấn on the back, and it made Tuấn smile. As he had walked down Bourbon, passing all the tourist bars, he was confident. Yet now on the corner of St. Louis, he couldn't even walk anymore. He collapsed and leaned on the trash can. Then an idea occurred to him: they didn't want to scare an old lady themselves, so they'd handed it off to him.

"Motherfucker," Tuấn said. He looked at his watch. 9:54. He took in another breath and let it out. His lungs burned.

It was cold. It was October, and nights would be in the fifties, maybe the forties. He bet it was warm in Wei Huang. He began walking. Wei Huang was the third store on the block. At the door, he paused.

Inside, Madame Wei counted money and wrote down her calculations on a piece of paper. Tuấn touched the door handle and pulled and, as in their plan, a bell rang.

Madame Wei looked up from her money.

"Oh, allo!" she said. "We about to close. Can I help?" She smiled and put down her pen and crossed her hands in front of her.

Tuấn licked his lips and tapped the bat against the floor. The steel made a hollow sound.

"I'm just getting back from baseball practice," he said and pointed to the bat. "I was walking," he continued, "and I'm hungry." He rubbed his stomach to let her know. "Can I look around?" He was speaking slowly and loudly like people sometimes did when they assumed he didn't know any English, and he felt ashamed.

"Of course," she exclaimed. "Take time!"

He began walking down the aisle. As he inspected the shelves, a pang of nostalgia came to him as he saw the foods of his childhood: haw flakes in red tubes, salted dried plums in small plastic boxes, White Rabbit candy. When he was out of Madame Wei's sight, in the back near the refrigerator, he took one of the bags of White Rabbit candies and stuffed it into his pocket. He slowed his pace.

He knew what lay in the end. He bit down on his lips. The store looked smaller. It seemed, almost, to collapse onto him, all of it—the walls, the shelves, the packages of food with gold Chinese characters.

Soon he was back to the front counter again, but this time Madame Wei was gone.

For a second, Tuấn was relieved. He imagined what he would say. "She just up and disappeared," he would tell Quang, and everything would happen according to plans. The store would disappear and he would join the Southern Boyz. *Easy!* Tuấn told himself. *Piece of cake!*

A microwave signaled, a steady beeping sound.

Madame Wei came out of the back room. She held up a Tupperware container. The sides were fogged up and he couldn't tell what was in it.

As she walked to the counter, Tuấn saw that she had left the money there, next to the cash register, out in the open. She uncovered the container and steam rose out. "For you," she said. "Here, here."

At first Tuấn didn't understand. "No," he said. "No."

"But you hungry," she said. "Here, here." She pushed the container toward him until he was forced to hold it. He looked down and saw noodles and pieces of vegetables and thick cuts of meat, all in a brown soup. "Here, here," Madame Wei said again. She handed him a plastic fork. "Eat, eat," she said.

"But," Tuấn said. He smelled the broth. Beef. Like phở but not.

"Eat, eat," she repeated.

Finally, he dug down the fork, lifted it to his mouth, and chewed. It was nothing special. It was not salty enough and needed more pepper. But it was warm and he drank all of the broth before slurping up the rest of the noodles. Madame Wei smiled the whole time.

When Tuấn was done, he didn't know what to do, so he gave her a five-dollar bill and left, dragging the steel bat behind him.

Outside, Tuấn felt the chill of the air. The temperature must've dropped five or ten degrees, somehow, in minutes. He pulled his hood over his head, held the bat under his arm, and placed his hands in his pockets. Not wanting to go home, he sat on a bench in Jackson Square.

He woke up near midnight and opened his eyes to a woman and her kid in the distance. He saw only their silhouettes, but they were the same size as his mother and brother. For a second, his heart stopped. He was thinking it was them, that they had found him out. She would grab him and drag him home, screaming and yelling and embarrassing him. (She did that once to his brother in a church. For a month, all of Versailles gave them mean stares, and she told Tuấn and Bình what they thought didn't matter because they weren't family.) He stood up, prepared to run, and as they came closer, he saw he was wrong. He ran away anyway, and the mother pulled her son closer to her, out of the way, away from danger. Running down the streets of the Quarter, he realized he was nearly disappointed it wasn't them. He took a bus home.

Tuấn would avoid Quang and the others that night and the next night and the entire week.

Later, he would go to Quang to confess. The woman was old and fragile, he would say. He couldn't do it. He wouldn't do it. They shouldn't do it. He had good reasoning, too, he would say. The old woman would die very soon. She had no family. The business would die. There would be no more Chinese in the Quarter, perhaps in all of New Orleans. The Quarter could be Vietnamese territory.

But Quang would have found out about it already. He would have taken care of it by then, too. Quang, with a smirk on his face and beer bottle in hand, would stand over a bonfire and tell his story: how he made that old hag cry, how he drove her out of her own store, and how, to make sure she would never come back, he smashed everything—the display case, the shelves of food, the neon sign, the window. And he took the money and he walked out.

"The old lady just left it there on the counter. That stupid cunt," he would say. "Here's the thing . . ." And he would see Tuấn from the corner of his eyes and he would shake his head and stop talking. Everyone else would quiet down, too. He shared secrets only with family, Quang would say then, and Tuấn wasn't family.

Ben

That summer, Addy wanted to join the swim team. In her front yard, she'd stretched like a swimmer, straightening her legs and touching her toes before racing across the grass as Ben watched from the porch.

"Imagine that's me in the water," she would tell him.

By July, she was ready for the pool, all the way out in Gentilly, and Ben followed along despite not knowing how to swim.

He sat on a vinyl lounge chair off to the side with a book and watched boys jump off the diving board, each yelling playfully before hitting the water.

"I get seasick just looking at it," he told Addy.

"Don't, then," she said.

"I can't help it."

Another boy hit the water and Ben imagined himself doing the same, but instead of popping up on the other side, he'd drown and die. He shook his head and returned to his book. There was summer reading to do, and he was already ahead, with two of the three books done. He read a chapter before deciding it was a good time to stop. He let the book lie open facedown on the chair and left for the concessions stand.

By the time he got back, a skinny, older white boy and what must have been his father sat in their chairs. The father had a bad, uneven tan that made him look like he was wearing a pale shirt. The boy was just pale all over. Ben's book sat on the concrete, closed.

He ran over. "Hey, hey, hey!" he yelled. He waved his arms in the air to get their attention. "Don't you see our stuff?"

"What stuff?" said the boy. His voice was sharp and it sounded like he was chewing gum or had something in his mouth.

"Our stuff," Ben said, then to clarify, "our bags, our towels, my book!"

"Where?" The boy held his arms in the air and shrugged his shoulders, cool—Ben would remember later—as a glass of lemonade. "Where? Where? Where?" The boy was mocking him now. And his father, having set down his glasses, walked away.

"There," Ben said.

The boy looked under the chair and picked up the book. Water had splashed on the cover; a dark patch stained the front. "Oh," he said. "These?"

"Duh, those!" Ben reached over and grabbed his stuff with such force that everything fell out of his hands and scattered on the ground. He picked it all up and began to leave.

"Hey, you! Hey, kid!" the boy called after. His voice was loud, tightly coiled, controlled. "You forgot something."

Ben looked around and saw the boy waving Addy's shirt and shorts, both hot pink. He turned his head toward the pool. Addy was still doing laps, oblivious to what was happening. He imagined what he'd tell her. "This white boy . . ." he would begin with a smack of his lips, the way they always began when they told stories about

145

the crazy white people they met—*This white man thought I stole something from his store; this white lady thought I was someone else because apparently all of our kind look the same. . . .*

Ben walked back and grabbed them. "My friend's," he huffed.

"This white boy . . ." he said to himself. Addy would enjoy his story.

Addy came up and, without drying, took a seat next to Ben. Her body squeaked against the vinyl.

"What happened?" she asked. "Why you change seats? Took me a good minute to find you."

"So this white boy took them," Ben started, putting his book down, "when I was getting snacks."

"You shouldn't leave our stuff alone, Ben," she interrupted. "You know how folks around here are."

"But our stuff was there."

"But nothing. You know how people are."

Addy was raising her voice; he was raising his. He imagined people looking at them, assuming they were a couple. He felt embarrassed and looked down at his hands.

Addy smacked her lips. "Just be careful. That's all I'm telling you. That's all I'm saying."

She dried herself and he returned to his book, though he couldn't concentrate. He read and reread the same sentence over and over a dozen times before Addy started talking again.

"Can you help me with this?" she asked. He looked over and Addy held out a bottle of waterproof Hawaiian Tropic. "I'm supposed to reapply every hour. It says right here on the bottle."

He grabbed it and Addy turned away. He squeezed the lotion onto his hands and spread it across Addy's back, first with only a finger, then, hesitantly, he used both hands until her entire back was all white and pasty. Under the sun, the chemical scent of the

Hawaiian Tropic intensified. It reminded him of cleaning supplies and made him gag. He tried to think of something else, anything but Addy's skin and the smell and texture of the lotion until he spotted the boy sitting where they'd sat. Shirtless, the boy stretched out on his chair, faceup, his sunglasses reflecting the sun. Even from this distance, Ben saw his breathing.

"Make sure you don't miss a spot," Addy interrupted. "I don't wanna get cancer."

"You're not going to get cancer. Who gets cancer?" he said. "Done. I'm gonna wash my hands in the bathroom."

"Just use the pool," Addy said.

He looked at the water, then back at Addy, and nodded and walked to the edge of the water, where he bent his knees into a squat. As his hand broke the cool surface, Addy dove in. The drops of the splash scattered in the air, and for a second Ben saw a rainbow. He let his hand sit as she became smaller and smaller the farther away she swam. Soon the pink cap was out of sight. His eyes wandered back to the boy, but his seat was empty. He let out a quiet sigh—of relief or disappointment, he wasn't sure—and, when the lotion was gone, headed back to the chairs. To his surprise, the boy was there.

Ben couldn't help but smirk as he ran. "You again," he called out, trying to sound serious and angry, but all he wanted to do was giggle. "Do you take everyone's seat? Is that your thing? Is that what you always do?"

"Are you new here?" the boy asked.

"What?"

"I'm here every summer," the boy continued. "Been coming here every summer, and it's just—I've never seen you before." He took off his sunglasses to reveal serious blue eyes.

"It's 'cause I live in New Orleans East," Ben said. He felt himself blushing.

"Don't you have your own pools there?"

Hearing that, Ben felt offended. He looked around. He and Addy were the only nonwhites here. He straightened his posture. His chest tightened and the hair on his skin stood up.

"It's a free country, you know. Anyone can go anywhere if they want to. It's written in the Constitution. It's, it's . . ."

"Relax," said the boy. "Relax. I'm from Metairie. There's no pool there, either. No good-quality pools anyway. There's no pools in New Orleans East, either?" The boy barely moved his lips when he talked. It must be the reason for his accent—part mutter, part muddled melody.

"Yeah," Ben said, calming down. "There's nothing in New Orleans East. There's one stretch of highway, strip malls, then there's the apartments and homes. Not the most fun place."

"Metairie isn't, either."

They agreed that neither New Orleans East nor Metairie had much going for it. The boy stretched out on Addy's chair and Ben found himself watching the boy, examining him. Ben took a seat himself, and his muscles relaxed.

"Name's Howie," the boy said.

"Ben." He looked out into the water, trying to find the pink cap.

"What brings you here?" Howie asked.

"Here?"

"This summer, I mean. Today. Right now."

"Oh," Ben said. "My friend's out there. The pink cap? She's trying out for the swim team. Wesley High has a swim team."

"You go to Wesley?" Howie asked.

"We're both going to Wesley," Ben said. "Freshmen."

"It means we're supposed to hate each other."

"What do you mean?"

"I graduated from Caddo last month," Howie said with a wry smile. Dimples appeared on edges of his lips. The lips themselves were full and red, swollen in the prettiest of ways. Ben stopped himself from staring. "We're rivals," Howie continued. "That's what you should know. Cowboys and Warriors? They don't get along. Never have and they never will."

"What?"

"Wesley, your mascot's a cowboy. Caddo, we have Chief Red Corn. You didn't know that?"

"I don't go there yet," Ben said. "We haven't even had orientation."

"Well, cowboys and Indians don't get along."

"Of course they don't. The cowboys stole land from the Indians. I read that in a book somewhere."

"Well, you're a cowboy now."

"What?"

"You're a cowboy, now, white man." Howie put on a thick, ridiculous country accent. "You gotta get over that."

"Hey!" Ben reached over for a friendly shove, but his body began to fall. Howie miraculously caught him. How strong he was, how his muscles bulged, and how they didn't even shake holding him up.

"Whoa there, cowboy," Howie said. "Be careful, now, you."

Because of Addy, they went to the pool every day. And every day, to Ben's surprise, Howie was there, too. Ben and Howie sat by the pool and talked as Addy practiced her breaststroke and butterfly, her backstroke and freestyle.

Ben told Howie about his love for books and writing. His favorite writers were Charles Dickens, John Steinbeck, and that guy who wrote *Lord of the Flies*. He felt he was smart for saying all this and wondered if Howie was impressed. Howie told Ben he never got into reading. When asked what he liked to do, he said he played sports. Junior varsity football freshman year, varsity baseball sophomore through senior, wrestling during junior.

Ben said he couldn't imagine being finished with school and that Howie was lucky, at least for being done with high school. It wasn't that he didn't like learning. He liked books and the feeling of knowing more about the world around him. He went to the library every week and could finish a regular-sized novel in three or four days. All the same, his classes were slow and he became bored. Teachers mistook this for stupidity and laziness, and one summer, even, he'd had to retake seventh-grade math.

It disappointed his mother. "The son of a teacher has to retake classes," she said and shook her head.

And the teacher, a short, elderly man who wore a cowboy hat and a handlebar mustache, said if he was struggling with home-work, "just ask your pa for help. I bet he's a smart man." Ben didn't correct him. "Orientals are very good at the mathematics. Just ask him for help. No shame." It wasn't worth the effort, any of it.

If it were up to him, he would skip the whole rigmarole and travel the world and learn from that instead, maybe even write a book.

"Like Jack Kerouac," Howie said.

"Like who?"

"He's a writer. Was a writer. Dead now."

"Never heard of him." He took out his notebook and penciled in "Jack Carrot."

"You'll read him in tenth grade," Howie said. "*On the Road* or *Going on the Road* or *In the Road* or something like that. I don't know. I'm not that smart, you see." He laughed. "Anyway, he went everywhere and wrote about all the places that he went."

"Where did he go?"

"I don't know," Howie said. "I never finished reading it."

"Oh," Ben said. He closed his notebook, leaving the pencil in as a bookmark.

"He drove from Boston to California or something. But this was in the fifties, when cars weren't that good, so it was a big deal, I guess," Howie said. "My point is there's a whole country out there."

"Tell me about it," said Ben.

"There's an entire world."

"Yes, there is."

When Ben asked Howie what his plans were after summer, Howie told him he was going to Lake Charles for college. "Undeclared for now. Until I figure it all out."

"Will you ever figure it all out?"

"Maybe." Howie said it confidently and pulled down his sunglasses. Ben reached for his, which he'd bought at a souvenir shop only after meeting Howie. They looked at each other conspiratorially.

When August began, Howie told Ben he wanted to teach him how to swim. "All this time here," he said, "and you don't even touch the water!"

After Howie led Ben to the pool, he told him to lie down.

"No," Ben said. "Bodies don't float. Unless they're dead."

"Don't be silly." Howie held his wrist. "Relax. *Relax.*"

"How can you be from New Orleans and not know how to swim?" Addy asked. Ben almost forgot she was there. She lay in the water to demonstrate. Howie did the same, and they both floated effortlessly, arms out, legs out. Ben wondered if, from above, they looked like floating flowers. The two moved their arms, and slowly their two bodies started to move more purposefully. Ben looked one way and then the other. His eyes settled on Howie.

Howie made him nervous. Numerous times he found himself shaking when he talked to him or was close to him. Yet it wasn't an uncomfortable feeling. He liked it. He wanted it to linger.

Ben turned his head to where Addy was and she was gone. He looked around.

"Addy?" he called out. "Addy?" Where was she?

Suddenly, something latched on to his leg. By reflex, he let out a scream. What was happening? He shook his leg, but it moved laboriously, sluggishly. He couldn't swim and he would die. He tripped and went under and in an instant everything became blue and there was no air. He began moving his arms, karate-chopping the water. But he wasn't going anywhere.

In the next second, he was above the water again. He breathed in all he could. Addy held one arm, Howie the other. When he realized he was alive and safe, he remembered what had happened. *Addy had disappeared. Addy pulled me under.*

He stared at Addy, furious. "Addy! Why you do that for?"

"I was just playing," she said.

"That wasn't funny," Ben said. "Why would you do that?"

"I was just joking." She let go and took a step back.

"It wasn't funny. It's not funny, *Adelaide Toussaint.*" He took his arm from Howie's grasp and left the pool.

That night, Ben returned to the pool with Howie. He told his mom he was going back to the pool and wouldn't be home until late. When she asked him who he was going with, he said a friend.

He was going to learn how to swim. He felt determined. The reasons for knowing how to swim were numerous: Addy wouldn't be able to make fun of him anymore; it was an important skill to have in case the city sank—because it was below sea level, he read somewhere, and the water could just pour in like in a bathtub; he was Vietnamese, and Vietnamese people are supposed to know how to swim. And Howie had offered to teach him.

The pool glowed. At the entrance, Howie motioned his head to the fence. "Climb," he said.

"I can't climb," Ben replied.

"You can try."

Anything for Howie. Anything.

Ben held on to the metal and stretched an arm upward. Next, he took a step up. With another movement he slipped and gasped aloud, but, to his surprise, Howie caught him and pushed him up. After some more struggle, he found himself at the top and dropped down to the other side. He landed on his feet. Howie followed after.

Together they walked to the pool's edge. At the shallow end, Ben removed a shoe and sock and touched the water. At the cold shock, he pulled back. Howie began stripping off his jeans and T-shirt.

What surprised Ben was that, though he had seen Howie shirtless—nearly naked—countless times, it always gave him a sense of—what word was there for it? Awe? Excitement? Wonder? The sight of Howie's skin made Ben's heart stop for a second, then the next he would feel it beating too fast and catching fire and burning him alive.

It felt strange, but he didn't want to feel any other way. Soon it began to make sense: the way boys were supposed to want girls was the way Ben wanted Howie. *Wanting*—what a strange feeling, what a queer idea to have toward another person! You could want food, you could want rest, you could want safety, and—it dawned on him—you could want a person, too.

He was terrified. What had he become? What would his mother think? ("The son of a teacher . . ." she would scoff with enough shame in her voice for their entire family, his dead father—the college professor! the hero! the martyr!—included.) Or his brother, the tough boy—no, a man now—who hung out with the Southern Boyz? The realization had scared him, and he couldn't look at himself in the mirror for the longest time until the day Addy pulled him under and he nearly drowned. He'd left the pool in a huff and headed for the locker room to change. There, he passed a mirror and he couldn't avoid it, that image of himself. He looked at his reflection and it was like he saw himself—*really* saw himself—for the first time. There had to be a word for that, too.

"Dunk yourself in first," Howie said when they were hip-deep in the water. "Get a feel for it." When Ben didn't answer, didn't move, he added, "It's just water. Good ol' H-2-and-O. Remember that. It's just water."

"It's just water," Ben repeated.

"The whole world is covered in it."

"Yes," Ben agreed.

"I think we're made of it, too."

"We are."

"On the count of three. Okay?" Howie said.

"Okay."

"One. Two. Three."

Down.

Ben had expected a trick, had anticipated the feeling of Howie's hand on his head, pushing him down, but he bent his knees and he opened his eyes and he was underwater and still alive. Everything was blue and bright, but now it wasn't scary. There was a strange serenity to it. A strange but peaceful silence. He stood back up.

"Good," Howie said. "Very good."

They would try to float next. When Ben said he was unsure, Howie laid his own body in the water and Ben watched as he floated.

Howie had a beautiful body. Ben wanted to say it aloud. *Beautiful.* He mouthed the words instead. Like a secret. Then he, too, lay down. He was prepared to sink, but he didn't. To his astonishment, he floated. More than that, there was a feeling of weightlessness, of floating in not water, but air.

Looking at the sky, Ben saw himself reflected in space.

And there it was: he was wrong. From above, they didn't look like flowers. Not even close. They were both stars, the two of them. Together in the water. Floating. Free.

A kiss. A kiss getting out of the pool, walking toward the edge of the pool. Walking and still up to the waist in water. A kiss in the pool with water at the waist. A kiss in the pool at night with water and hands at the waists, wet hands on the waists, as they stand in the pool, standing to kiss, to try—because I have never done this before—but really it is nothing—but have you kissed a *boy* before—but I have kissed plenty of boys before—but plenty of boys, plenty of boys in pools? plenty of boys in pools?—of course plenty of boys, but never plenty of boys in pools—so I'm your first boy, your first boy in a pool—yes, you're my first boy in the pool, ha-ha—okay—ha-ha, you're funny—a kiss: a kiss in the pool. Two boys in the pool: two boys kissing in a pool.

After the swimming lesson, Ben and Howie went out for ice cream in a place in the Quarter with a cow on its window and its doors propped open because the AC was always broken. Howie said it was the only place to get ice cream in New Orleans because they had more toppings than anywhere else and their scoops were fist-sized huge.

They took their bowls to a secluded booth in the back. A light-bulb with a stained-glass cover hung above the table, making the shadows green. After they ate a spoonful of their sundaes and tried each other's, Ben asked Howie how long he'd felt *that* way.

Howie nodded. "Since I first saw you, honest," he replied, and they both blushed. When Ben asked Howie how long he'd felt any-thing, Howie recounted one winter when he was a junior at Caddo.

The boy was named Anderson. Anderson was a senior. Ander-son and Howie were both on the varsity wrestling team. One time after practice, the two of them stayed behind to work on a take-down. For it to work, Howie had to take hold of Anderson behind the knees and push him up, then slam him down. The problem, he said, was that Anderson was bigger; he'd hold his ground.

"Anderson," he said now, pushing his spoon down into his ice cream and picking it up. He placed it gingerly into his mouth and swallowed before continuing. Ben watched his Adam's apple jump.

"He was all big muscles. Pecs the size of grapefruits, I swear; calves bulging like baseballs. Sturdy, built guy. Beautiful." Howie spoke nervously and his eyes twitched back and forth, watching and waiting for something. Then he set down his spoon when one of the shop's employees started to clean the next booth over. She took her time wiping the table with a white rag in slow, large circles. Ben and Howie sat silent, moving spoons in their sundaes but not eating.

When the worker left, Howie went on. "At Caddo, we had open showers, a square room with showerheads lining the walls. Usually, only the real buff seniors like Anderson used it. I stayed away from that." He fidgeted with his spoon and Ben leaned in closer, feeling himself sliding off the vinyl seat. "Anyway," Howie said, "when we were done that night, we hit the locker room. I was gonna change and drive on home, but Anderson started to tease me. 'You're gonna stink up the highway. . . .' he says. 'I swear that's you smelling up Route 10,' he goes. 'I always thought that was road-kill or something,' laughing all the time. He grabs my shoulder and play-shoves it and goes off to the showers. I hear the water turning on, the sound of wet feet on tiles.

"I didn't want to admit it to myself, but even then I knew Anderson was . . . he made me feel a certain way, you know? So maybe it was that, or maybe I really did stink or whatever, but I go and strip off and walk to the showers. The whole time, I try to keep my eyes on the floor, you know, and go to my own showerhead, far, far away from him. And I'm soaping myself up when I start feeling a hand massaging my neck."

Ben filled up his spoon with melted ice cream, lifted it a few inches, and dropped it back into the bowl. He didn't know how to respond, anticipating what happened next. He did it four or five times before Howie began talking again.

"We did stuff in there, us. And we did it for the rest of the season. And the rest of the year, though we both played different sports. In

my mind, we went steady, but he was thinking something else. I
don't know. He moved off to college, went up north or something.
He hasn't kept in touch. We haven't been talking."

"I'm sorry," Ben said. He felt sorry and saw the hurt on Howie's
face even if he was trying to hide it.

"Nothing to be sorry about," Howie said. "Nothing at all."

"Do your mom and dad know?" Ben asked.

"No. Yours?"

Once, his mother found his journal. In it, he had written his
innermost fantasies: stories of boys holding hands under moss-
cloaked oak trees; men kissing on camping trips in the woods;
men touching each other out in a secluded bayou at night. She
showed it to him and asked him what it was. She had an angry
frown, and he had never seen her like that before. He told her it
was all fake, it was something for school, and that she'd misunderstood everything because she didn't know English anyway. He
threw away the journal that same night.

"My mom? No," he told Howie.

"What about your dad?"

"Dad? My dad's gone." He didn't want to say "dead" because it
always made him look pitiful; he was tired of pity. It was the same
reason he never said aloud that he would have wanted to know
more about his father beyond the vague descriptions his mother
gave, to have just one glimpse—for curiosity's sake, of course. But
people would pity him for that and he would be embarrassed for
their pity, would not know what to do with it. "But my mom's boyfriend lives with us," Ben added.

"What would he think?"

"I don't know," Ben said, trying to imagine what Vinh would say.
"What he thinks doesn't matter. He's not my dad."

"My parents would rip me to shreds. My dad especially," Howie
said.

"I'm sorry."

157

After ice cream, they walked around the Quarter, which was quieter than Ben expected. Howie pointed out a used bookstore ("Because you said you like books"), a candy shop that specialized in pralines ("'Cause you sweet!"), and Club Paradise, a gay bar ("I've been there once or twice or maybe more," he said and broke into a boyish laugh). As they approached Toulouse, Ben got them to turn around because he didn't want to pass his mother's work, though he knew at this time of evening no one would be there. They ended the night watching ferry boats in the Mississippi, and Howie drove him back to Versailles.

When he got home his mother was sitting in the kitchen in her pajamas, writing what looked like a letter. She stopped him on the way to his room to, as she said, check up on him. His brother wasn't home much anymore, and she was checking up on him now more than before. She asked him how the pool was. He said fine.

"Are you trying out for the swim team," she said, "now that you're learning how to swim?"

"Swim team?" Ben asked. He'd forgotten all about it. His mind was floating elsewhere. "Yes. Yes, I guess. Maybe. I don't know."

"Your father," she said, folding up the letter she was writing, "was a good swimmer, too. Not when I met him, but eventually he learned. He learned quick, your father. Like you."

He didn't know why she kept bringing him up. He was tired of this father he'd never met, though she talked about him as if she didn't want him to forget. But he wasn't there to remember anything in the first place; what, then, was there to forget? The man played no role in his life, and Ben resented always being compared to him. Perhaps if he had known him, had memory of him, it would be different. Perhaps then he would say to himself, "This is the man I want to be." But that was never the case. To want anything more, anything else, seemed useless.

He asked her what that had to do with anything. She said she didn't know. He closed his room door harder than he'd meant to.

———

Ben wanted to call Addy to tell her everything, to confess it all.

He was gay. Gay. He said the word over and over in his head. He was gay, he would tell her, but it was something he needed to say in person. It needed a human touch. After the light in his mother's room turned off, he got his bike.

When he arrived, the lights were out except for the uncovered bulb attracting moths on the porch. Even from the sidewalk he could see them. Somewhere, an owl hooed.

He stood in her front yard, thinking about other things. About what book he would read next after he finished his summer reading. About the fact that he wasn't afraid of the water anymore, at least not like before. About how Howie helped with that. He wanted to think about a million other things, but he looked up and he was still on Addy's front lawn. He rolled his bike across the dry grass and opened the fence into the back. Mr. Toussaint must have oiled the hinges, because it was not a week ago that they squeaked. The silhouette of the swing set looked ominous, and so did the back fence. In the dark, it felt like a different, unknown country.

At Addy's window, he threw a pebble to get her attention. Because there was no answer, he did it again, creating a slow rhythm of small rocks pinging against glass. After a few more pebbles, Addy opened up and, squinting, looked down.

"Ben?" she asked into the darkness. "Is that you?" She left the window open, disappeared, and came back with a flashlight. It looked big in her small hands. "Ben?" she asked again.

Did I wake you up? he wanted to ask. *How long have you been asleep? Am I bothering you?* He wanted to say anything and everything except what he'd come to say.

"I need to tell you something," he whisper-shouted, but still, inside his head, his voice sounded loud and booming. He leaned his bike against the chinaberry tree, and there was a soft crunch as the metal touched the bark. "It's kinda important. Can you come down?" He scratched his head, then his hand. He felt restless. "So I can talk to you?"

"It's late, Ben. It's like eleven." She faked a yawn. She hadn't been sleeping, he could tell. He imagined her lying in bed all this time, waiting. She stood at the window watching him and he looked up, watching her. They heard a bird fly away.

"Okay," she said.

The next minute, Addy stood outside. She wore her pink paisley-printed nightgown, though in the dark, under the night sky, it looked white. Her pajamas were always pink. He remembered their childhood sleepovers. It seemed so long ago now—a history's worth of time had passed. She hugged her body as if she were cold, though it was humid. The air conditioner hummed.

"Addy," he said. He took a step toward her.

"What is it?" She sounded impatient. "What happened?"

"Addy," he said again. Her name hung in the air—*Add-dee*—and he heard his teeth chatter. Maybe it *was* cold. He tightened his jaw to stop it. He remembered how Howie's jaw always looked tight, too, how square and strong it seemed. He shook the image out of his head.

"What is it?" Addy asked again. She began pacing and circling him. Her eyes were aimed at the ground as if she were searching for something she had lost and come out to look for specifically. It made him more nervous.

"Stop moving, will you? I'm trying to say something."

She stopped and pressed her back against his. He faced the house as she faced the back fence. He felt her breathing and, automatically, he synched his breathing with hers like they were one.

"The moon is so big tonight," she said. "You should see it."

Ben shook his head. "I want to tell you something."

"It's beautiful," she continued. "The way the moon makes the other houses look. Look! You have to look."

"I want to tell you something. It's . . ." He felt his hands shaking. He held them together.

"What are you talking about?"

"The thing I'm trying to tell you is this," he said. He rubbed his hands together. There were words in his head; they repeated themselves over and over again until all it sounded like was the buzzing of bees in a small, compact space.

Shhh, he said in his head, *quiet down, quiet.*

"What is it, Ben? You know I'm always here for you. Whatever happens, I'm always here."

Ben said, "We went to the pool tonight. Howie and me."

Addy stopped breathing, and so did he.

"Just me and Howie, at the pool," he said, "and there, that's when I realized something. Something about myself."

Addy said nothing.

"Addy," he said. Then, "I kissed him. We kissed, Addy. And I liked it. I liked kissing him. Imagine that, I liked kissing him. I liked kissing Howie. Addy." He took a breath. Addy did not. "I like Howie the way I'm supposed to like girls. Addy, I like boys the way I'm supposed to like girls."

Addy released the breath she held. He heard her take a step. Then another. Soon, he turned around and saw her circling back to the house.

"Addy?" he asked, though it didn't look like she was listening. He grabbed her elbow before she passed him, clutching it with all his strength. When she yanked away, he let go and she nearly fell, as if she were expecting him to keep holding. After steadying herself, she took another step.

"I think you should go home," she said.

"Addy," Ben insisted, "are we cool? Are we still friends?"

"Sure, Ben, sure." Her voice trembled.

"Are you sure, Addy?"

She looked at him as if she wanted to reach out and touch him, but didn't. "But the people at school, Ben."

"What about it?"

"You know," she said. "They're not gonna like you."

"But you like me, don't you, Addy?"

"Sure I do," said Addy. "But just imagine this." She stopped herself as if gathering her thoughts. "Imagine us walking down the hall and everyone knows this about you. And then they see me. What do you think they're gonna say?"

"Are you embarrassed of me, then?" He couldn't believe it. "Is that what's eating at you?" He felt himself getting angry.

"No," she said and began walking away.

"Addy," Ben called out.

"I have practice in the morning," Addy said. "They're not gonna let me on the team. If I don't practice."

"Addy," he called out again. He tried running after her, but the door closed before he could get to her, and he was left alone again, under the stars and the moon and the branches of the tree and not even the owl was there now, not even the moths.

His mind was everywhere all at once, replaying everything that had happened that day at lightning speed. He pedaled as fast as he could until his legs burned and gave up and, exhausted, he let the bike fall out from under him and onto the sidewalk. The wheels spun as he rested on someone's lawn and listened to himself panting and watched the stars shine down. The stars, their lights glittering, lulled the images in his head. The words in his head quieted.

In school, one of the teachers had a poster of constellations on one of his walls. They had names that reminded him of the Greek myths he learned about in English. Sailors, he remembered reading, used to look at the stars to find their way back home or whatever their destination was. It was a map written in the sky. When he said this in class, the teacher told him this was science and that he was off subject. The other kids laughed. He didn't think it was funny. He spent the rest of the class period drawing stars, and he failed the pop quiz because he was too angry to think.

Weeks later, after Howie left for school and the pool closed up and the August heat gave way to cool September air, he thought about how the stars, too, were once used to tell the future, like the words to a story written in dots, holding everyone's fate. How he wanted to run his fingers across those stars and read what they said, every single word, every piece of light.

August 1994

The weather woman on TV says it's going to be a real scorcher today and even the cartoon sun is sweating. The heat wave, says the weather woman, will last all week, maybe into the next. Stay inside, pull down the shades, and turn on the AC, because it's going to be hotter than hot. The temperatures keep rising: 100, 101, 102.

"It will feel like a hundred and fourteen today," says the weather woman, smiling. "Because of the Code Red, RTA will be providing free bus rides."

Hương runs her hands under the kitchen faucet and splashes her face with cold water. The AC is broken. Again. She wishes Tuấn still lived with them; he was always the one who fixed things. But now he lives in Tremé (out of all places!) with his girlfriend, the one she doesn't like. She tries to visit every weekend if she can but doesn't like seeing the girl. She is on the cusp of asking him to choose—his own mother or some cheap, thrill-seeking girl. That is something she never thought would happen.

Hương fills up a glass with water and drinks it all in one go. Vinh says he's tired of news of hot weather and changes the channel. *Maury* comes on. "And you are not the father!" Maury says. Vinh changes the channel again.

Hương wants to go for a swim, submerge her body in water, but the bayou's too dirty and, she swears, it's disappearing. She stuck a stick by the shore, marking the water level with a permanent marker. Yesterday morning the water was lower again.

It must be happening all across the state, she says. She thinks of the fishermen, how in the heat wave they must be struggling.

"We're disappearing," she tells Vinh. "The water keeps this place alive—the crawfish, the crabs."

"The shrimp," adds Vinh.

"The shrimp," Hương says. "Soon, everything will be gone." The words sound melodramatic, something a soap opera wife would say. An infomercial pops up on TV; they're selling life vests. "I mean, we'll have to move somewhere else. You can't live in a place without water."

Vinh says, "You can't live in a place with too much of it, either."

Vinh sits at the kitchen table. Today, like any other day, it's rice noodles and fish sauce with sliced-up lạp xưởng for breakfast and Hương is at work. He wishes she didn't work so much. Work is overrated. Anyone can do work, but it takes a man to let it all go.

"It's the American dream," said Hương, "to earn a living, to provide for yourself."

"What about the Vietnamese dream?" he asked.

"This is not Vietnam," she told him. She had a point.

It is a Friday and his job is to find a job. When he first came to New Orleans, they let him sell cars, but he was "let go" because he was "too friendly." He moved on to a factory, managing and repairing machines until he was fired because he didn't know what he was doing. (He'd thought it would have been more self-explanatory.) For a while, he stocked canned foods at Langenstein's, but eventually they laid off some of their workers. He has the worst luck. He flips to the classifieds. The pages are littered with red pen marks from Hương.

> Cemetery ~~Foreman~~ Quán lý: *Provide leadership to cemetery staff to accomplish goals and objectives while working within company guidelines . . .*
> ~~Fabricator~~ Người sận xủất: *The job requires the employee to fabricate from piping drawings. The ideal candidate must be able to operate all equipment used in the fabrication department.*
> CDL ~~Driver~~ Người lái xe: ~~Candidate should have experience with . . .~~ *You'll drive a truck, Vinh.*

At the very back is a full-color ad with masks and beads and frosty mugs of beer with foam spilling out. A festival, it says. *Southern Decadence.*

It's been a long time since he's taken Hương out. He means *out* out, not the Chinese restaurant they go to once a week and order the same thing and never finish it, eating the leftovers for breakfast the next day. Last week the fortune cookie said: *Pick a path with heart.*

He decides: he will pick a path with heart. Tonight, the Southern Festival. Tomorrow, a job.

The heat is too much; where is that fan?

Ben lies in bed watching TV: *Paris Is Burning* on VHS from the library. It's the second time he's checked it out and it's two days past due. He can't get enough.

It was Georges who said he should watch it. Behind the bar

at Club Paradise, the bartender rattled off everything a gay boy needed to know—what movies to watch *(Paris Is Burning, The Boys in the Band, My Beautiful Launderette)*, what books to read *(Tales of the City, The Boys on the Rock, Giovanni's Room)*. Ben has spent plenty of time at Paradise over the past month, skipping summer school (remedial algebra) for, in his mind, a different type of education.

For the past year, every time he was on Bourbon, he'd made sure to find the establishment and observe it from a distance. He thought *homosexuals* (the word always made him gasp in his head) would have had more shame than to go there so openly in the daytime. It eased his own guilt. It was only within the last couple of months that he found the courage to step inside.

That first Saturday afternoon, there was a bodybuilding competition of some sort. Men in Speedos walked onstage and flexed their muscles to the cheering crowd. Everyone was smiling. Ben wandered in and sat for an hour before anyone noticed him. They were supposed to kick him out, but Georges—bald, tattooed, fatherly—said, in his lisp, "The youths need to know, Veronica" (Veronica being the lesbian who owned the place). "How else will they ever know?"

Georges teaches Ben everything he needs to know about being gay: say no to drugs, say yes to safe sex (though Ben has never even had drugs or sex); if your family kicks you out, build your own—no one needs a bad-vibe familia, Bambino. (He calls Ben "Bambino.") Everyone else at Paradise calls him the bar cat, the baby gay, the one-day-you-will-turn-eighteen boy. They are a friendly bunch. Unlike everyone at school.

Once high school started, everyone seemed to stop being friendly with one another and started hanging out with people more like themselves. There were the jocks, who always gave him threatening scowls and called him a fag. And there were the geeks, who no one wanted to hang out with except other geeks, and Ben knew you couldn't be both a geek and gay because that was social suicide. And there were the art kids, who got high all the time and didn't pay attention to anyone.

Addy, his best friend all throughout elementary and middle school, was with the jocks because she swam. She didn't swim too well, but that seemed to be beside the point. She was on the team and ate lunch with burly football players and thin cheerleaders every day. Ben saw her between classes or after school, but they had a hard time finding what to say to each other. And by the time one of them was ready—perhaps just a simple "Hi"—one of Addy's new friends would guide her away, leaving him alone. *Another reason to skip classes,* he thought.

Onscreen, Venus Xtravaganza says, "You're just an overgrown orangutan!"

"You're just an overgrown orangutan," Ben repeats and laughs.

Tonight is the kickoff for Southern Decadence, and he has it in his mind to go. He wants to be *fabulous.* He wants to be *fierce.* These are the words everyone in Paradise throws around, and he has started adding them to his vocabulary, whispering them in front of the mirror.

Outside, his mom and Vinh are getting ready for a night on the town. (Vinh's words, not his: "a night on the town.") Even with his door closed, he can hear her going through her closet while Vinh paces the hallway.

"I made reservations," Vinh calls out.

"Almost ready," says his mom. More shuffling.

Soon his mom's out and Vinh is saying, "Let me take a look, just wait one sec, let me take a look." Ben imagines his mom spinning around, her arms in the air. "Price tag," Vinh says, followed by the movement of feet, the opening of a kitchen drawer. *Scissors,* Ben thinks. Snip, snip.

The door opens. Ben lowers the volume. No one knocks in this house.

"We'll be home around ten," his mom says. "Maybe nine."

"Ten." Vinh leans in.

His mom looks around the room. Her face screws up as if she's thinking about saying something but doesn't know what.

Last night, he came home late. He tried to sneak in before his mom stopped him. She had been in the kitchen the entire time; paperwork littered the table.

Her torrent of questions: *Where have you been? Why were you out? Do you know what time it is?*

She had sniffed the air and found the smell of cigarette, the smell of alcohol, the smell of Paradise and the Quarter and New Orleans. She walked up to him and felt his shirt. Dirty.

"And your father, if he saw you like this," she went on, "he'd roll over in his grave. Times like this I wonder why we even came here. This wouldn't happen in Vietnam. We should've stayed in Vietnam."

Something snapped in him and the next thing he knew, he was yelling, "This is not Vietnam. Fuck Dad and fuck you!" All his life, it felt like she was trying to shape him, to mold him like a piece of clay into the man he's never met. Didn't she understand he was his own person? That he had his own flesh and blood and mind? That he was unique, one-of-a-kind? Why couldn't she see that? He stomped off to his room and slammed the door. Something, somewhere—a picture, a decorative bowl of plastic fruits, a vase— fell down. He heard her sweeping up afterward. He took a breath and bent down to look through the keyhole. It was a picture on the hall table. She was bent over sweeping the bits and pieces into a dustpan. She paused for a second, squatting there on the floor.

Now her face softens. "Be good," she says and leaves. As she closes the door, Ben swears he hears her sigh.

Thảo is here somewhere, in the sea of people and the rap music shaking the floor. She said seven o'clock. It's ten past seven.

A man grabs him by the shoulder. "ID," he says.

Tuấn reaches into his pocket and realizes it's with Thảo. Thảo needed ten bucks that morning (for something), and he'd told her to just grab his wallet. They share a place together, a duplex in Tremé; what's ten bucks? Tuấn pretends not to understand the bouncer. He cocks his head to the side. *I no undohsten?*

"ID or you're out, little guy."

Little guy? The fuck?

"He's with me."

"Thảo!"

"This way."

"Where've you been?"

She doesn't answer, just pulls him and walks. Any other man would have demanded an answer from his woman, but he and Thảo don't work like that.

The bouncer goes away, too, and tries to disappear among all the bodies, but he can't. He's just too big, too bulky. Who needs that much body, anyway? Not Tuấn!

Together Thảo and Tuấn move, slick as snakes, to the third floor, to a balcony overlooking the dance floor, and the whole gang's already there. They've been waiting a very long time.

It's seven o'clock and still very hot. Hương's dress sticks to her legs, and though she didn't want to go out (her back is killing her), she humors Vinh. She feels like eggrolls tonight.

He drives out of Versailles. He passes their usual Chinese restaurant.

"Where are we going?" she asks.

"The Quarter," he says.

"No, no, no!" She waves her hand to tell him to stop.

"What? What is it, *hun-ey?*" He's never called her "honey" before, but saw it on a TV show, a husband calling his wife "honey."

Now is as good a time as any to start using it, though they're not married. Yet.

"I just came from there," says Hương. "Why would we ever want to go there?"

He stops at a red light. "But it's different at night. Parties, music . . ."

"Did you know New Orleans is one of the most dangerous places in the country? I read that in the *Thành Phố*. The store across from me was robbed just last month. And they sold Mardi Gras masks! *Mardi Gras masks!*" she says. "Nothing is safe! Mardi Gras masks!"

Then there were the tourists. Loud, drunk, obnoxious tourists. She had plenty of them during the daytime. That morning, for instance, she found a tourist asleep in front of the salon, a puddle of neon vomit around his head. She had to ask one of the city workers for his hose.

The light turns green. The car accelerates.

"Turn back," she says.

"This is going to be fun." When Vinh sees he's over the speed limit, thirty-five miles per hour, he slows.

"Tell me this: What are we going to do out there, anyway?"

They drive under a small overpass. A wad of green gum falls down and sticks to the windshield.

"Stop the car!" Hương yells.

Vinh brakes. There must have been something in the road, but then he sees Hương stepping out, head turned upward toward the bridge.

"You kids!" she yells. Her voice can be shrill if she wants it to.

One kid wears a football jersey—not the Saints (that's the important part, Vinh notes). Another one drops a Styrofoam cup. Blue ice splashes everywhere. It splatters onto her shirt. The smell is astringent. A hurricane daiquiri, for sure.

"You go home!" she says. "We don't want you here!"

They laugh.

"You think this funny?" she asks.

Vinh doesn't know much English, but he knows she has an accent.

"You go away," Hương continues. "Go home. This not your city!"

"Hương! Hương!" Vinh runs and leads her back into the car. "You're ruining a good evening, *dear.*" "Dear" is another word he heard on TV. Since moving to New Orleans, he's had a lot of time to himself. He takes napkins out of the glove box and presses them on her dress where the slush splattered.

"Those kids!" says Hương. "They come here and make the city dirty. They don't belong here."

Tuấn's in the backseat of Sáng's car (stolen, he is sure), speeding down Royal Street, though you shouldn't speed through the Quarter, not even if a stampede of gators is chasing you. The roads are made for horses, not cars.

Tuấn bites his lip and Thảo pats him on the knee. "Lighten up," she says.

Up front are Quang and Sáng, and Sáng is driving with one hand. He presses down on his horn and a lady standing on a corner yells at them to slow down.

"Mẹ mày," he shouts out the window. Then to his friends: "In Vietnam, they used to speed like this in their Citroëns and motorcycles. I mean, have you ever seen pictures of Saigon? We người Việt don't care about speed limits," Sáng says.

Tuấn doubts it. He's beginning to doubt everything Sáng and Quang and even Thảo say. They all came to America as kids and spent more time in New Orleans than Saigon. How much could they remember? There must have been a limit, a moment of transition when they were more American than Vietnamese, and there was no going back. *Maybe they were fighting that,* he thought, then he wondered what the point of fighting it was.

Quang passes a bag of Cheetos to the back. His arm is hairless like a boy's but has the SBZ tattoo, a bit faded like it's on an old T-shirt, not as vibrant and attention-grabbing as it used to be.

"Where you taking us, anyway?" Thảo asks. She laughs. She laughs because the speed is fun or funny.

"You'll see!" says Quang.

"Anh Quang sạo quá!" Thảo exclaims.

The Cheetos are spicy and taste like cigarette butts.

When Ben hears the car start, he runs to the window to see it back out and drive away. He waits there for a full minute before knowing for sure they're gone. It's seven. If he can get ready quickly, he can leave by seven thirty, get to Paradise by eight thirty at the latest. He told Georges he'd be there by eight to help with some setup. He might run late, but Ben doesn't think Georges will mind; he wants Ben to experience the gay life, he wants to have a positive influence on the youths. After all, Georges always said, children are the future.

"Southern Decadence," Georges had told him, "is like gay Mardi Gras."

"What's more gay than Mardi Gras?" Ben asked.

"Southern Decadence!" everyone within earshot said. They swung their beers and cocktails in the air as Madonna's "Vogue" played. All the liquid sloshed around, spilled to the ground. A guy in roller skates passed by as he framed his face. A chubby drag queen chased a muscular woman into the back room. Someone came in and asked if anyone had seen their dog—a purple-hued poodle wearing a leather vest with fake diamond studs who answered to the name Martha. It was only noon.

They sit down on the patio of a restaurant named after a captain. It has a big fish above its name. The fish wears an eye patch. Everything in the Quarter is in bad taste, Hương thinks. Even the salon has a fleur-de-lis sticker on the window. She wanted to take it off, but Miss Linh said it made the salon more authentic, more New Orleans. ("They don't want a Vietnamese manicure; they want a New Orleans one.") It almost made Hương laugh—the fleur-de-lis on the window, Miss Linh's Buddha statue in the corner, the smell of sewage and alcohol that wafted in from outside. What mish-mash was this? Who was responsible for this mess gumbo?

That was what Bình smelled like last night, she remembers. Sure, she was mad that he was coming home late (he'd been doing that for a while, and as long as she knew where he was, she was satisfied), but the smell of the Quarter told her something else. He was heading off the rails (just like his brother!). She imagined him coming under a bad influence that was distinctly New Orleans (which, she'd learned only recently, was also called the City of Sin) and rued the day she came to this city. Where did she go wrong and what could she do?

As an exercise, she wrote to Công. She never stopped writing to him. Writing was the only way she'd survived the last fifteen years, a way to put down her thoughts, make the world make sense. On loose-leaf paper, she'd put down the date and write the words *Dear Công* and all her thoughts would flow out, organizing themselves or at the very least making themselves apparent. *Dear Công, Another day in New Orleans . . . and our sons are in danger.* She could have used anybody's name, she convinced herself, but old habits do not die.

Hương looks over the menu.

They'll have dinner and after that they'll make their way down to the festival, Vinh thinks. The ad said there would be music and performers and drinks. He decides he will not drink here. They'll find a bar where they can share a daiquiri.

"Too expensive," says Hương. "I can cook this at home for a third of the cost and we could feed the entire family, too." She eyes Vinh.

How are we paying for this? say her eyes.

"Don't worry. You're worth it, *darling!*" says Vinh.

Credit cards, Vinh has learned, are the bricks of the American dream. The trick is to have several cards, so you can pay each off with another. Borrowed money, borrowed time, borrowed country.

"What do you think Bình is doing right now?" asks Hương out of the blue. Maybe she should be gentler with the boy. She is always angry, she's beginning to recognize. She uses the menu to fan herself.

"Do you want to end up like your brother?" she had asked when she learned he had to retake a class (again!).

"And what's wrong with Tuấn?" Bình huffed.

"Everything!" she huffed back. She hadn't meant to say that. She had meant to point to one or two things. But "everything" just came out, and she couldn't take it back. She felt flustered. "He just went down the wrong path," she said. "I want to save you from that."

How unrecognizable America had made them, she was thinking, all of them. If Công were here, he would not know any of them, would not even know her. At times like these she missed him the most—how life would have been different if he hadn't stayed behind. Thinking about it made her mad at Công all over again.

"I should check on Bình," Hương says to Vinh, rising from the table. "I'm sure they have a phone I can use. I'll be right back."

The outfit comes together better than he'd planned: blue jeans, a white tank top, a sprinkling of glitter on his face, a bright blue feather boa he got at a thrift shop. He looks at himself in the mirror and smiles. They'll take his picture, he's thinking, for *Out on the Town*. But something is missing. Something more. Lipstick, perhaps. Lipstick—of course! The clock says 7:20, so he hurries to his mother's room.

He checks her bathroom. Nothing. He checks her drawers: a

stick of ChapStick and a compact mirror. Not useful. He goes to the closet. The first box (a tin for butter cookies) he sees is full of sewing supplies: spools of thread, a cushion for needles, loose buttons. He stands up to see where else things might be and sees the top shelf lined with shoeboxes. It is already 7:26. He must hurry up!

He's too short, so he stands on tiptoes. When that isn't enough, he begins jumping with one hand reaching out in the air. He jumps and he jumps and he jumps. He's almost reaching the shelf, just so close, so he pushes off the floor even harder and reaches out his pointer finger. And then—*bang!*—they crash to the floor, all four boxes plus a Polaroid camera that flashes when it falls to the floor, a scattered mess. But the task is almost complete. It is 7:28.

One box spills out important documents, passports, and citizenship papers. Another is completely empty. One of the smaller boxes holds what he needs—unused blush, eye shadows in sealed plastic containers, tubes of eyeliner, a bottle of perfume, and two tubes of red fiery lipstick. He reaches for the lipstick, but it's the box that fell behind it that catches his attention. A box of letters, a postcard, pictures, cassette tapes.

It is 7:31. The phone rings.

Sáng slams on the brakes. A parade.

"Fucking parade," says Thảo.

"Fucking queers," says Sáng.

"Fucking fags," says Quang.

Tuấn peers over the headrests of the front seats but sees nothing but people and flags waving high. One is the Louisiana flag with its pelican, the other has stripes of colors like a rainbow.

"Where *are* we going?" asks Thảo.

"The Lot," says Sáng.

"But look at Bourbon," says Quang. "It's always Bourbon."

"We should just take Canal," says Thảo.

"Canal has traffic."

"I hate sitting here." Thảo opens her door. "Park it and walk it, boys," she says. It amuses Tuấn, a Vietnamese girl with a southern accent. "I said park it and walk it!"

They park it and they walk it.

"Bình," says Hương, sitting back down, "isn't answering."

"Boys will be boys," says Vinh.

Boys will be boys, she repeats in her head. It's stuff like this that makes Hương believe Vinh could never be a father. Too unserious. Too immature.

"Do you know how hard it is to raise children?" she asks him. "Did I tell you about that one time I left the boys home alone and they threw an entire box of bang snaps on top of the Phạm girls, and . . ."

"And those girls had sand in their hair for a week and smelled like fire." Vinh completes her sentence. He likes completing her sentences. It's what couples do.

"And the little one had to get her hair shaved off. Trời ơi, it was months before she grew it back."

"That was ages ago. Tonight, relax!"

"And last night the boy comes home late! What's a mother supposed to do?"

"Relax, Hương."

"I can't relax. It's hot and look at all these people, listen to all this noise. It's all giving me hives!" She takes a sip of water but stops when she sees something in the distance. "They're having a parade or something tonight," she says.

"Yes," says Vinh. "Exactly."

"The Lot is past Bourbon," says one of the guys.

"What do you need there?" asks Tuấn.

"Someone owes me money," says Sáng. "Three Mexicans." Sáng is not looking where he's going because he's busy eyeing Thảo. Tuấn has an urge to push him or punch him, but the guy bumps into a tall lady with an overwhelmingly pink wig.

"Dahling! Be careful!" says the woman. "A boy like you, someone will snatch you up!" It's now that Tuấn notices it's a guy in a dress.

"Faggot!" says Sáng, offended or scared or shocked or surprised. The word comes out like a gasp.

"Hey, keep your voice down," says Tuấn. He doesn't want to get into a fight. He always loses fights.

"What he means," says Thảo, "is to shut up, Sáng."

"Who's calling who a fag?" someone yells in the crowd.

A set of beads with a gold medallion on it flies toward them. Tuấn sees it clearly. It sparkles in the light of the streetlamps. Like a shooting star. He sees it coming until it slams down hard on his face.

"Who's a faggot?"

"Where's a faggot?"

"There's a faggot!"

"We're all faggots here!"

All the letters are in Vietnamese, the whole stack. Ben can't read it, but he can tell that much. It's the squiggly marks on top and below the letters. Each piece of lined paper starts with "Công." Each ends with a signature that starts with jagged mountains that become rolling hills. There are fewer envelopes than letters. The envelopes are stamped RETURN TO SENDER.

There is one postcard. The picture on it looks like a place in Europe: cobbled streets, old buildings, moody sky; a man in the background strolls with his hands in his pockets. A couple sits outside a restaurant eating pastries and drinking coffee. The postmark, though, is Bangkok and the date says 25-04-1980. The message is in Vietnamese. The signature at the end is a squiggle that looks almost like a snail unraveling itself.

The photographs are what shake Ben the most.

There's one with a man holding a bicycle between two buildings, an empty alley. Laundry lines hang between the buildings. Ben sees in the distance a shirt, a pair of pants. The man in the photo wears neat pants and a button-up shirt and sunglasses that look too big. The corners of his mouth curl up but only slightly, as if he's not in the mood to get his photo taken. This photo, says his face, is a favor. The man lifts his eyebrows, waiting. Ben imagines him tapping his foot.

The same man is in the next picture, though he's maybe a few years older and this time he's kissing a woman. It's a wedding. They are wearing *áo dàis*—is that what they're called? Very traditional. This must be in Vietnam. It's an up-close photo. The man holds the woman's face. The woman holds on to his shoulder. They're both smiling, even as they kiss. They are the happiest, perhaps the happiest they've ever been and will ever be. Ben looks closer and feels like he's seen this woman before, known her all his life.

In the last picture the man is a bit older again. He's standing in what looks like a classroom—a chalkboard in the background, a desk in the center. A briefcase lies on the desk next to a small stack of books. The man holds his hands in front of him, holds them together. His posture is relaxed, and Ben can tell he's comfortable here in the classroom. His face is serious—he's not smiling. But his eyes, they light up. Ben swears he's seen this man before, too, known him all his life.

They walk toward the parade. Hương carries a plastic bag of the food they didn't eat around her wrist. How does anyone finish a "surf 'n' turf"? Bình will like it. He's American and will like this kind of stuff. This, she imagines, is a peace offering.

"What's this here?" she asks when they get closer to Bourbon.

"It's a parade!" says Vinh. "A celebration of something Southern or other. You know the people here have parades for the smallest reasons."

"It's New Orleans." Hương shrugs. "It's what we do," she says like a true New Orleanian. When someone asks her where she's from, she tells them New Orleans, and they always say, "No, really."

It's when they reach Bourbon that Vinh realizes he's made a mistake. He didn't understand something in the advertisement. A word was missing. This wasn't what he imagined: the half-naked men holding each other; the drag queens riding floats, waving like they're Miss America; a woman with short hair and a leather suit whistling at Hương.

"Not bad," says Leather Suit.

"Do you remember where we parked, Hương?"

"What do you mean? We just got here."

Vinh takes her hand and they turn around. He pulls her and walks faster.

"I don't understand. You said you want to take me out, so why don't you take me out?"

"There was a mistake," Vinh says. "There's been a huge mistake."

"Who's a faggot? Where's a faggot? There's a faggot! We're all faggots here!"

It's the face. The man's face. His tall nose, his eyes, his serious lips. Where has Ben seen it before? He has a suspicion.

He runs into the bathroom (his mother's) and gazes into the mirror. His glitter-speckled face stares back seriously. He holds up the picture of the man standing by the desk. His eyes move back and forth—two seconds on his own reflection, two seconds on the man, two seconds here, two seconds there. He runs down the hall to his own bathroom, turning on all the lights on his way there. For a second, he's sure the other mirror's lying to him and this one, the one he's used to, will not.

He holds up the picture. He looks at his face. *Uncanny,* he thinks.

In the chaos of high heels and leather boots, Tuấn is on his hands and knees. The bruise on his right eye, where the gold medallion hit him, aches, swells. He closes it and crawls forward with one eye open. He's trying to find Thảo. His heart pounds. His forehead is soaked with sweat. Someone steps on his finger.

"Fuck!" he screams, though no one hears him. "Fucker!" He could get trampled on tonight and die and no one would care. He stands up and tries to maneuver through the street. An empty beer bottle falls from above. He trips over a blond girl barfing into a bag. Her friend rubs her on the back. For a minute, he finds reprieve outside of a closed cigar shop. The window is polished and, somehow, still clean, no smudges or oily marks from hands. He sees himself reflected there and doesn't recognize what he sees—a black eye, unkempt hair, baggy clothes that make the wearer look smaller than he actually is.

And what *was* he, exactly? Who *is* he? He tries to straighten his hair, which is greasy with gel. He licks a finger and cleans the dirt off his cheek. He remembers, years and years ago, his mother dressing him up (for what, he doesn't remember), wiping his face with a thin cloth and combing his hair. When was that?

Out of nowhere, Thảo grabs his wrist.

"There you are!" she says. "What a party! What a parade!" She laughs and slaps his back.

"Let's go," he says and pulls her out of Bourbon toward Dauphine and then Canal. He sees the tall business buildings ahead, the palm trees on neutral ground, the cars stopped at a red light. Someone throws a bottle, and it crashes on the ground in front of them. They step over it and Thảo is still laughing. Laughing with her mouth wide open, air pushing out from the gut. She's laughing and can't stop because everything is so wickedly fun, so wildly funny. *What a party, a parade!* she keeps saying. Tuấn's mouth, meanwhile, has gone all dry.

Ben lays everything on the kitchen table and gets the boom box out of his room. He plugs it in and pops in the first tape. His mom's voice, unmistakably *her* voice, goes:

A lô, anh Công? Em Hương đây. Em và các con đã tới Mỹ. Đang ở New Orleans. Trước đó, em và các con ở Singapore trong nhiều tháng, ở trại tị nạn chật ních thuyền nhân. Thuyền nhân, boat people, là cái tên họ đặt cho những người có hoàn cảnh như em . . . Em nhớ anh vô cùng. . . .

He doesn't know what's being said, but he remembers the words, remembers what was happening when she said those words. It's less an actual memory than an impression of a memory, many memories: shadows moving in soft lighting, a quiet clicking of a spinning tape, the feeling of buttons with their small indentations for fingers, the smell of new plastic.

Tuấn and Thảo wait at the bus stop. Thảo is still laughing.

"What the hell happened there?" Tuấn asks.

Thảo keeps on laughing. Every time she tries to answer, she can't help but laugh some more, louder.

"Thảo," he says. He says it several times to get her attention. "Thảo, maybe we should stop—"

Thảo leaps to his lips. She tastes like Cheetos and cigarettes and alcohol and lipstick. He pushes her away.

"No," he says.

"What do you mean, no?" she asks.

"This"—he points to himself, his clothes—"it's not me. None of this"—he points to her tattoo on her arm—"is me."

A bus comes, stops, then continues on its way. It is a hot New Orleans night.

The car pulls into Versailles and Hương is still giddy.

After they turned away from Bourbon, they found a jazz bar on Burgundy. Surprisingly, barely anyone was there and they stopped in for a drink. A brass band played music from the seventies and they, nearly alone, danced. The whole evening made Hương feel young again and unleashed a side of her she'd almost forgotten was there.

Hương and Vinh walk up the stairs to the apartment hand in hand. From outside, Hương sees all the lights are on. She looks at her watch. Eleven o'clock and he's still here. She unlocks the door, pushes it open.

Then her voice.

A lô, Công?

She looks up, and Bình's standing over the kitchen table. His dented boom box sits in the center.

Em Hương đây. Em và các con đã tới Mỹ.

The boy presses Stop. Her voice clicks off.

It's now that she notices the letters scattered across the table, the pictures, the postcard. She runs to grab them, but in the same instant Bình takes them in his hands and throws them out the back window. They flutter down and scatter on the ground.

"You lied to us," her son cries. "This . . . it's proof," he says. He reads, "1980."

"I can explain," says Hương, steadying her voice.

"1981. 1982. 1983. 1984. He wasn't dead."

"I can . . ."

"1991, 1992 . . . What is this? He didn't die."

". . . explain."

"I had a father and you kept him away from us."

Things got complicated, she wanted to say. You don't understand, and she is twenty-five again. It is 1978. And she is on a boat, she is on an island, she is on a plane, she is living with the Minhs and Mr. Minh smashes a lamp and the lamp shatters into hundreds of pieces and they are yelling all night and she is staying up all night then she is living in a motel then she is living in a church then she moves to Versailles then she's trying to contact him, trying to contact their father. . . .

"Your father . . ." she says.

"You were talking to him. See? See?" He balls up more letters and throws them out the window.

It is 1978 and she is twenty-five again. She's writing letters. She's recording messages. The letters, the packages, they get returned until the day they are not.

It is 1980 and she is twenty-seven again. *Please don't contact me again,* his message reads. *It is the best for the both of us.* It is 1980 and she is twenty-seven.

"Are you listening to me?"

In this new country, by herself, all alone in the world.

"I was all alone . . ."

He ejects the cassette tape and throws it out. He takes the entire box and throws it out, too. The contents splash into the bayou, into the mud, the receding water.

". . . trying to protect you, Bình; the truth . . ."

"What kind of life are we living? What else are you keeping from us? What else?"

"Just let me explain, Bình. Let me explain. Your father aban—"

"What else?"

"Us. What else was I . . ."

"What else?"

". . . to do? To say."

"What else?"

"L-Let her explain, son," Vinh stammers.

"Don't call me that. You don't get to call me that. Don't call me that!" He pushes Vinh. Vinh stumbles back. *It's true,* Vinh thinks, *he's not the boy's father.* It hurts him all the same. He tries not to let it show.

"Bình," says Hương.

"Leave me alone."

"Bình."

"Who are you, even?"

"Son."

"No mother . . ."

"Son!"

"You're no mother."

It's as if her body is acting on its own then—her hand reaches out and strikes his skin. The smacking sound of flesh on flesh echoes in the air, hangs in her mind.

"Son?" Hương says.

She doesn't know what's come over her. She sees herself from far away. What has she done? What will she do now? She peers into his eyes and there it is—a burning, hot look, a mean, scolding look. She touches her own impossible hand.

What has happened? they all think. *How did we get to this point? And what will happen now?*

Ten miles south, Tuấn sits with his head in his hands. Thảo is thrashing about, knocking stuff down, packing up her belongings, making the most noise possible.

We should stop seeing each other, he had said. *You should leave.*

Fine, she said, *but say goodbye to the life you've had.*

She knocks over a chair (several chairs) and breaks a lamp.

SBZ will come after you, she says.

She flips over a table, kicks away the couch.

We will ruin your life.

On the way out, she grabs a bat, takes it through the front window. And then she's out, slamming the door, and there, on the wall, a family picture falls down, the crash the sound of a cry.

In the ensuing silence, he thinks of his mother, he thinks of his brother. They are lying on the floor under broken glass. He wants to check in on them now, give them a call. Yes, that's what he'll do; he'll do that and go to sleep. He picks up the phone and dials home. It rings and no one picks up. Yes, this will calm his rapid heart, he is thinking as he waits, he is sure; this will calm him down so he can sleep. It rings and no one picks up.

Yes, everything will be okay; he just needs to hear their voices, it's everything he's ever needed, all this time, why didn't he think of it before, he's so stupid. . . .

The phone rings and everyone just lets it ring until it stops ringing.

Hương steps back, lets out a breath. Her hands shake.

"We're not the bad sons," Ben says. "You're the bad mother." He feels a weight lifted off his chest.

"Mẹ xin lỗi," she says. *Mom is sorry.*

It is calm like before a storm. She remembers her first days in Versailles and a hurricane alarm howling out of nowhere, without warning. How frightened she was, but also how prepared: grab the boys, run, and escape. *Escape.* It was later that she realized there were no wars in New Orleans: no wars, not here.

The last war was on a different shore, with different people, in a different country, and there's no going back, back to that life. She realizes this now, but that doesn't make it ache any less. In fact, the ache grows. It grows into two boys, and the two boys grow into two sons, and those two sons grow to look like their father, uncannily like their father in their moods, their movements, their voices, so that it's always like she's losing him again—to the world, to life, to fate.

She reaches out a hand, but he turns, walks away, closes his door. She stays frozen where she stands, not trusting her own body, what it would do, what it's capable of doing.

And a gentle breeze blows in from the window. And the gentle breeze is cool. And she realizes how strange it is on such a hot day in the middle of August in the middle of the night. Chilled, she wraps her arms around her body and starts for her room. The night is silent.

IV

Ben

Tuấn rented one-half of a duplex house in Tremé. It sat off Highway 10 and rumbled every time trucks passed by. Ben had visited only once and could not remember where exactly it was, except that it sat off the highway, somewhere on Ursulines. The bus let him off half a mile away. When he got there, he walked up and down the street, trying to remember what it looked like. Start with the color of the place, he told himself—was it a white house or a yellow one? What sat across from it—another house or a gas station?

By eight, his shirt was sticky with sweat as people left their houses for work. He fanned himself with a magazine and dragged his suitcase across the sidewalk until he saw his brother kneeling on a front porch, sweeping up bits of shattered glass. It was a blue house, the only blue one on the block.

"T!" he called out. At first his brother didn't hear him. He walked up and tapped him on the shoulder. When he turned around, it was the bruise on his brother's eye that Ben noticed first.

"Is something wrong with mẹ?" was his brother's first question.

"No, nothing," Ben replied. "Why would you ask that? What happened to you?"

"She didn't pick up last night. I was calling and no one picked up."

Ben pointed at his brother's eye. "You're too old to get into fights, aren't you?"

"What? This?"

"Is Thảo here?" Ben realized he had to deal with her now. "Should I go? I can go." He didn't want to go; he had nowhere else to go.

"Thảo left. We broke up." He held up the broom and pointed at the shattered glass.

"Oh, God, geez. I'm so sorry, T," Ben said, though he didn't mean any of it. "Wow. God. What happened?"

"Look, I don't want to talk about it, okay? Why are you here, anyhow? It's like almost nine. Don't you sleep in? It's Saturday. You don't even get up before ten."

"Well, you wouldn't believe it, but"—Ben walked in and settled his suitcase on the sofa; he sat down and took off his shoes—"Mom went crazy."

After Tuấn cleaned up the shattered window, he made breakfast (cereal with soy milk from the can) as Ben told him about the cassette tapes with their mother's voice, the photos of their father ("Undeniably him," Ben said. "Looks kind of like me, but exactly like you"), and the fact that their mother had been writing to him all this time.

"She lied to us," Ben said. "All this time she said he was dead and here she was, writing to him. What was she trying to hide, that's what I'm thinking."

Tuấn paused, then shrugged his shoulder. "There are many

things we won't ever understand," he said. He finished his cereal and walked to the sink.

"Why didn't she—" Ben grasped for words with his hands as if they were right in front of him but he couldn't catch any of them. "Tell us?" was what he settled on.

"There was a war, Bình."

"*Ben.*" He stood up and followed his brother. The sun streamed in through the window over the sink; there were no blinds there.

"Ben. There was a war, *Ben.* Things go horribly wrong during wars. Even without wars, things go horribly wrong all the time. You pick yourself up, you move on, be glad with what you do have. That's the best we can do sometimes."

Ben stood by his brother's side as he washed the dishes. There had to be a better explanation, he felt. What was his own brother hiding from him? And how could he stand there so calm?

"Aren't you angry?" Ben said then.

Tuấn went on washing; the water was now steaming. It fogged up the window, so he leaned forward and wiped it with a sudsy hand.

Ben continued, "It's like, I don't know, I've been seeing a ghost my entire life and now I finally see him, have proof of him—but I can't grasp him, can't show him to anyone else. But that ghost is more than just some dead man, some stranger. It's me. Or part of me. All my life it feels like a part of me has always been gone, a ghost."

"I know what you mean."

"And she could have stopped that from happening. But she didn't. She didn't, T, she didn't!" He heard his own whiny voice and hated it. He changed his tone. "You knew the man—don't you wanna know what happened?"

Tuấn let the water run and looked out the window, into the distance. He squinted and Ben thought he must be hurting his eyes and wondered why he was doing that, what he was looking at, out there beyond the bright morning sun.

"I don't go into people's business. I'm over that," Tuấn told him finally. "I don't question anybody anything. Everyone has to make choices. Sometimes there're only bad choices, all of them, each way you look it's a sea of bad choices, and we just have to pick one, the best one, or maybe just any one."

Ben balled his hands into fists, then he let them go. "You don't understand," he said, more sad than angry.

"There was a war," Tuấn said. "*You* don't understand."

Ben looked at his brother then and swore he saw tears welling up in his eyes. The sight of his brother on the cusp of such sadness nearly frightened him. He took a step back and felt embarrassed for coming, for bringing any of this up.

Later that morning, their mother banged on the door. As Tuấn went to answer it, Ben hid in the hall closet. Tuấn's black eye didn't seem to reassure her of anything. They were speaking in Vietnamese, which made it hard for Ben to understand, but she sounded angry nonetheless. She left just as abruptly as she came, probably because of work. The last thing Ben heard his brother tell her was "Whatever happened," something more in Vietnamese, and the word "family."

"What you tell her?" Ben asked when she was gone.

"I pretended I didn't know what she was talking about." Tuấn looked at his own watch. "She's upset," he said and began getting ready for work.

Over the next month, Ben stayed at Tuấn's. Tuấn thought he'd be helpful because he could stay home all day and be on the lookout for Thảo and the Southern Boyz, who were mad at him for wanting to leave. For two weeks straight, they came and asked where Tuấn was; Ben answered the door and told them he'd moved away and they weren't in touch anymore.

Ben, meanwhile, planned what he would do next. School, he

felt, was out of the question. He hated it and it hated him, and if his brother did fine leaving, he, too, would carry on the (only) family tradition they had. (Tuấn said he hated that he called it that, and Ben said it was true.)

He scrapped the plan to move to a different city for now—too expensive, even if he had a job. He kept the idea in the back of his mind; it was always a possibility later.

A job was a good place to start. His brother worked as a busboy at an oyster house in the Quarter. He couldn't work in the Quarter since his mother worked there, too. (For the same reason, he stopped going to Paradise altogether.) One afternoon, Tuấn came home with a flyer he found stuck in the window of a coffee shop. MISSING it said on the top, and under that showed a picture from last year's yearbook. They were plastered all over the Quarter, his brother said. "I feel like I'm housing a felon here."

He started job hunting by circling ads in the newspapers. He'd visit the place before he applied to make sure he liked it enough, and if he did, he asked for an interview. With all the time in the world now, he encountered places in the city he never had before. The old clutter of Tremé and the Quarter gave way to the rundown housing projects in Iberville, which transformed into tall, clean buildings in the Business District, which was a world away from the Garden District and its opulent homes behind iron fences.

The large white house on St. Charles Avenue with purple trimming and a wraparound porch was the address the man on the phone gave him. They were a couple: two professors at UNO who were too busy, the man said, to pay attention to the smaller but necessary things of life. They were looking for someone to do housework—cleaning the mildew from the shower; laundering the clothes (his word, "launder"), the bedsheets, and kitchen towels; some light food preparation now and then. They'd placed an ad in the *Times-Picayune*. Ben did not usually read the *Times-Picayune* but one day, on a whim, decided to get a copy.

Ben walked up the steps. He tightened his tie. How odd, he was thinking when he reached the door, that this was the first time he'd ever seen a doorbell. None of the apartments in Versailles had them. Neither did any of the homes he visited in New Orleans East. He knew this was an embarrassing fact, and he swore he would not say it aloud in case they would think of him differently. He pressed the doorbell.

The man, Mr. Lars Schreiber—no, Professor Schreiber, or was it Doctor Schreiber?—opened the door. He wore a polo shirt tucked into his pants. His arm muscles bulged under the shirt's tightness. The head of thick hair was already graying, matching his mustache.

"Early," he said, pleased. "Come in!" The professor led Ben to his library. Wood shelves lined the walls, each filled neatly with books. Two leather wing chairs sat near the window, which looked out into the street. Between the chairs was a large marble globe. It was what Ben expected from a professor.

The interview commenced. What experience did he have with cleaning? Did he have experience in housekeeping? Laundry—did he know not to wash clothes on Hot? Why was that? Did he know how to treat a spot? The man had a light accent. It was vaguely European, not English or French, but something else that made his words topsy-turvy. What has he cooked? No real matter. Could he follow directions? That's what this all really is: directions. When could he start? Great.

"Great," Ben said, shaking Schreiber's hand. He had a strong grip, and Ben was tempted to squeeze back even harder, though he knew he couldn't. Up close, Ben noticed, the professor had a strong woodsy, earthy scent, some type of cologne. "Tomorrow, then."

"Tomorrow," Schreiber repeated as he waved goodbye and closed the door.

Ben arrived at Schreiber's every weekday at eight in the morning. The first day, he was given the key to let himself in. On the kitchen counter, a note would be left telling him what needed to be done. Sometimes the Schreibers would be gone; often they were still getting ready for work. Over time, the job turned out to be more than housework. Sometimes, they had him outside doing yard work. Other times, they had him help with their research. Mrs. Schreiber—Elaine—was an art history professor and asked him every now and then to go up to NOMA to take photos of art or look up books at its library and photocopy pages. Schreiber, on the other hand, was a literature professor. When he asked Ben to go to the UNO library to check out a few journals, Ben told him he couldn't: he wasn't a student, being a high school dropout and all. Schreiber said he would take care of it and the next day gave him a library card to UNO. It had Ben's name and a barcode, and under it all, Special Assistant/Guest of Faculty.

"You've been, how they say, upgraded," Schreiber said.

Because the library was bigger than any other he'd ever been to, Ben used the card to his advantage. As he checked out archive copies of *The Comparatist* or the *Journal of Modern Literature,* he also borrowed books he meant to read: *Jane Eyre, A Portrait of the Artist as a Young Man, Germinal*—books assigned to seniors in high school. He could enjoy them now. He went through them at his own pace without having to wait for the dumb students to catch up. He read them during his lunch breaks in between mopping the floors and having to catch the bus to the museum to take a photo.

Schreiber didn't even know about his reading habits—Ben didn't feel he needed to know—until nearly a year after hiring him, before the start of the fall semester, when Ben had to return to the professor's house; he'd left his copy of *Madame Bovary.*

He rang the doorbell, and Schreiber answered. They were about to sit down for dinner. The professor asked if he needed anything. Ben didn't answer (they were at that stage of their relationship, employer and employee, but also friendly and casual—Ben did clean their bathrooms, three of them, after all), but walked past the professor and into the library. He searched the desk, then the chairs.

"Did you leave something behind?"

"*Madame Bovary.* I left *Madame Bovary* behind."

"Oh, I shelved it," said Schreiber, walking over to the bookcase. His fingers glided over Faulkner and Fielding and Fitzgerald and stopped at Flaubert. "I thought it was mine."

"The spine sticker should've been a giveaway," Ben said. He took the book and threw it in his backpack. Before he left for the door, he said, "Sorry."

Ben would read several pages each night. Each morning, before heading off to work, Schreiber would ask him how the reading was going, what he thought about this aspect of the book or that, what kind of ideas did he have about what it was trying to say and how it was going about saying it. What *was* it saying? He must have seen him as some type of novelty, Ben thought: an immigrant boy who dropped out of high school who cleans houses (one house) and reads books. He was not a novelty, he was not some monkey. It reminded Ben of the tourists in the Quarter, pointing and staring at everything. The professor was no better. Ben answered the man's questions. When he finished the book, the professor gave him another: *The Sorrows of Young Werther, Crime and Punishment,* and, for the sake of diversity, the *Lyrical Ballads* by Wordsworth and Coleridge. By the end of the year, when Ben was looking at the instructions for putting up a Christmas tree, Schreiber said: "You're an intelligent young man. Very intelligent. You shouldn't be here."

"Your house?"

"Putting up a tree. Sweeping kitchens. Laundering." He was drinking whiskey, but he was not drunk.

It was the first time anyone had called him that: *intelligent* and *young man.* "Don't waste a life. Let me help you." Schreiber said.

With Schreiber's help, Ben passed his GED test after his eighteenth birthday and got into Delgado Community. Two years later, he quit his position as the professor's assistant and started at UNO as a junior, thanks to Schreiber's pulling of a bureaucratic string here and moving a stack of papers there. Ben came to UNO with a scholarship for gifted literature scholars with Schreiber his strongest advocate.

Ben remembered thanking the professor so many times when he learned about being accepted into UNO. He felt silly—"embarrassed" was more the right word—for being overly thankful. But he was.

"No one has ever cared so much," he wrote in a Hallmark card. He never had a chance to mail it off or give it to him. It sat in a drawer in his desk in his dorm—his very own room, the first in his life.

At the end of his first semester, Ben was invited to Schreiber's year-end dinner. It came as a surprise to Ben: the dinner was just for the professor's graduate students. He was the only undergraduate, but Schreiber said, "You're on their intellectual level."

He arrived at Schreiber's place early, a tub of store-bought cookies under one arm. He thought it was important to bring something.

There was one other student when Ben arrived, a girl who had curly brown hair and orange freckles on her pale cheeks. The frames of her glasses made her eyes look bigger than they really could have been and her turtleneck shirt made her look skinnier and taller than she was.

Schreiber introduced her as Stella and then he pointed at Ben with his hand and said, "The junior I've been telling you about," which made Ben blush. Elaine was explaining to Stella about the art they collected. While her specialty was modernism, she collected Asian art—ceramics, lacquerware, woodblock prints. Ben followed them around the living room as Elaine talked about her collection.

The doorbell rang and two other students came in. They introduced themselves and were pouring bottles of wine when the doorbell rang again and another student entered. All of them were white, and Ben had trouble telling them apart. For the evening, he noted a particular feature each had and in his mind called them that. The guy wearing a blue cardigan was called "Cardigan." The other guy who had a nose ring became "Rings." And the girl wearing knee-high, multicolored socks was named "Socks."

"Tati is not feeling well," Cardigan announced. Ben could not imagine anyone among them being named Tati and assumed it must have been short for something else.

They had all come from across the country to work with Schreiber. Most of them were studying poets and their works. Rings and Socks were both doing their dissertations on Emily Dickinson, while Stella interjected to say that she didn't care for Dickinson that much.

"Take away my feminist badge!" she trumpeted. "I don't like her experimentations. It just isn't my taste. If you're gonna say something, say it straight, don't stay it slant, for Pete's sake." Stella, Ben learned, was a second-year PhD student, and she was the outlier out of all of them. Her dissertation was going to be about more contemporary writers. She liked the dirty realists most of all. ("I would let Raymond Carver fuck me," she would say later that night.)

Cardigan, who threw away his research and was starting all over again on something about Flannery O'Connor, held up his wineglass to say that he agreed and that he didn't like the political correctness of the day and that it hindered good, serious scholarship. If only Bob Dole were president, Cardigan said. He'd voted for Bob Dole, and life would have been different if Bob Dole had won. Sometimes he called Bob Dole "Bobby."

The dining room was set with eight plates for the six students plus the hosting couple. Elaine took away one set since Tati wasn't able to make it, which she said was "a shame." The smell of what must have been roasting chicken drifted out from the kitchen as both Schreibers ran back and forth between the kitchen and dining room, each time carrying a bowl or plate of food for the table. When they got up, Ben felt, as if by reflex, he had to get up, too. The first time he did it, Elaine patted his hand.

Before dinner started, Professor Schreiber said he wanted to have a word.

"Every year at the end of the first semester, I love to bring together my best pupils for a dinner celebration. A life in academia is not easy. It's thankless work. And obscure work!" Here everyone laughed. "But we are doing important work. We're adding some great and necessary thinking to our fields, and the canon will be better for it. This dinner celebration is not only for what we have done but what we will do."

"Hear! Hear!" someone said.

"To the stuff of life!" Schreiber said, and everyone raised their glasses and drank.

It was not the first time Ben drank alcohol, but it was the first time he tasted wine. It surprised him how sweet it was, how very unlike the beers he'd had. And with that, the dinner began.

At one point, after the main course but before the dessert—a choice between pecan and apple pies, frozen because the couple still didn't have time—Cardigan, who wasn't wearing a cardigan anymore, asked Ben what it was that he was studying.

"You're the undergrad he's always yakking about in class. The one doing comparative lit," he added.

"That's him?" Rings asked. "I didn't know that."

"We've read your paper, you know," said Stella.

"I remember the title: 'False Temporalities in Flaubert's *Madame Bovary*: The Misuses of Time and Realism and the Advent of Postmodernism,'" pronounced Socks.

Ben blushed. Outside of the library, outside of Schreiber's office, it sounded ridiculous. Who out there cared about *Madame Bovary* or Flaubert? His mother had wanted them, Tuấn and him, to one day have proper, practical jobs. Ben would be a lawyer, she told him, and Tuấn would be a doctor. They would use their minds and skills to make the world a better place. None of that happened. Nothing ever happened the way you wanted.

"I only liked the title," Cardigan was saying.

"It was a bit underdeveloped," said Socks. "I mean, it seems clever on one level but then unsubstantiated on another." She used her hands as if to diagram the situation in question, her right one atop the left.

"But it was good enough for the SCMLA in March," Rings added.

Someone gasped.

"Oh," said Stella. "He's bringing you?" Her mouth was open, shocked, it seemed, but also disappointed. "I didn't know that. I didn't know he made a decision yet." Her hands shook as she set down her half-empty wineglass.

"He did," several chimed in.

"He did?" Stella asked again.

Socks said, "He did," and held her hand.

"Yeah," said Cardigan and finished his wine. "We should be happy. Very, very happy. Ben is so lucky! We should congratulate him. Congratulations, Ben! Congratulations! Everyone should congratulate him. C'mon, now!" He pointed his empty glass at Ben. When no one said anything, when he was greeted with complete silence, Cardigan yelled, "Everyone, congratulate him!"

Everyone laughed and Cardigan put down his glass violently. "And it seems like his kind is always lucky. I mean." He laughed. Socks touched his arm and told him to take it easy. For a second, she held both of her friends as if they were in a séance. But he pulled away, knocking her arm off the table.

"They're everywhere these days, you know," Cardigan continued. "These Chinese kids. And you'd think they'd just stick in the sciences and math and all that junk and you think just because you're an English major, you're safe because these kids, these always-lucky kids, don't even know English. It's not even their first language. But Ben here, Ben, buddy ol' boy—if that's even his real name—he proved us wrong! He got a scholarship ride here, and now he's going to South Central!"

Socks pulled Cardigan's empty wineglass away and stood up. "I'm going to check in with Schreiber. The pies," she said, then went off.

"Your paper isn't worth shit," Cardigan said. He banged his hand on the table and got up. Ben stood up and backed away. Everyone else gasped.

"I don't know what you want me to say," Ben said. He tried to steady his voice. He took another step back.

Cardigan's face was red and sweaty. "You know you're not supposed to be here. You and I both know that. Goddamn, everyone here knows that."

Just then the kitchen door swung open and Schreiber yelled, "Enough of this!"

He stood at the top of the table and held on to his seat. "This is supposed to be a celebration," he continued. His accent came out more noticeably. German, Ben remembered Schreiber telling him. "A *celebration*, and I will not have anyone criticizing anyone else's work. This is a dinner. We leave academics out of this. We leave politics out of here."

He paused and looked at each of them. "Ben is as intelligent and hardworking as anyone in this room. He is probably more civilized than some of us."

Cardigan put on his cardigan and walked out of the room. They heard the front door slam shut and a car start up.

Then, looking uncomfortable in his own home, Schreiber called to his wife, "Are the pies ready yet, Elaine?" and left for the kitchen.

"This could be a Raymond Carver story. It has everything. It could definitely be a Ray story," Stella said later that night, smoking outside after dessert, as zydeco music—something celebratory, Schreiber said—played inside. "I'm gonna write that story."

The night ended with a slurry of apologies and goodbyes. No one had touched Ben's cookies, and he went back inside to get them as everyone left. Schreiber followed.

"Thanks for sticking up for me out there," Ben told Schreiber. "You didn't have to."

Schreiber shook his head and laughed. "Those students. They get into a PhD program and they think they're better than everyone else. Even *me,* sometimes—you should see some of them in class or department meetings! But, like I always tell them, talent isn't limited. Anyone can be talented. It's about nurturing. And you, you, Ben, you shall be my legacy." He pointed at the cookies, and Ben let him have one.

"Thank you," Ben said as he was about to leave. "I wouldn't know what to do without you, where I would be."

On the bus ride to campus, Ben wondered how long he had to be grateful in this type of situation and if gratefulness amounted to outward expressions and actions or if it was simply a state of one's mind, a feeling. How much did he owe this man and what did this man mean to him? He wondered if this was what having a father felt like, though he wasn't looking for that. His father, dead or alive, was out of the picture, had been out of the picture for a very long time. Any idea he had of him was null. And his mother, too, as a matter of fact. As the bus let him off, he reminded himself to write to his brother. He tried for a postcard each month but had been too lazy lately.

The entire student body was gone for winter break. The campus was empty. A cloud covered the moon. It was cold, but not too cold. His hands slipped into his pockets as he walked through an empty parking lot and then into his dorm building, up the steps, and down the hall to his room. He didn't bother turning on the light or closing the blinds. Just slept off the feeling.

Hương

1998

There was a boy," Hương said, closing the bedroom window. She had been late coming home and Vinh was already in bed, a newspaper folded in his lap. She wanted to tell him why she was late. "There was a boy" was the only way she could have started. On the drive home through torrents of rain, his dejected face was all she remembered.

"It was fifteen minutes to closing," she said. "I was sweeping up, wiping down the tables, totaling the sales. Miss Linh was gone, of course. I was the only one. No one ever comes in at that time. You can't do much with nails in fifteen minutes except maybe trim them."

She closed the door and sat on the bed.

Outside, the rain came down slanted, the wind was so much. It was always like that here. Tomorrow morning there would be pools on the road and water running like small streams in the gutters. The bayou would be engorged for a week then shrink back to its normal size.

"Then I saw this boy coming toward the store. He must have been about nineteen or twenty, and he wasn't from around here."

"How did you know that?" asked Vinh. "That he wasn't from around here?"

"He looked . . . odd," she said. "He was wearing a coat like he was cold, but you know what the rain's like here." Wet but hot. At times violent, at times dreamy, even in October. "He didn't know what the weather's like around here, is what I'm saying. That's how I knew. And besides, he had this look on his face like he was lost. Like he wasn't sure where he was, and, spotting the shop, didn't know if he should come in or not.

"At first, I tried to ignore him. A guy like that wouldn't want his nails done anyway. But he came closer then, and he put his hands around his eyes and he leaned into the window. I was sweeping and he was looking in, this boy in a coat. We both stared at each other for a minute. I didn't want him to come in because it was nearly closing and I had Khánh Ly playing."

Vinh threw the paper to the floor. It smacked the wood and startled Hương.

"But then he moved toward the door and came in. What could I do then? What else could I do?

" 'How are you?' I asked him, leaning the broom against the front desk. All of a sudden, I felt ashamed of the music and the broken store sign and the Buddha in the corner. What was this boy doing here? This boy in a nail salon on a Thursday night? It didn't make any sense.

"But then I saw his face. He looked familiar, like a face I've known before, like when you watch a movie and you know a face but you can't name it. His face reminded me of Vietnam."

"How could a face remind you of Vietnam?" asked Vinh, turning to her now. "He was either Vietnamese or he wasn't."

Even Vinh's face didn't remind her of Vietnam, didn't bring to mind the dirt paths, the bicycles, the wild barefooted kids of her youth, the wet smell of a river, so unlike the dirt smell of New

Orleans. She had lived *here* for so long now, but she would always remember *there*.

"I don't know. He looked like người Việt. He had the bone structure, the broad nose, the round face. Yet he wasn't người Việt, either. His hair was cut close to his head. It would curl, I could tell, if he'd let it grow out. He was part Mỹ đen.

"He was pretty in a way," she said. "A pretty boy. Pretty in the way a child should be. When you hold a child in your arms—he was that kind of pretty. Anyway, you wouldn't understand. You don't have any children."

Here she paused to see if Vinh changed his face. When he didn't, she sat down on the bed.

"He didn't answer, so I pointed to the clock and told him we might not have enough time for a manicure because that's the only thing men get if they come to get anything, and they don't come in by themselves. I told him what I would've told anyone else: that we would open the next day at ten, and we'll have more people there to help him with anything he wants. I should have continued sweeping to show him I was busy closing up, but then he unzipped his coat and took it off.

" 'Maybe you can help me,' he said. 'I've been walking for a very long time. Since this morning.'

"I then remembered that it had been raining all day. I hadn't noticed because I was inside the whole time. And he didn't have an umbrella. Poor boy! No umbrella! That was why he was wearing the coat. The coat was soaking wet.

"It was then that I walked over and took his coat. Up close, I saw he had beautiful but sad eyes. His nose, it was either runny from a cold he was getting or it was the rainwater. I wanted to get a tissue and clean him up, but I told myself one thing at a time. First, the coat.

"It was still dripping so I took it in both hands and twisted it, this big thing, wringing the water out, the way we used to do laundry, you know. And all this rainwater became a puddle on the floor."

Hương looked over at Vinh, who had already stretched out under the covers, his head pressed into the pillow. His eyes were closed.

"I'm still listening," he said. He opened his eyes. "All ears. I swear." He reached over and turned off his lamp. Hương turned hers on.

"Listen," she continued. "After I hung the coat on the rack, I came back, and he was still standing there, listening to the music. It was that tango song about a girl who wants to dance, but she can't find a partner and it's getting late and she has to return to her poor village. It must have sounded like gibberish to him, this song. I wanted to turn it off, tell him sorry. I didn't turn it off, but when I told him I was sorry, he didn't answer, so I walked closer.

" 'I'll stay a little late,' I told him. 'Manicures don't take too long.' "

If he wanted a manicure, she would give it to him. If he didn't, what else could he want? Hương had heard of homeless people coming into stores at the last minute, begging for a place to stay. She knew, looking at this boy, that she would have said yes.

Hương went on. "He took his hand and wiped his nose and then looked at me as if he just noticed I was there. When he saw me, his eyes lit up like he remembered why he was there in the first place, like this was the place he was looking for all along and I was the woman he needed to help him. Without waiting another second, he dug into his pockets, trying to find something.

"For a minute, he looked like he was lost in his own pockets. Like he didn't know if what he was searching for was there. I was standing, trying to guess what it was, like it was a game. Would he pull out a map? A piece of paper with an address? Then he pulled it out. It was in his back pocket."

Hương smiled; the best part of the story was coming.

"And I was right, in a way: it was a piece of paper. He unfolded it and I saw it was wet, too. This boy, he was wet all over. And it was at that moment that I felt I wanted to become his mother. I wanted to sit him down, make him cháo like I used to make the boys when they were sick. I wanted to tuck him into bed. Tell him everything was all right. Whatever it was that was troubling him, it couldn't be that bad. You just had to look at it a different way, I wanted to say."

Her own boys were older now and away. Tuấn lived in Tremé. When he moved, she had begged him to stay: "We don't have much family," she was telling him as he packed. "We're not like those white people with aunts and uncles and grandparents. You, me, your brother, that's all we have. That's why we have to stick together." More than the troublesome girlfriend, more than befriending the wrong people, she feared her sons' going away, leaving her, abandoning their family. She implored Tuấn to stay, but all he did was smile and laugh. "It's only Tremé, Ma! I'll come and visit. You can come and visit." *Ma,* instead of má or mẹ, told her everything.

Her youngest, though, Bình, he ran away. She woke up one morning and he was gone. She didn't even have a chance to say goodbye. At first, she kept quiet about it. She was thinking about the neighbors and then her own shame—How could she not control her own son? Didn't she teach him to respect his elders? These questions soon became: Why wasn't she a better mother? How could she hurt her own flesh and blood? She stapled missing flyers around town, until Tuấn came to her one evening with a bundle of them ripped off from telephone poles.

"Enough, Ma," he said.

"You've found him? Where is he?"

"No, Ma. He's fine. He's doing okay. Trust me. He's fine, he's happy." Over the next few months, when she brought him up again, Tuấn was prepared. "Look," he'd say and pull out a postcard. He had his father's handwriting.

She decided then: If being away from her brought him happiness, who was she to stand in his way? Who was she to say no to her sons? That's what it came down to when it came to raising children: their happiness.

Yet at times she wondered, with a sense of dread in the pit of her stomach, what they were doing and how they were feeling, the both of them. Did they get enough to eat? Were they in good health? She had only ever wanted to protect them and prepare them for what's next, whatever that might have been. In Vietnam. Aboard that boat. Those first days in New Orleans. It was why she'd hidden their father from them. Whatever happened to Công, whatever his reasoning, the fact was his love did not hold up, he was never coming, and that was what he chose. How could she tell her sons that? Wouldn't they be hurt—devastated—to know they weren't worth the journey? Better if they knew a comforting lie, she thought, if that lie meant a kind of shelter.

"It reminded me of a conversation," she said to Vinh. "A conversation I had years and years ago with Tuấn, before Bình was even two years old. He had this frog, you see. We caught it in the bayou. He named it Toto. We kept it in a Tupperware container with tall walls but never sealed it, so he could breathe. But then one day, Toto was lost. He must have hopped out, jumped out the window or something. I remember Tuấn cried so much, like he had just been shot or someone had died. We looked all over the house, but Toto must have escaped, I told Tuấn. I told him that he was free somewhere, that Toto wasn't really lost, just free."

She had wanted to tell the boy that story. Perhaps it would make him feel better. Perhaps he would leave with a smile. Perhaps all his problems would be solved.

"So the boy unfolded the paper," she said. "And he came walking toward me. I began to ask him: 'Did you lose something? Was it a cat? Was it a dog? A frog, maybe?' I was convinced it must have been one of these things. Then he handed it to me.

"It was a picture of a man. A Black man in a clean marine uniform with brass buttons and a white hat. An American flag in the back. I stared at it for a second and then looked up at the boy."

Was he looking for his father? An uncle? No, it must have been his father. They looked nearly identical—that was undeniable. Did his father live here a long time ago, before Miss Linh bought the building and made it into a nail salon?

"'Have you seen this man?' the boy asked me.

"At first, I didn't understand. I saw many people; how could I remember just one of them? Then the boy said he used to live in New Orleans. He and his mother, he said, used to live in government housing on the outskirts of the city. He said he remembered a bayou in the back and how dirty it was. He said he remembered the metal gates in the front. It sounded like Versailles, very much like Versailles, but he didn't say Versailles.

"But if he had lived here, I would've remembered him, wouldn't I? If someone was from somewhere you lived, you would remember them, wouldn't you?

"I didn't tell him any of this, though. I was quiet. I kept listening. So he went on.

"'I was born in Saigon,' he said. 'I never knew my father, but my mom was sure he was from New Orleans. Said she remembered it in a conversation one time or in a letter. That's why she moved here after the war. But she gave up. We moved to San Jose then to be with my aunt.'

"I looked at the photograph then back at the boy in his rain-soaked clothes. Did he fly here? Did he drive? All that effort! I mean, some things, they're lost, but what was lost is perhaps best forgotten. The past is the past. Most of us know this. I know this. You, Vinh, you know this. But this kid—why didn't he know that? What made him come back?

"At the same time, I wanted to tell him that his father was around in the city somewhere. It was a gut feeling. It's a big city, but it isn't that big. When it comes down to it, New Orleans is the type of place where everyone knows someone else you know. It's possible to know everyone here in that way. But I couldn't tell him that," said Hương. "I couldn't be cruel.

" 'I don't know. I'm sorry,' I said. 'I don't know who this is.'

"I handed the picture back, and he looked at it longingly one last time before folding it and placing it into his back pocket.

" 'Thanks anyway,' he said.

"I went to get his coat and he left. It was only after he left that I remembered his name. I remembered him as a child, so small and quiet you sometimes forgot he was there. I remembered his mother."

Sitting on the bed, Hương remembered how he always scowled as a boy. That, along with his shyness, made everyone in Versailles somehow suspicious of him, mean to him, though he was only a child. Once, she remembered, she found him out back by the bayou in the middle of the night. He was holding a large cardboard box, something that once held a large appliance. She asked him what he was doing, and he told her he was trying to get back to his Vietnam: they left on a boat and he thought they could go back on a boat. His response took her breath away. She didn't know what to say to him then. So she just shook her head and told him he had to go home. She remembered that scene now and wondered what she could have said, what she should have said, and if that could have changed the outcome of things.

"What do you make of all of it, Vinh?" Hương looked over and saw Vinh was already asleep.

It was still raining outside; the wind had picked up some more.

Hương wondered if the boy was still walking around New Orleans now, head down, pushing against the falling water. She wished she could have helped him, could have picked out the father he'd lost in the crowd.

She imagined the reunion—the tears, but also the questions that needed to be answered. Why had he left? Why had he never come back? Where was he all this time?

In another life, the boy would find his father and they would be happy. In another, he would find him and everything would be ruined: his father had left him in Vietnam, never thought about him in the last twenty years, resented him. In yet another, it would have been the father who came to her that night.

She imagined her own sons flying to Vietnam and wandering the streets aimlessly. How lost they would be. How disappointed they would become. What sadness they would encounter that she could not protect them from.

Hương

A Vietnamese woman called Hương with the news. She told her her husband had died.

"Husband?" Hương was confused. It was five in the morning. The sun was not yet up.

"Chị Hương," the woman said. "You were the first wife. You must come. He will not rest."

Later that day, a thin white envelope arrived by express mail from Vietnam. Inside, Hương found a small clipping, only a few inches wide, from a newspaper glued to the front side of a postcard, covering a picture of a government building:

Professor Trần Văn Công, 43 years old, of District 2, died of lung cancer. He is survived by a wife.

Hương read and reread the obituary on the airplane. She reread the date: August 4, 1999. What was she doing on August 4, 1999, just a few days ago? What was she doing when Công took his last breath?

"He started smoking," she said to no one in particular. Tuấn slept in a seat across the aisle, and Vinh had been angry and silent since the letter came.

Hương told Vinh he didn't have to come, but he insisted—for her own safety, he said—though she was sure he was jealous. Hương said that she wasn't in love with Công anymore. Công was married to someone else. And she had him, Vinh.

She opened her window shade and was surprised to see water. She wanted the water to be blue, like in the maps. In her memory, it was blue the first time she flew over, a fluorescent blue that was strange and wonderful and alive. On the boat ride, she remembered the water being black and threatening. The water was black now, too, but flat; it looked plain and boring. Disappointed, Hương closed her eyes and tried to remember what Công looked like and why this woman, his wife, had called to tell her the news and ask her to come.

"I feel his spirit," she had said. "He will not rest." The woman made it sound like Hương would be doing *her* a favor.

As they walked through customs, people swarmed beyond the glass that separated the inside of the airport from the outside that was now Ho Chi Minh City. Hương felt like one of those celebrities she saw on TV, greeted by screaming fans as they stepped off their planes.

Lan, Công's wife, would be among them. Lan had said, over the phone, that she was a short and simple woman, whose hair was stringy and flat so she tied it in a bun. Her clothes were simple, too.

"Not extravagant clothes like you have in America," Lan said. "They're simple clothes. I'm a practical woman, chị Hương—có hiểu không?"

Lan might as well have been describing everyone in Vietnam. They all looked the same: small, tired, dirty. Hương felt pity for them, then she felt guilty for feeling that way. They were her countrymen, and she was returning.

Her eyes scanned the crowd as a customs agent inspected her bag. He tapped her shoulder and held up a makeup purse. Plastic and transparent, it looked as harmless to her as anything else. Its contents—her compact, lipstick, a brush, a small pack of ear swabs—couldn't hurt a fly if she tried.

"Cô," said the customs agent. "You can't bring these in here. These are illegal."

"What do you mean illegal? It's makeup. Women everywhere—"

"Cô không phải đang ở Mỹ. Rules are rules here," he replied with a smirk. He had a sloppy way of pronouncing words. He had too-thick eyebrows and oily skin. Then she realized how young he was. Perhaps Bình's age, this boy was born after the war. "Rules are rules," he repeated, raising his caterpillar eyebrows.

Vinh pushed her aside. "Here, take it." He threw a crumpled American bill at him, grabbed her bag, and moved her along. Tuấn followed behind.

They passed through the doors and an old woman grabbed her. "Phương? Phương? Is that you? It's your Auntie Bích!"

"Không," said Hương, pulling back her arm. "I'm not your niece." She walked on.

Another woman, a younger one, grabbed her wrist. "Is that you?" the woman asked.

Hương stopped. "Are you Lan?" she asked. "Are you Công's wife?"

The woman paused. "Yes," she said. "This way; I have a taxi waiting for you." She pulled Hương through the crowd, pushing anyone else who got in her way while Vinh and Tuấn trailed behind.

When they reached the curb, the woman let go of Hương's hand. "Five American dollars, please," she said. She stuck out a palm.

"What?"

"I walked you through this crowd, didn't I?"

"Who are you?" Hương asked.

"How about one dollar? I have two kids to feed."

"Get out of here," Vinh yelled, shooing her away.

"Who asked you, anyway?" the woman said to Vinh.

"Đi!" Vinh said, and the woman ran back into the crowd without another word. "Panhandler," Vinh said.

Hương turned back. "Lan?" she yelled through the crowd. "Lan? Lan?"

At last, she spotted a poster board sign: *Chi Hương va Gia đình từ New Orleans.* She rushed over.

"Lan?" Hương asked the woman.

"Chị Hương?" The woman looked at Hương intensely, then her eyes opened widely in recognition: *Yes, I do know this woman.* On the walk to the waiting van Lan told Hương, "It's like I've known you in another life. Yes, that's what it must have been, why you look so familiar."

Công had settled in Ho Chi Minh City, across the river, in An Lợi Đông, District 2. His wife kept a calm voice as she directed the van driver down a long stretch of highway and down smaller streets. Behind, the city—its buildings still under construction—faded.

"I'm sorry I was late," Lan said. "The funeral preparations. We're behind on everything. *I'm* behind on everything." The body had been cremated the way Công had wanted, but there was still more to do. She had not yet notified all the extended family, had not yet sent out the mourning garments, the white headbands and the thin tunics. She had trouble deciding which poems and prayers to have read at the memorial ceremony. Decisions were so easy with someone else. Now, alone, she told Hương, everything was up to her.

Remembering her own first days in New Orleans, Hương almost said she knew how Lan felt but stopped herself from saying it.

"You must be strong, Lan," she said instead.

Lan said she had not even given Công a posthumous name for his afterlife yet. She was afraid if she didn't choose a tên thụy soon, his spirit would not leave. He would show up every time someone called his name and his family would suffer the consequences of a restless spirit. Think of not being able to go home, Lan said; it could make one mad. Lan didn't believe in much, but she believed in this: that life was a temporary stop, and death a journey home, wherever that was.

Công never cared much for religion and neither did Hương. She asked herself how Công could have fallen in love with this type of woman.

The van stopped on the side of the road. Lan hopped out with a flashlight. Together the four of them walked a dirt path that cut through a thicket of trees.

"You see these trees, Tuấn?" Hương asked aloud. "These are rubber trees. Like in your shoes or tires." She had to look back to make sure Tuấn was still there, he was so quiet. For half a mile, they walked until the path ended and they came to a clearing and a house with marble steps. Lan slid open the front door.

Inside was spacious, bigger than Hương's Versailles apartment. Compared to Versailles, Lan's home was a palace. The polished wood floors led to polished, clean rooms, several of them, immaculate with neat beds, white sheets, and bamboo art panels on the walls. It felt like an insult, this house. What you could have become, who you could have been, where you could have lived. As Lan led them to their rooms, she told them it was built for the entire extended family. With the family wealth on her side, she wanted a family home, where everyone could belong. But no one ever made it to the house. After she showed Tuấn his room, Lan walked Hương and Vinh to theirs.

"Sorry it's a small bed," Lan said. "We usually don't have guests. Maybe a family friend, but no one else." She turned on the light and wiped a finger on the sheets as if checking for dust. "You need more pillows," she declared.

"Don't," said Hương. "We couldn't have asked for more. Thank you, Lan. Thank you." Hương shut the door. There was a long pause before Hương heard footsteps walking away, bare feet slapping the floor, repeating until they faded behind another door.

The next day was Wednesday. The memorial would be held Saturday, the most auspicious day, according to Lan. They would walk, along with Công's lifelong friends, through the neighborhood to a creek at the edge of the woods, where they'd let his ashes float.

When Hương woke up, Vinh was gone, though she heard his voice outside. He stood leaning against a doorway in the back of the house. "You and me have a lot in common, then," she heard Vinh say when she got to the door.

Outside, Lan squatted in front of a hole in the ground where a grill rested over a fire. She placed a wok over it and threw in minced garlic.

"Chị Hương," Lan said. "Did you sleep well?" She fanned the fire. The garlic sizzled. She added more oil.

"I slept well enough," Hương answered.

Lan smiled and threw in vegetables and meat. The frying meat sounded like electricity until it was put out with fish sauce and steam rose from the wok. She tossed the vegetables and used chopsticks to turn over the pieces of meat.

In another life, they would have been rivals, vying for the same heart and the same lives. But in this life, Lan had won, and a pang of jealousy came over Hương. It was unjustified, she knew, though it didn't make her feel any of it less.

"Let me," said Hương, walking over the threshold and toward Lan. "You look tired," she said. Then, looking at Lan, Hương realized she *did* look tired, not a sleepless tired, but a gripping weariness that seemed like it took hold weeks or even months ago and did not let go, did not give any sign of letting go. "I'll finish cooking breakfast. You rest."

Lan fussed but gave in. When she was gone Hương asked Vinh, "What do you think about her?"

"What is there to think about?" he said. "What do you think?"

"I don't know what I think," she said. "What *should* I think?"

After breakfast Vinh and Tuấn left for a city tour, leaving Hương and Lan to plan the memorial. They walked through the house and out into the backyard where Lan had been cooking earlier. Beyond the sheltered outdoor cooking space, there was a small plot of land with a clothesline hanging between two wooden posts. Beyond the clear plot, thick trees blocked out the rest of the world.

Hương looked up into the sky. A gray cloud bloomed into a bigger one. A flock of birds flew past.

"It's supposed to rain today," Lan said, squatting down over a basin of water. She poured in soap and began scrubbing. There was plenty to wash.

"I met Công while he worked at Open University," Lan said. "We were both in the Humanities Department, though we taught different things." She told Hương about the classes she had taught. A folk poetry class, a class on folk songs. "The trick," she told Hương, "was to tell the officials you were teaching about Vietnam's honorable peasant history. But then in the classroom, you do something else completely different. Hồ Xuân Hương didn't just write about peasant things, you know." She laughed and Hương tried to do the same, though she had no idea what Lan was talking about.

Hương found herself, in her mind, competing with this woman. She imagined she was in a race, but when the gun went off she realized someone had strapped cinder blocks to her feet. She told herself that she could have been teaching folk poetry—or a foreign language or even chemistry—if only there hadn't been a stupid war. Had they thought about that when they started the war, she asked herself, that they were ruining so many lives? Yet she knew this was a lie. She was a housewife from a small village. She would have always been a housewife from a small village.

"He never told me about you, you know," Lan said. "He told me he had a wife who went away after the war with his child." Hương thought she heard an accusatory tone in her voice, but decided she was imagining it. "But it was his mother who told me your name." She shook a pair of chopsticks to dry them off and moved on to a spoon.

Hương's eyes lit up. "Is she still alive?" she asked. "Is his mother still alive?"

She remembered Công's mother now, an especially tall woman with a long nose and tiny eyes. She didn't want them to leave the country. She didn't want *Công* to leave the country.

"No, she died last year," Lan said.

Hương remembered the night on the beach. She remembered feeling his hand one second and then, the next, it was gone. He hadn't let go, she had concluded, but he had paused. And she, in the mad rush, in the chaos of the night, must have gone on without him. Yet still, he hadn't followed them, he hadn't followed her. After years of contemplation, she was sure it was because of that woman, his mother. He could not leave her behind. That was at least part of it. At moments Hương hated her, but then she understood his love for his mother, a different kind of love that bonded them, and Hương admitted to herself that she would have wanted the same from her sons.

She had to ask Lan then, "Did he stay because of her?" Her throat felt dry and scratchy. "We, all of us, were supposed to escape together. But he stayed. And we lost contact, of course. Was it because of her? Did he stay because of his mother?"

Lan paused. A look of thinking came upon her face, and she licked her lips before continuing.

"The truth is," she began.

Hương stopped breathing for a second.

"He said his feet stopped moving at the shore," Lan said. "The coldness of the water was a shock to him and he couldn't move." She finished cleaning a plate and dried her hands on a towel. Hương did not understand.

"Let me begin again," Lan said as if realizing a mistake. "He told me, years into our marriage, about the reeducation camp after the war. In Lăng Cô, the officers were these skinny boys from the countryside and they hated Công. They called him *the Professor*, locked him up in a cell by himself. During questioning, they asked him the question he most dreaded. What did he think of French literature, the literature of the colonizers? He knew, when he entered that camp, they would ask him that question. He had thought about it ahead of time, but none of the answers he came up with would have satisfied those prison guards. What could he have said to make them happy? In truth, nothing. So, he told them the truth," and here Hương imagined Công, younger, idealistic— the way he always was in her head—but also afraid. "Công told them art transcended boundaries, beauty crossed borders. He said, one can't contain life and the stuff of life. It was impossible, he went on, to imprison that; it was impossible, he said, to imprison beauty and truth, no matter who was in charge of Saigon—no person, no ideology, no misguided boys.

"He believed that, Công did."

Hương agreed. He would have said that; he would have believed it.

"The prison guards, they laughed at him then and spat on him. The spit hit his cheek and before he could wipe it off, they grabbed him by the arms and took him away from the cell. Outside, they dragged him through the fields. Tied his hands together; his legs, too.

" 'Confess!' they shouted at him. One of them kicked him.

" 'What?' Công asked, because what did he have to confess?

" 'Confess!' they continued. But he had nothing.

"They left him for an hour. When they came back, they were carrying buckets of water. They started pouring them on him. The water kept coming. Bucket after bucket. Wave after wave. Like magic, they did not run out. He barely had time to breathe before the next one came down.

"They would do this for days, he told me," Lan said. "For weeks. Can you imagine? Weeks? Two weeks into the regimen—that's what they called it—they stopped feeding him. They only gave him this rice water. But even then, he was so afraid—scared of the water—he could scarcely drink it. He endured this for a month before he found a way to escape with a group of other men. There was a hole near a fence. He escaped by foot."

Hương remembered Công knocking on their door after five months away. He'd collapsed into her arms. Her hands still remembered those bones. Even now, she felt them on her skin. He had told her nothing. Her eyes welled up.

"He decided he had to leave. All of you—him, you, the boy." She looked up and around, as if afraid to speak. "Vietnam, he said, was no place for a family. He would get you out. He had to get you out. So . . ."

"He planned everything," Hương interrupted.

"Yes, yes he did. But at the edge of the water, when his foot hit the ocean, something came back to him. Memories," Lan said.

Memories, Hương repeated in her head.

"He remembered—he told me—about his trip to France once. It was before he met you. He was studying abroad for six months. He thought he would love Paris. He thought he would have wanted to move there. But it was so different from everything he knew: the food was difficult on his stomach, it was always cold, the people were rude.

"One night, he was walking the streets of Paris alone after class. He was tired and he sat down on a bench. He fell asleep. When he woke, he forgot where he was and couldn't find his way back. He flagged down a small old French woman to help him. 'Where am I?' he asked her, 'I am far away from home,' but she, seeing who he was, started screaming. *'Un Chinois!'* she called him. *'Un Chinois!'* A Chinese. She started crying for help. No one came. She spat in his eye and ran away. That was one of the memories he saw as he stepped foot into the water.

"Then, another memory rushed back to him: the reeducation camp. The water falling over his head. Those breathless moments. Those men laughing with revenge in their eyes.

"He said he became another man at that camp. Something, he said, in his soul broke. How could he ever return to his previous life after all of that? That was the question he asked himself as his body froze on the shore, on that water.

"Chị Hương, you have to know this: all he ever wanted was here, in Vietnam, among his people, in the life he had always known. He realized he couldn't have it then. Not ever. He had become a different man. He could not be the husband you needed. He was not the man you loved. His life was over, he said, but at least *they* could start again, *they* could become something—the two of you—and it will be beautiful and that was all that mattered. That was all that mattered to him, chị Hương: that you escaped, that you survived."

He would be captured again. When he was released, he was put under house arrest. That was when he sent the letter, Hương realized. That vague letter. *Please don't contact me again. It is the best for the both of us.*

She wiped her eyes with the back of her hand. She wanted to be back in New Orleans suddenly, she wanted to be in her own bed, someplace to nurse her own grief, hold it tight greedily, let it engulf her.

Lightning blazed the sky, followed by a strike of thunder. Suddenly, rain poured.

"The clothes!" said Hương, getting up, glad to have something else to talk about.

"Don't worry," said Lan. She motioned with her hand for Hương to sit back down. "They were wet anyway. And I have more clothes inside besides."

Hương sat down and watched the clothesline sag. Lan left and came back with a box of tissues. Lightning flashed again; the wind picked up a little. Water pelted the ground into mud. It reminded Hương of hurricanes. Though it wasn't as strong, it was still frightening. Lan continued washing. Every few minutes, she stopped to massage her hands.

"I'm sorry you have to hear all that from me, Chị Hương," she said. "In a way, I'm jealous you knew him before. You knew the real him." She started washing another spoon.

"Let me help, Chị Lan," Hương said after drying her tears. "You must be tired. Let me help." They switched places. Hương cleaned the rest of the silverware and then the plates and then the bowls before she found what else she wanted to say, what else she must say.

"There was another baby," Hương started. "I was having pains before we fled. I didn't tell him." But she did tell him and she remembered thinking what life they would have together—the four of them—in another country. She continued, "I had to stop so many times. We were running through the jungle to get to the beach."

The rain came down harder. Hương watched as the wind blew at the clothes. A solid yellow shirt, a pair of brown pants—simple clothes swaying mournfully. It felt like a terrible, lonesome place to stay during a storm.

After the funeral, they would celebrate Công's life. There would be, she was sure, loud music and food and alcohol. The kids would have a table, the adults their own. They would talk over each other, each proclaiming he knew Công the best, could give evidence of his great life. *Remember when he did this, remember when he did that, wasn't he a kind man, a smart person.* All of them would wear white mourning bands around their heads, half smiling in remembrance. By the end of the night, they would be too drunk to feel the pain of loss.

"Anyway," Hương continued, "we decided long ago one of the children would be named Khoa. Công wanted to name Tuấn Khoa, but I argued against it." She had thought it was an ugly name, and, in the end, he surrendered to her. It was like him to do so, she remembered that; he liked her happy. "When I gave birth to Bình at the refugee camp, I had forgotten about Khoa."

Hương repeated the name. "Khoa."

Now, she realized, hearing the rain and the water stroking a porcelain bowl in her hands, it was a lovely name. Indeed, the loveliest: the way a short, abrupt sound from the throat rushed sharply to the lips to be held lovingly before it left to become a word and disappear in the storm-time air: Khoa, K-hoa: *K-hwaah*.

"Công should have that name," said Hương, standing up. "His tên thụy. He would like that name," she said.

When Hương was finished with the dishes, they both went inside. Lan gave Hương the mourning garments and showed her the map of the procession—how they'd pass the library, the temple, and a school to get to the creek. There they'd scatter the ashes into the water. Công would ride the current into the Saigon River, then into the Nhà Bè. From there he would be led out to sea. At some point, she thought, he might even see the Gulf and Lake Pontchartrain and then perhaps the Bayou Versailles, where she'd lived all these years.

Tuấn

Tuấn wanted to see his old home. After his mother gave him the address, and after Lan checked the maps to give him the right street name (because all the streets were renamed), he and Vinh headed out into Saigon together on a motor scooter. Vinh sat up front because he knew how to drive, and Tuấn held on to the seat.

Since his mother told him they were going to Vietnam, he'd started dreaming about the country again. In those dreams, he walked through the maze of Saigon. The city was wrapped in morning haze, and he couldn't see much ahead. He'd take a step forward and immediately forget where he was. When he got close to something—a store or a restaurant or a church—he couldn't make out the words on the sign and became frustrated. He needed to get back to Vietnam; that was what those dreams meant.

They passed the large concrete compounds of the suburbs and made their way onto busier streets, stopping at a wide boulevard.

Scooters and motorcycles and bikes and the stray car crisscrossed the road.

Vinh paused and laughed. "I remember!" he said.

"What do you remember?" Tuấn asked.

"The traffic. The awful traffic," Vinh said. "Just hold on tight." He revved up the engine and pulled ahead.

Tuấn let go of the seat and held on to Vinh. "Fuck," he said.

Everyone else, it seemed, wasn't bothered by the reckless traffic. A woman was eating a stick of meat as she sped past them. A child sat sidesaddle as his bike pulled forward. A motorcyclist popped up his bike and rode on one wheel before disappearing ahead. Finally, Vinh slowed into a right-hand turn and then a left and the traffic faded. They rode straight for another five minutes before stopping at a block of storefronts. Some were closed and had their aluminum doors slid down shut. Others were open, but it didn't seem like many people were in them. It was nine in the morning.

Vinh parked the scooter and they both hopped off. Tuấn reached for the piece of paper with the address.

"This can't be right," Tuấn said more to himself than to Vinh. "We lived on a block with other houses. There's only . . ." The store signs told him nothing; he couldn't read them. A woman came out of her restaurant and set out small red plastic chairs and several matching plastic tables. She held a cigarette in her mouth the entire time until she noticed them and took it out.

"Are we lost, brothers?" she asked.

"No, no," Vinh answered. "The kid"—he pointed at Tuấn—"he's looking for his old home. Before the war. We're from America."

"There haven't been houses here in ages," she said. "At least as long as I've been here."

"How long have you been here?" Vinh asked.

"'Ninety-one or '92?" she said. Tuấn looked disappointed. "Do you remember if it was at the end of the street?" She pointed to the far end, a couple of yards away. "Or was it closer to the park?" She pointed behind them at a gated field. A lone boy dribbled a soccer ball.

Tuấn tried to think. He pictured a narrow, tall building with a balcony. He remembered that much. He wanted to see if he could get up on that balcony and take a photo looking out. It was what he remembered most, the place where he waited for his father's arrival home. "I don't know," he said.

"Well, I can tell you this," said the woman, "when I came here these buildings were new."

Tuấn walked past the woman as if not hearing her and down the street.

"Thank you," Vinh said, following after.

No, this couldn't be the street, Tuấn thought. He turned around. It was exactly like his dream—cruelly, a dream come true. Except nothing was covered in fog. It was all clear and he was still lost.

The funeral was more like a party than a funeral. After they walked to the creek, where Lan let him throw a handful of ashes into the water, the procession walked back to the house. Food was already laid out and a man was filling an ice cooler with beers. Music, reedy horns that reminded Tuấn of bagpipes, blared from speakers. Everyone gathered in small groups for conversations. Tuấn, not knowing anyone, stood to the side. At one point, Lan took his arm and walked him around. *Công's son,* she would say, and they would comment on how strong and smart he looked—a spitting image of the old man, they'd say—and they would tell him how sorry they were. He wanted to tell them he didn't know the man. To him, his father had died a long time ago. He'd grieved already. Now it just felt like everyone was catching up to the fact, fifteen years late.

By three everyone had left, and Lan cleaned everything up.

Tuấn and his mother tried to help, but she seemed determined to do it alone, so they went back inside and began packing. They would leave tomorrow morning.

"Did you see the old house?" his mother asked him.

"It wasn't there anymore."

"A shame."

"They must have torn it down, built over it. Nothing but shops now."

His mother sighed with a defeated look. Her wrinkles seemed more defined now. She was quiet and still for a while, as if she were remembering something, and Tuấn wished she would say it aloud, so they could both remember it together. "A shame," she repeated and shook her head. Her lips trembled. Tuấn reached out to hug his mother and she leaned in to him. "Another shame your brother's missing all this," she said.

"I know. I tried to get him to come," Tuấn said. "He's not ready."

"Not ready for what?" She let go and began packing again.

Ready to be back with his family, Tuấn thought, *ready to face the death of a father he never knew.*

When Tuấn had called him with the news, his brother had shrugged it off—"People die every day, T."

"But he was your father," Tuấn had said.

"No, he was *your* father. There's a difference."

"You should come. It's the right thing to do," Tuấn insisted.

"Have fun," his brother had said.

Tuấn didn't tell any of this to his mother, and now she added, "You can't expect to be ready for everything. Sometimes things just happen whether you're ready for them or not. Haven't I taught you boys that?"

Before they left, Lan gave him some of his father's things. "I wouldn't know what to do with them. It would only make me cry if I kept them."

When they landed, it was already ten at night in New Orleans.

As Tuấn turned on his phone, he saw he had five text messages. All from his brother.

"I need to talk to you," said the last one. "TONIGHT," it read. It was from yesterday.

He hoped it wasn't an emergency. As his mother dropped him off, Tuấn couldn't remember the last time he had talked to his brother face-to-face. For a while, they lived together in his one-room house in Tremé. It was almost like they were kids again, with beds on opposite sides of the room. Then he got into UNO, which made Tuấn really proud—his own brother, a college student!—but also somehow suspicious. How did he pull it off? Who was the professor he hung out with: Schultz? Schmidt? Scheibe? When his brother came out, that was what Tuấn worried about: that some older man would take advantage of him. (Or AIDS, which the newspapers were always talking about, that gay cancer.) Was that the case? From his dorm, Ben would send him postcards semi-regularly, the kind you could buy at tourist gift shops. As time passed, the message would become vague: *Doing fine,* he would write, or *Am fine,* he would say, or sometimes just *Fine,* which Tuấn thought was an amazing waste of paper, and their mother thought so as well.

"What's wrong?" his mother asked him when he got out of the car.

"Nothing, Ma," he said through the open window.

"Was that your brother? On the phone?"

With his mother and brother not talking to each other, Tuấn was their mediator. The role tired him sometimes. They were both adults now, and Tuấn had no idea why he had to be in between their issues. But he hated seeing his mother's mixture of anger and anxiety, hated to see it simmer.

"No, Ma," he said. His heart sped up for a second and then slowed down, the way it always did when he had to lie. He looked at her to see if she could tell.

"Oh. Okay" was all she said. As his mother got older, Tuấn

noticed, she put up less of a fight. A resigned dignity came on her face and she nodded. "Take care, okay?"

"Okay, Ma."

"Zup?" Tuấn texted back after he set down his luggage. He set the phone down and got something to eat. The only thing he had was Lucky Charms. He ate it dry. It was Ben's favorite cereal growing up, and over the last couple of years he himself had developed a taste for it.

An image popped into Tuấn's head then: His car sat outside their Versailles apartment and he was standing there with the hood open. It was the radiator that needed fixing. It was, for a long time, the radiator that always broke. He was taking a look at it when Ben ran out and, out of nowhere, said he wanted to take the car for a drive. Tuấn must have been nineteen or twenty then and Ben fourteen or fifteen, about to start high school. It was the end of August—'92 it must have been—and his girlfriend at the time, Thảo, was away at Catholic camp, where she worked as a camp counselor (funny, he would think in hindsight). Ben smelled like a pool. He was always going to the pool back then, at first with his friend but then the two of them stopped being friends and Ben had to ask for rides or take the bus.

"Why?" Tuấn asked. "You don't even have a license. You're not old enough." Tuấn filled the radiator with water. *It was always heating up; it needed a way to cool down,* that was his thinking.

"Please," Ben was saying. "Just one time. I just want to know what it feels like to drive."

Tuấn remembered smirking. "Fine," he said. He threw the keys at his brother, which flew past him and landed in the dirt. He was never good at sports.

———

Within five minutes, Tuấn finished what was left of the Lucky Charms and his phone glowed green and vibrated. The power of the vibration made it jump off the table. His brother was calling now. Tuấn took hold of the phone and, deciding he needed to air out the staleness of the house, walked outside.

"Finally," Ben said. No *hi* or *hello*. "I've been calling you all week."

Tuấn leaned against the house. His legs felt like mush; funny how sitting for so long made your legs tired. He slid down and looked up at the moon, and the air around it bent like the mirages he saw in films.

"T, are you listening?" he heard on the phone.

"Oh. Yes. Yes. What's up?"

"I'm leaving," his brother said. He sounded far away, like the phone was on speaker and he, for whatever reason, was whispering.

It made Tuấn whisper, too. "Where you going? And for how long?"

When they were teenagers, his brother kept a map by his desk. He always wanted to travel. When the chance came up for him to go to Vietnam, Tuấn was surprised he didn't want to come. During the entire trip, he kept thinking how his brother should have been there and how he would have enjoyed it. And how having his brother there might have made him feel less out of place.

Tuấn rubbed his eyes and looked at his watch. Eleven.

"I'm *leaving* leaving. Out of the country," said his brother.

"What?" He rubbed his face. "What do you mean? When?"

"Soon," he said. Then after a pause, he added, "Meet me at Daisy Dukes. Now. I'll tell you everything you need to know."

There was a long silence before Tuấn began talking again. "Why don't you just tell me what's going on right here on the phone?" he said before realizing his brother had already hung up.

Tuấn got his bike from inside the house and began pedaling toward the Quarter. By the time he got to Daisy Dukes, Ben was standing at the entrance under a flickering neon sign. He wore an UNO hoodie and jeans, though it wasn't too chilly outside, and greeted him with a casual two-finger salute army-style as Tuấn slowed down and got off. Tuấn locked up his bike and, wordlessly, they entered the restaurant.

"Long time no see," Tuấn began as they were seated.

"I've been busy," Ben said. He scratched his head and looked down at the floor. Tuấn looked down, too, trying to see what Ben was seeing, but he saw only scuff marks and french fries and napkins and straw wrappers. He looked up and saw a waitress taking a couple's orders.

"Hey, do we know her?" Tuấn asked Ben and pointed with his chin. "She looks familiar. But I don't know where I know her from."

Ben turned to look and quickly pulled the menu over his face.

"Fuck," he said.

"What?"

"Addy Toussaint. I went to school with her. I didn't know she worked here. Shit."

Tuấn remembered now. Addy. A small girl, Haitian, liked chewing gum and Coke. She came over sometimes on her bike and waited for Ben. He remembered she was close enough friends with him that his mother was comfortable having her wait inside the apartment.

He looked at her now. Obviously, she grew up, but her smile was still childish. The word that came to Tuấn's mind was *innocent,* like she wouldn't hurt a fly. He wondered what ever happened to the two of them, Addy and Ben. He was quick to think it was Ben's fault.

"Tell me when she's gone," said Ben, still hiding behind the menu.

"Not yet, not yet." He tried to hold in his laughter. How childish they were being, like teenagers hiding from their crushes.

Addy looked over at their booth, and for moment she paused. She looked like she was about to walk over, but another waitress called her and she walked away.

"Now," Tuấn said and let out a laugh he couldn't help.

"Thank goodness!" Ben said.

"What you ever do to her? You couldn't have possibly broken her heart."

Ben didn't answer. A waitress came by and filled up their water glasses.

"So tell me about things," Tuấn said now, sighing. "How's school going? You got that degree yet? What's it in?" He looked at his brother, who was still small—always more of a boy than a man— and tried to find any changes. When people haven't seen each other in a long time, there was always a comment on how different one of them looked. He searched and searched, but couldn't find anything different about his brother.

"English," Ben said. Then, as if to clarify, "Books and reading and writing. That kind of stuff. I just graduated, actually."

"Congrats, my man. I'm proud of you. I am. I always wanted to go to college, you know," Tuấn said, though they both knew it was a lie.

"Yeah?" his brother answered.

"Yeah. Learning and stuff. A man can go far."

After they ordered—a bacon cheeseburger and fries for Tuấn and a veggie burger and a pickle for Ben, who said he was watching his weight—Ben told him where he was going.

"France," he said. "Paris. To be exact. There's a school there. It's a summer program." He looked out the window and took a napkin from the napkin holder.

"But you're done with school. That's what you said."

"I am," he said. "I am. It's something extra. You wouldn't under-stand. But it's important, you see?"

"Do you need money? Is that what you need, why you needed to talk to me? Or are you asking for permission?" He pictured his brother on the streets of Paris. Tuấn had never been, but he'd seen it in enough movies and on TV. It was always cold and rainy. There were cobbled streets and old cafés and expensive apartments. He pictured his brother lost and unable to speak the language, unable to survive. *You shouldn't go,* he wanted to say now, *you're being ridiculous.* "You always do what you want."

"It's what Dad taught," Ben interrupted him, "wasn't it? French literature? Or language? Or something like that?" He unfolded his napkin and began tearing off pieces.

The question caught Tuấn off guard. Now he remembered his father's wife and her library of books, all in different languages, not just Vietnamese. It occurred to him that some of those might have been his father's and not his father's wife's. It made more sense, somehow, in his head.

"Yeah," he said. "I think he did. In Vietnam he had this big library."

"I wonder," said Ben, "if he's read anything I've read."

Ben drives cautiously but above the speed limit. He holds the steering wheel with both hands and bites his lip; still, he pushes down hard on the gas. Tuấn wants to tell him to slow down—the car's engine's not in good condition—but his brother seems very focused. *Maybe he's afraid of driving,* Tuấn thinks. Ben slows down when they reach Seabrook and turns in to Wesley.

"Ol' Wesley," Tuấn says. "Haven't been out this way in forever." He had dropped out in the middle of senior year. He was always getting in trouble with everyone there. He was living two lives back then: one in school and one outside of it. He had to make a choice and at the time he was proud of it, but sitting in the parking lot with his brother makes him question it.

Ben is looking around as if he's anticipating something.

"Why'd you drive here?" Tuấn asks.

"Wanted to see it in person before school started," he says. He rolls down the window and turns off the engine. The humid night air seeps in. Cicadas hum in the bushes. Tuấn unbuckles his seatbelt.

"How does it feel," Tuấn asks, "to drive? It's freeing, isn't it?"

"Sure," Ben says. He opens the door and walks out to the front. He looks out into the empty parking lot, dimly lit by a single lamppost. Four or five parking spaces away, two crows fight over a slice of pizza.

Someone was here not too long ago. Tuấn pictures teenagers hanging out and listening to music and eating pizza. He wonders what he missed by dropping out. He opens the car door and stands by his brother, who is now sitting on the hood, staring into the night sky.

"I'm so glad we don't live in the city, downtown," Ben says. "You can't see the stars down there. Too much light."

Tuấn looks up. His brother's right. He'd never noticed it before— all the stars spotting the sky.

"Did you know," Ben says, "sailors used to use the stars to find their way home. They're constellations, you see, and if you knew what group of stars was what, what you were looking at, you knew where you were. Isn't that neat?"

"Neat," Tuấn says. (Looking back at this memory, Tuấn will think of his brother's inheritance: the intelligence of a man he never met, the ability to hold on to facts, a pure love of knowledge.)

They sit silently.

Whenever a car passes, Ben stiffens and watches it drive by. When it's gone, he lets his body relax and looks disappointed. Tuấn doesn't know what to say, so he says nothing.

"I wanted to tell you something," says Ben, breaking the silence, "but I forgot what it was."

"It probably wasn't anything important," Tuấn jokes.

"Probably."

After a few more minutes, Ben tosses him the keys.

"He was right," Ben says out of nowhere, pointing to the school's emblem. "It *is* a cowboy." They get in the car and Tuấn starts the engine. He drives.

He's exiting I-10 when the car starts to smoke.

"What's wrong?" Ben asks, shouting his words over the sound of the sputtering engine. "Something's wrong."

"Not sure," Tuấn says. There's a grinding sound he hadn't heard before. He pulls off to the side of the road, across from a shopping center.

Tuấn pops open the hood. The smoke makes him cough, and he waves his hands to get it out of his face. It's smoked up before, so this doesn't surprise him too much. He had gotten the car extra cheap from a friend of Thảo's. At the time, it felt like a bargain. Now, everything makes sense.

Ben rushes over with a bottle of water and Tuấn pours it over the engine to cool it off. "Thanks!" he says when the smoke clears and the bottle is empty.

"It was for *you*," Ben says. Then, "You were coughing." They look at each other, then at the car, and laugh.

Tuấn plays around with the engine before he turns and sees a Kmart across the street.

"They might have something we need," Tuấn says, already beginning to walk.

"Like what?"

"Something. We can see. Maybe coolant. I should've used coolant in the first place, not water. I'm stupid."

"Nah," says Ben, walking with his brother. "Just bad luck."

The four-lane road is empty. They walk over. Once on the other side, though, they realize it's too late—the store's closed for the day.

"They close at eight," Ben says after reading the store hours. "Who closes at eight?"

"One hour late," Tuấn said, looking at his watch.

Tuấn leans his head against the window. He could break in. He's done worse things in his life. He could list them all in his head, but when he looks over, Ben's heading toward the shopping carts in the parking lot.

And when he's there, he takes one, begins running, and lets go. The cart flies a few yards until it hits a lamppost at the end of the lot and falls over, the metal banging against the asphalt. They both laugh, though Tuấn doesn't know exactly why, or what is so funny.

He says only, "Hey, I have an idea!" and runs and gets another cart.

It is Ben in the cart first and Tuấn at the handlebar. Pushing the cart down the street, Tuấn laughs and Ben says this is ridiculous. He exaggerates the word: *ree-dic-coo-liss!* He waves his wrists in the air and his hands look like they're about to take flight. *Not too fast, not too fast—but not too slow, either, not too slow!* says his brother. Tuấn listens and does the opposite of what his brother wants: fast means slow and slow means fast and everything is fun. Tuấn pushes for a few minutes, then it's Ben's turn. He's small, but what he lacks in strength he makes up in energy. They switch back and forth, riding the cart until Versailles is on the horizon and they make it home.

After they finished their meals, Tuấn told Ben to come home with him.

"For a quick second," he said. He let Ben ride his bike as he followed behind.

"Where do you live now?" Ben asked as they went down the streets.

"Same place." Tuấn trailed behind as his brother took the lead.

"Working at Royal Oysters still?"

"Nah. Now I'm a guide for Swampland Tours. It's an okay gig."

"You gotta learn a lot for that, don't you. A lot of history and geography and stuff like that."

"I guess so. But I've lived here for so long. You know, you kind of just absorb that sort of stuff."

"Look! No hands!"

"Don't do that. You'll fall. Quit it!"

They turned onto Esplanade and made their way toward Claiborne.

"I've lived here all my life, and I still don't get it," Ben said. He stood up on the bike and stomped down on the pedals. The front wheel zigzagged down the street.

"New Orleans is not for everyone," Tuấn said, "but it's home."

"Yeah," Ben said, like that was all he had to add. Then, "How was Vietnam? How was the funeral?"

"Everything changed," Tuấn said. "I tried to find our old home."

"Yeah?"

"But it was gone, built over. Even the street names changed. Our street used to be named after a type of flower. Now it's named after some guy."

"Bummer."

They turned down a dark street. Ben slowed down, so Tuấn took the lead.

"And our father, he was married to this woman. Another professor. He became a professor, you know, at a state-sponsored university. It was the same building he worked in before, just a different name. She works there, too, his wife. Very nice. Quiet. Younger than Mom."

"Is that so?"

"Yeah. It made me wonder."

"Wonder what?"

About what we hide from each other, Tuấn wanted to say, about what we don't know about the people closest to us. "I don't know." Then, "There was a war. Things happen."

"I know," Ben said.

They went two more blocks before Tuấn pointed out his house.

"Still blue, I see," Ben said, pointing at the stoop.

"Fresh paint," Tuấn said. "Stay here," he said at the door. "I have something for you."

It had occurred to him while they were eating that there was something his brother needed to have, something of their father's—a necklace with a gold coin engraved with some other language. With the way it looked, it was probably from France or somewhere in Europe. It didn't belong in Vietnam. It didn't belong anywhere in Asia. Maybe their father had been to France and brought it back. Maybe Ben would know more about it, find it useful in his travels. It belonged to Ben, Tuấn felt; it was already his.

He rummaged through the pockets of his suitcase until he found it and ran outside, feeling the small metal chain jingle in his hand. When he opened the screen door and let it swing closed behind him, he found his brother wasn't there anymore. The bike leaned against the house and next to its front wheel sat an envelope. Tuấn picked it up. It felt heavier than he'd expected. Inside were a few fifty-dollar bills and some twenties. About five hundred altogether. Tuấn looked out into the streets and there was nothing. The night was silent. No cars, no people, no animals, no Ben. Ben was gone. Ben disappeared. Like he wasn't even there, like he never was. Not a trace. He was so much like his father.

Ben

2000

rofessor Schreiber told him history happened in cycles. One thing happens, something reacts to it, it all disappears from consciousness only to return later. His mother came to the United States to escape the Communists. It seemed fitting, then, at least to Ben, that—years later—he would leave New Orleans and fall in love with a communist—in France.

The communist was named Michel, and Ben was stunned by his ruggedness and energy. There was a wildness in him, in his eyes especially, that made him seem out of place in a city as sophisticated as Paris.

He reminded Ben of the construction workers he saw in New Orleans. They had rough hands, sun-tanned skin, and bulging muscles from work. For months, there was construction work across from Paradise. Ben would watch them work diligently and marveled at the way their muscle, visible beneath their skin, moved—machinelike but at the same time somehow erotic. The men would come over and ask to refill their bottles of water. When they learned it was a gay bar, they seemed embarrassed, but it didn't stop them from coming over.

Michel could've been one of those men—easily. Surely, Ben thought, he couldn't have belonged to *this* world, a dimly lit bookstore in Le Marais, counting money and chatting with customers.

That Wednesday night, Michel stood behind the counter, talking intimately with a girl who must have been maybe Ben's age, twenty-two at the most, with bobbed hair and a light spotting of freckles that did not make her look unattractive. Michel wore a beard that made him look older, though he couldn't have been that old. Ben pegged him at no older than twenty-five or twenty-six.

They were laughing, the two of them, at something one of them had said. It was so funny the girl had to cover her mouth with both hands and catch herself from falling backward. Then the girl looked at her watch and her eyes opened wide.

"*Tard, tard,*" she kept repeating as she gathered her shopping bags. "Late, late." They pecked each other on the cheeks and she ran out the door.

Ben had planned to stay in the city for as long as he possibly could. He had graduated in May of last year, and with money from the extra student loans he took out for living expenses, he was in Paris before he knew it. He chose Paris because after reading Henri Murger—a used hardcover of *Scènes de la vie de bohème* in English with yellowing pages—he knew it was where he was meant to be. And then there were the news reports always announcing riots and protests over little things—an increase in stamp prices, taxes, changes in school curriculum. Parisians, he was sure, cared more than Americans, who were too content for their own good.

When he was nearing graduation, Schreiber sat him down in his office. He asked Ben what graduate schools he was applying to.

"I have a good friend up in New York," the professor said. "Their doctorate program is world-class. And you'll have all the resources you'll need at your fingertips as well as a sizable stipend, if you're willing to teach."

"I think," Ben said then, "I'm going to take a year or two off."

Schreiber was surprised, perhaps even shocked. "You have a bright career ahead of you," he said. He furrowed his brows. "Why would you do this?"

To me was what Ben thought he would add, but the professor didn't.

For the last four years, Ben had been grateful for all that Schreiber had freely given to him. Yet there was the feeling of incurring debts—debts that he could never repay. It was unfair to the professor, who acted like a father to him. It was unfair to his own father, who he never had the chance to know, who never had the chance to know him.

Ben told Schreiber it was time he got some life experience, to spread his wings on his own, to fly.

"And what is your plan? How do you plan on surviving?"

Ben told him he would travel to Paris and find a job and settle down. From there he would live and write.

"That's more than a year or two," Schreiber said. Then, "As long as you're writing, I guess that's at least something!" Schreiber threw his hands in the air; he was being sarcastic—he was mad. In the past, when they had arguments, they were always theoretical, philosophical, abstract. Ideas were involved but never people. Now it seemed personal.

"Remember," Ben said. "You, too, moved to this country with a dream."

"Go to Paris, then," Schreiber said. "Go to Paris and be a writer!"

Yet when he got to Paris, he hadn't a clue what to write! His words failed him. He was waiting to be inspired, though he found himself in bookstores like *Livres avec des amis*—with its charming hand-painted store sign, its book carts scattered on the sidewalk— more often than not. It surprised him that, after several months of living in the city, every other day sitting in the aisles of his favorite bookstore, skimming the pages of a book he had no intention of buying, he had *just* noticed Michel.

At closing time, while the customers emptied from the store, Michel and the manager reshelved books, rang up customers, and dusted the shelves. Ben stayed and fingered the same pages of an antiwar novel he'd been reading for three days.

The manager whispered something to Michel and pointed to Ben. Ben went back to his book, anticipating the tap on the shoulder and the notice that they were closing in *cinq minutes*—those lips saying *cinq minutes* and those fingers pointing to a clock or the door or a watch. Ben heard footsteps.

Then *"C'est trop tard. C'est presque minuit."*

Ben cleared his throat. *"Cette,"* he said, holding up the book.

Michel smiled and took the book with him to the cash register.

"A good one," Michel said. When Michel spoke English, his words glided in a way a native speaker's words wouldn't, like he was preparing to sing. "Tourist?" Michel asked Ben.

"I just moved here," he corrected Michel. He felt like he should have added something—where he was from, why he was in Paris, what brought him to the bookstore today. He dug into his pockets and fished out a few crumpled euros.

"Where from?"

"New Orleans," Ben said. Then, as if to clarify, "America."

"I have friends in America," said Michel, smirking. "Have you heard of Peter Johnson?"

"No."

"Johnson Peter?"

"No."

"You must know Pete Johns, then?"

"I'm sorry."

"I'm just joking with you. I do not know any Americans."

"We're not that bad."

"You're not that bad."

Ben blushed and took his book. When he was out of the store, he realized he'd forgotten his change. The manager locked the door. The bookstore lights flickered out.

"Fuck," he told himself. He took out his wallet to count his money. He had to be careful. The cost of living here was high. Everything was double what it was in New Orleans. In addition to that, he had yet to find a job.

He began walking. The January air was cold and made his skin ache with dryness; he held his hands in his pockets. Though it was late and winter, the bars and brasseries were still busy. Passing by, he saw tourists huddled around wine bottles. He could tell the tourists from the locals now. Tourists were more excited to be alive, to be in the moment, while the locals had a gentle melancholy about them. Both groups could be heard saying "Oh, Paris!" but one said it ecstatically and the other said it forlornly.

He heard a tourist group laugh through a window. Over at the next table, a waitress was texting on her phone.

Ben made his way through the small, old streets, leaving all the tourists behind, and headed toward the 10th arrondissement, a mile or so walk, but Paris was a walking city and he enjoyed that. He felt as if he finally understood why Vinh went on long walks. It gave you time to think, to be alone. And Paris was that, at its core: a lonely city.

When he arrived at the flat, he stopped himself. It was too early. The Austrians hated when he came home early, though he didn't understand why they should have a problem; it was his place, too. They were a boy and a girl, a couple, who came from Graz. Like Ben, they were artists, though not writers. The boy was a photographer, the girl a singer. Ben was excited to room with other artists. He believed they would be carefree, exciting, and passionate: *bohemian.*

Instead, they left dishes in the sink (they would do it later, they said), tossed their clothes every which way (they were their clothes to toss every which way they pleased), gave off body odor (deodorant is an American invention). And, despite renting the place together, they didn't like him there and tried to convince him he'd be better off elsewhere, if only temporarily.

For the first month, the girl left flyers on his bed for concerts and book readings and, on more than one occasion, postcard-sized pieces of paper advertising a gay club on the other side of the city. From anyone else, it would have been an act of kindness. But from the girl, it was her attempt at getting him out of the flat and out of the way. Ben could tell by the way she would clench her jaw, waiting to see if he would take her bait and leave. It was the lack of intimacy they had in such a space, Ben came to understand. They hated to see him home, their shared flat too small for even one person.

"Bean," they would call him, "why don't you go see the city more?" They'd smile crookedly and speak slow English, the words slurring into one another and then yanked in different directions. "Yes, Paris is a beautiful city." "They call it the City of Light." "You can see the light only at night." Afterward, the girl would say something in German to her boyfriend. They didn't bother whispering, the same way his mother spoke Vietnamese in public, which he always found too loud, too obnoxious.

That night, he had promised he would stay out longer. "Don't wait up for me. I'll be out late, *mes amis,*" he said, though he was sure they didn't consider themselves his friends.

"We will miss you!" said the boy.

"But don't make so much noise when you come back!" said the girl.

Ben looked up at his room's window. The Austrian girl was leaning out. She was wearing underwear but not pants or a shirt. She held the curtains to her chest, but they were paper-thin and Ben saw her small breasts anyway. She let a cigarette fall, and he sped away just in case she saw him.

Because it was a weeknight, those who were out in the 10th

arrondissement were walking home from their jobs, the homeless, or no-good teenagers. And then there was Ben, a foreigner away from the tourist center of the city, the historical sites, the hotels and hostels.

In America, Ben felt like a foreigner, too, but in a different way. He couldn't have explained it. In New Orleans, he couldn't have explained how he and his family got there. There was a boat, a wind led them this way, and, like pilgrims, they settled. Here, in Paris, there was some choice in the matter. It was not a familial myth—a story told and retold, each time a little bit different, each time a little bit more holy. His hero of a father sacrificed his life under Communist bullets while his mother played reverse Penelope, cast away from her homeland waiting for her Odysseus until the news of his death arrives and she is transformed into a tragic widow who weaved fables for her children (because that was what his life was—a fable, a series of twisted truths, outright lies). His immigration to Paris was a story made of flesh and bones written by himself, and no matter how horrible things turned out, he was the one who wrote it. That was the important part—to be the writer of his own story.

He walked into a convenience shop and bought a pack of cigarettes and a soda. The cashier, a brown-skinned man in a turban, was talking into his cell phone and held it on his shoulder as he counted the money. Outside, Ben lit up a cigarette and coughed out the smoke.

He was disappointed in Paris. When he thought of Paris, his mind drifted to independence and liberty. A European paradise of writers and artists. He knew the risks he took. He would be poor and there would be challenges of communication, but he'd find others like himself and they'd all be poor but happy.

Instead, the nights were cold, the streets smelled like urine, and the average Parisian was rude and just as idiotic as any American.

His first week in Paris, a beggar ran away with his backpack and, with it, his wallet, a pen, a French-to-English paperback dictionary, a plastic key chain in the shape of the Eiffel Tower, and a diary. Ben walked two blocks and found it dumped in a trash can. The wallet was gone; everything else remained.

When Ben finished smoking and found himself at a park, he sat on a bench and threw away the rest of the cigarettes. Murger lied, he thought. Madame Bovary was right: France was a bore. And Paris, for all its European sophistication, was not that different from New Orleans.

Everything was clear now. This was no place for him. He would leave soon enough. Somewhere else he would go, but here he would not stay.

"C'est le gars à la librairie," Ben heard someone say. He opened his eyes and sat up. Three silhouettes under streetlights. Who could they be? "It's you," the same voice said.

Ben readied himself to run, but when the figures came closer, all three of them wearing hoodies, one of them looked familiar— Michel, the bookstore boy.

Michel came up close and patted Ben's face lightly three times. "You are afraid?" he said; his breath was sweet. "Did I scare you?"

"Non," said Ben. "I was just lying down. You surprised me. That's all."

"You shouldn't sleep in the streets. It is very dangerous."

"Michel," said one of the other men. *"Qui est-ce?"*

"Un Chinois?" said the other.

"Non," answered Michel. "American?"

"Oui," said Ben.

"Américain," said Michel. The others let out a sigh jokingly, as if in relief.

Ben looked at his watch. It was midnight. He had been asleep for nearly an hour. He checked his pockets to make sure he still had his wallet, and, finding it there, he let himself relax. Then he said, "I have to go. Good seeing you again." He began toward his flat, but Michel grabbed his arm.

"Don't be afraid," he said. "We're not unfriendly. We're communists!" He laughed. The other men did the same.

Ben freed himself from his grasp and began walking again, but Michel ran to catch up to him and, to Ben's surprise, took a step in front of him.

"The night is young, *mon ami,*" Michel said. "*Que faites-vous ce soir?*"

"Going home, I guess," Ben replied. The Austrians should be asleep by now.

"Going home!" Michel scoffed. He chuckled. "*Il est trop tôt. La nuit est jeune! Nous sommes tous les jeunes!* Come, come!" He grabbed Ben's arm.

He tried to move, but Michel's grip was tight. He couldn't have run from this strong man even if he wanted to, and the realization made him smile.

"Where are you taking me?"

The other two left Michel and Ben alone. Michel lived fifteen minutes away. It was less of a proper flat than an abandoned apartment complex. A piece of plywood with *condamné* painted on it was nailed to the entrance.

Michel opened the door. "A perfectly good building," he said, "left here all alone."

Ben strained his eyes. There was no electricity, possibly. He saw the shadows of a wardrobe, boxes, a table, and on top of that, piles of something. Michel closed the door and Ben jumped as the darkness enveloped them.

"Something to drink?" Michel asked. He took out a lighter and pressed down on it several times before a flame jumped up and just as quickly disappeared.

Ben took out his book of matches and handed it over. Michel swiped a match against the book and a small flame appeared in his hand. He took a few steps forward and lit a candle.

"You live here?" Ben asked.

"*Oui.*" Michel took Ben's hand. "*Avec mes amis.*"

Together they walked, stepping over piles of books and bricks and boxes, and then a row of glass bottles. Michel led Ben to the far side of the room, where there was a table and, on top of it, a plastic cooler. He let go of Ben's hand and dipped his own into it. There was the sound of water splashing.

"*Merde!*" Michel said. He fished out a bottle and handed it to Ben. "Wait," he said. Michel took the bottle back and laid the capped top against the table. He held the cap in place with one hand and pulled the bottle away with the other. The bottle cap popped off and rolled onto the floor before settling. He opened another.

"*Salut!*" said Michel.

"*Salut!*" Ben repeated.

"To new friends!"

After the beer—two or three or four bottles more plus some type of hard liquor—they fell into bed passionately, or as passionately as two drunk men could. Afterward, Michel got up to wash himself from a tub of collected rainwater, because the building had no plumbing.

"We have our ways," Michel said, though Ben was too tired to remember all that was said.

When Ben woke up, one of the boys from the night before, one of Michel's friends, was shuffling cards. The sound seemed louder than it should have been. The boy said good morning, and then to Michel (still lying in bed, half awake from the look of it) said something about bringing outsiders over and about rules and agreements, and Michel mumbled sharply, *"Baise les règles!"* and the other boy replied *"Baise-toi!"* the word said firmly with a sly yet serious smile.

The other friend, sitting with a bottle of beer, said they should go get breakfast. At this, Michel stood up and stretched his limbs.

"Room 210!" Michel said.

"Room 210!" the others said in unison. They packed up their cards, their cigarettes, their beers, and ran to the door.

Room 210 sat across the hall. It was the same layout as the other apartment but less cluttered. It seemed just painted, and, indeed, Ben saw a bucket of paint in the corner along with brushes and a roller.

In Room 210, they sat at a kitchen table and passed around bread and jam and cheap wine by a window that looked out onto a street. Someone rode by on a bicycle. Pigeons flew on and off the window ledge of the building across.

"Who is this boy here?" one of Michel's friends asked.

"This is the American," Michel answered. "Ben," he said.

The boy shuffling the cards introduced himself as Mateo. His curly brown hair made him look young. He was twenty-three and a Spaniard but had come to Paris two years prior on a whim, hopping aboard a train and jumping off after they found him.

Across from Mateo sat a Russian named Sergei. Sergei was twenty-five and wore thin wire-frame glasses. His hair was red and wavy. At university, Sergei read about the Soviets, how the Revolution had failed miserably, and, learning of this and seeing the conditions now, he felt disappointed with his people.

"The Soviets didn't try hard enough," Sergei said.

Mateo said something about the general dimness of Russians, and Sergei pushed the table forward, knocking Mateo over playfully. Only Russians could make fun of Russians, he said.

Everyone spoke French, though bent with different accents. It sounded like a bus depot or an airport, a place full of travelers trying to find where they needed to go. At times, Ben couldn't keep up.

Mateo took out the cards again. "We want to change the world," he said. He shuffled the cards and dealt them. What they were playing, Ben didn't know; he picked up his cards anyway.

"What do you mean?" Ben asked. "How do you change the world?"

They did things, they said, for the betterment of society. They protested; they wrote pamphlets; they stole from grocery stores, department stores, and gave what they stole to the poor. Mainly themselves.

Once Michel, Sergei said, broke into Parliament at night. He was arrested, of course. He convinced the police that he was drunk and they let him stay in jail until he seemed sober enough.

But they weren't lawless, violent, *fou*.

Sometimes, for instance, they were a band. They played an acoustic guitar and tambourine in Place de la Bastille to bring awareness to revolution. Mateo ran into another room and came back with a guitar, strumming a few chords and singing off-key.

> *Ah! ça ira, ça ira, ça ira*
> *Le peuple en ce jour sans cesse répète*
> *Ah! ça ira, ça ira, ça ira*
> *Malgré les mutins tout réussira!*

It was a revolution song, Mateo said. Did Ben like it? Something by Edith Piaf, a little song by Edith Piaf, *the* Edith Piaf, Mateo said, as if there were multiple Edith Piafs roaming the streets singing revolutionary songs. *Ah ça ira. Ah ça ira . . . it will be fine, it will be fine.* Because it will be. Because they believed it. Because they suffered.

"We've all suffered," said Sergei, seriously now. They've never been in a war, but they've gone hungry, thirsty, sexless. And they've seen things—the very nature of humanity and human evil and what people were capable of doing and what people were incapable of having, which was, in the end, they theorized, the cause of all evil. They've seen it all and they concluded: they wanted no more suffering. For themselves. For the world. For the universe!

L'univers, Ben repeated in his head. *Pour nous-mêmes, pour le monde, pour l'univers!*

They passed a hand-rolled cigarette around. When it got to Ben, he inhaled and let the smoke stream out unhurriedly. As it passed his lips, he tasted something earthy and green, and it put him at ease and made his muscles relax. He didn't cough this time and it made him proud. He was becoming French. No, *Parisian!* Life was beginning again. Here was what he'd been waiting for.

"What makes you communists?" asked Ben finally after the cigarette went around the circle a second time.

"It's the belief that all men are equals," said Sergei. "You and me, we're the same. I'm not better than you. You're not better than me. We're all the same."

"Except for those no-good *putains* in the government!" Mateo exclaimed. He jumped up, joyous, and positioned himself in a fighting stance, hands up, legs ready to leap. "We should make them do work for us! Show them what hard labor is! If not, we ship them all to—"

"Siberia!" said Sergei.

"Siberia!" Michel repeated.

"Siberia!" everyone said. They lifted hands in the air and cheered, and Sergei stood with his hands on his hips and danced as if "Siberia" were an old folk song. He fell down when he was done and took a drink of wine as the others clapped—*Bravo, bravo, bravo!*

"And then we start from scratch," said Mateo. "We've suffered so much! This is what we deserve! We deserve this much! At the very least!"

Outside, the sun had risen fully. Ben heard cars starting, the squeak of doors opening, the hacking cough from an old man or woman. The pigeons were gone. The window behind the ledge was open. A woman leaned out with a cleaning rag.

The Spaniard gripped Ben by the shoulder. "*Mon ami,* we've all suffered here. Tell us, how have you suffered?"

How had he suffered?

The words repeated themselves in Ben's head, the sound of them swirling in a drunken haze. How had he *suffered*? How had *he* suffered? He had suffered, that was for sure, yet how—how had he suffered? How could he explain in a different language? He took a sip of his wine and went deep into his memory, a labyrinth of infinite clean-cut hedges, trying to find the moment he was most disappointed, most mad at the world. The images flashed in his mind. There were so many, but to pick *the* one—that was the challenge. He saw hues of flesh, mouths moving, stars shining faintly.

Then it struck him. *Of course,* he thought. It was a long story, but he could sum it up. Slowly, he conjured the words in French in his head, and, sloppily, he began to speak.

"My father," he said. *Mon père.* "*Mon père* was left behind in Vietnam." *Au Viêt-Nam.* "When we came to the States, my mom made these cassette tapes for him. She talked to him to tell him about life in America. She did this for years," he said. "For *years.*"

The others nodded.

Ben continued. "At the end of the tapes, she'd point to the recorder and tell us to say goodbye to our dad. I was still little back then, but for whatever reason, for the longest time I thought our dad lived in the recorder. I thought my dad *was* the recorder. It wasn't until I was in school that I knew what a father even was."

The wine came to him again, and he emptied it into his glass.

"A few months ago," Ben went on, "my dad died. My brother and mom, they board a plane to Vietnam. When they come back, my brother, he says our dad was married to this other woman.

This small, quiet, fragile woman who taught poetry and didn't have children or couldn't have any children, I don't know. Anyway, my brother said they lived in this big-ass house with marble floors and photos of the places they went to together and potted plants in every corner, all healthy and green. Nothing like how we grew up. Also, they had a lot of food. Tons of it. A whole walk-in pantry. They had giant meals each night and every morning and every afternoon. Nothing like we had growing up—canned soup, instant ramen. My mom—*ma mère*—worked all day cleaning people's hands, their feet, scrubbing calloused heels, inhaling fumes from nail polish removers. She'd come home tired, her head hurting. She couldn't take care of us. We had nothing growing up. Not a thing."

How he was doomed to be disappointed his entire life, Ben thought. And just when he was beginning to like the idea of his father! How his disappointment led him across the world. At the airport, waiting in line to board the plane, he was half tempted not to go. The reason he wanted to go to Paris was to know more about his father, a French literature professor, to connect with him in some deep way. But going, he knew then, would not get him what he wanted. As the flight attendant scanned his ticket, he told himself he was wrong for thinking this—wrong and stupid—and boarded the plane.

Now Ben looked out the window, then around the room. How empty it was here. How dusty and dark. He pictured his mother moving to Versailles and entering the apartment for the first time. How empty it would have been back then, too. How it would take a lifetime to make a place lived in. He remembered for the longest time they didn't have a kitchen table and how for some time they had only one bed and then his mother got a bed and he and Tuấn had to share one.

He wondered what Tuấn was doing now, alone in that duplex house of his, and how he'd made it a home in no time. When Ben lived there, he felt like it was home.

And now where was he? What had he chosen? That thought came to him often when he realized all of a sudden he was in another country, on another continent, away from where he grew up. But now the question—*What had he chosen?*—felt heavy, a weighted item you palmed. He should write to Tuấn, he thought. Why hadn't he done that since he got here? But then he realized he forgot the address; perhaps he never even knew it.

He felt sleepy. He finished the rest of his wine, stood up, and shook his head. He needed to lie down.

"Are you okay?" Michel asked, reaching out his hand.

"What? Oh, yes." Ben reached out his and smiled. "I'm fine. Just sleepy."

Ben and Michel became quiet lovers. Michel was a kind man who had grand ideas. The man gave Ben chills and made his heart drop, and he felt like it was love or something like love. For love, he thought, one would sacrifice anything. He would stay with Michel and his friends for the rest of the week.

They spent the mornings with wine and coffee and conversations. They went to work in the evenings—Michel, a bookseller; Mateo, a busboy; Sergei, a professional beggar. They kept their money in glass jars, plastic cups, bottles. Communists didn't trust the bank. The commune money was used only for certain things like supplies, revolutionary literature, food, alcohol, and cigarettes. Communists wanted revolution, but they also needed to eat. They had the entire four-story apartment building to themselves. There was a hole in the roof, and when it rained the top floor became soaked. When Michel said that he was sorry, that he wanted to give Ben a better life, and that he was working toward that, Ben said he grew up poor so it didn't make a difference.

"Of course! I knew you would understand!" Michel said, giving him a kiss on the cheek.

The apartment was all they needed. They were self-sufficient.

They had fire, food, shelter; they collected rainwater for showers and were conveniently a block away from a metro stop and a public restroom. They would survive, Michel was sure; they would thrive.

Ben, against all reason, trusted him, and, within two weeks, left the Austrians. They would miss him, they said. He had been so kind. The girl said she was happy he found love. She squealed gleefully when he told her and looked like she wanted to talk with him genuinely about it the way Ben imagined girls gossiped over boys in high school. Michel was happy to have not only a lover, but also, more important to him, another revolutionary.

"You will join us, no?" Michel asked one night, his head on Ben's shoulder. "Join us, the communists?"

It was funny. No one in America would have so happily called themselves communists. What would his mother think, his mother who ran away from the Việt Cộng, barefoot peasant revolutionaries who changed the course of a country and, consequently, the lives of millions? What would all those people think of this?

"Oui," Ben said, *"bien sûr."*

He lay back into the bed and closed his eyes.

He woke up later that night, hearing his mother's voice. It sounded like it came on the wind, like it traveled over land and water to tell him something—something important, something to be remembered and kept. But when he opened his eyes, there was only the wall lit by moonlight, a warm arm on his chest. The night was bitterly cold, and he got up to put more wood bricks into the fireplace. He got back to bed and bundled himself tightly, pushing up against Michel for warmth. New Orleans nights were never this cold. And what had he chosen?

August 2005

Bà Giang will not leave her apartment. Vinh and Hương stop by on their way out. In a moving box, they've packed only what is necessary: food, bottled water, a family photo album, ID cards, passports, the boys' birth certificates, and all of their naturalization papers.

"I can't. I'm too old," says Bà Giang. "These bones!" She pushes down on her cane to get up from the couch. It is the same corduroy couch she's had since moving to Versailles. The color's faded from navy blue to dirty cobalt. With her other arm, she holds her cat, a rescue kitten named Đường—*Sugar*. It's white, though Bà Giang swears she's only that way because her last owner dropped her in a tub of bleach. Đường can't see, either.

"And besides, Đường can't travel. Bác sĩ says so," Bà Giang adds. "She's losing her hearing, too!" She holds up the cat adoringly.

"But the news reports!" says Hương. "Haven't you heard? What are you watching, Bà Giang?"

Hương pokes her head inside and sees an old *Paris by Night* video playing. Women in áo dàis dance with pink umbrellas and sing, *Sài Gòn đẹp lắm, Sài Gòn ơi! Sài Gòn ơi!*

Hương walks in, turns off the VCR, changes the channel. The weather reporter wears a poncho and holds his microphone with both hands, though nothing is happening yet. The screen cuts to a map of the Gulf with a spinning red disc moving toward the boot shape of Louisiana.

"There!" says Hương. "It'll be here tomorrow, Bà Giang."

"Oh, a *hurricane*," replies Bà Giang, like she dropped a handkerchief and Hương was kind enough to pick it up. "I've seen plenty of those. It'll just pass."

"It's getting stronger; the weatherman says so."

The screen cuts back to the weather reporter. He has a different hat now. It's red and doesn't match his yellow poncho.

"Those men don't know a thing. But if you're worrying about me, I'll tape the windows."

"Bà Giang!"

Outside, Vinh presses down on the horn. It's nearly midnight. They are going to pick up Tuấn and his girlfriend, who gets off her job at midnight. They are planning to go to Baton Rouge.

"Hương ơi! I've survived the collapse of a country. I'll survive this. I'm sure I'll survive anything. Believe it or not, người Việt are like cockroaches. We'll survive a nuclear bomb!" She laughs, turns the VCR back on. The singing, dancing women spin, spin, spin!

The horn sounds again.

"We have to go, Bà Giang. I can't leave you here. I couldn't live with myself."

"You'll live just fine," says Bà Giang. "I promise."

Addy pedals faster. Tuấn had called her at the restaurant.

"My mother says it'll be a direct hit," he said.

"Really?" She was folding napkins, holding the phone on her

shoulder. She eyed the television. A cartoon was playing. Goofy the dog.

"Just to be safe, she said she's coming to pick us up."

"Where would we go?"

"Baton Rouge. We'll get a motel."

Addy turned down the volume and plugged a finger into her ear. "What? I can't hear."

"Baton Rouge," said Tuấn. "We'll get a motel."

When Addy asked Sebastian if she could leave early, he refused. "You know how long my family's been here?" he asked.

"A gazillion years, Sebastian!" Addy answered. She'd heard it too many times. Sebastian was a proud New Orleanian, but Addy never understood being proud of coming from a place: you didn't have any choice in the matter, it just happened. "A gazillion fucking years!"

"Close. Two hundred," he said. "We don't let no freakin' hurricane drive us out. We'll be fine. This city floats. We're practically a rubber duck."

She went back to her napkins. There was only one table of guests. Outside, the streets were empty. She tried to remember if any of the animals were acting strangely. A documentary on TV once said animals had a sixth sense about the weather.

"Watch the animals," said a Utah park ranger, a canyon yawning behind him. "They know everything."

She looked out the window. A plastic bag drifted by and disappeared around the corner.

At midnight, when the restaurant closed, she rushed out, a baseball cap her only shield from the rain.

Now Addy slows as she approaches Mr. Franklin's Grocery. From the street, she can see him in there alone and standing behind the counter with a book.

Some bottles of water to bring with us, she thinks. *A little water wouldn't hurt anybody.*

———

The water comes rushing at him. At first he tries to swim, but the waves push at him, forcing their way past his lips, down his throat. He tastes the sea and the salt; he tastes it all. On the water's surface, in the distance, a boat. He whips his arms in the water. He needs to move or else he will die.

Ben wakes up panicking.

It was just a dream. A dream! Thank God! Thank all the gods, any of them! Another dream. He sits up and flicks on the light.

He'd been having dangerous dreams all week. They always involved water. They felt so real that, for a split second, between the dreaming and the waking, he confused them for memory.

In this dream, he was on a boat.

"Sacrifice, sacrifice, sacrifice," they were chanting. Someone had to be sacrificed for the safety of the others. In the middle of the chanting, he—a small boy—was dropped into the ocean.

"*Ça va bien? Qu'est qu'il se passé?*" asks Michel, massaging Ben's back. He touches Ben's forehead, then goes to the bathroom. Ben hears the squeaky faucet turning on, then off. To think they lived in an abandoned apartment without water or electricity for nearly two months before the city found them and kicked them out. That he put himself through that seems silly now, perhaps even dangerous. Michel comes back with a wet towel. He places it on Ben's head. "*Fièvre,*" he diagnoses.

"*Impossible,*" says Ben. "I don't get sick. It's the nightmares. They get me worked up."

Michel gets ready for work as Ben goes to the window, opens the shutters. It's so quiet and his dream was so loud. The water, especially. But it's an ordinary day here now, safe and ordinary.

Michel comes out of the bathroom, tightening his tie. "Today is your day off, *non*?" he asks.

"*Oui. J'irai au marché. Nous avons besoin des pommes, des*

27

oranges, et des tomates." Ben has to undo the knot and retie it. Because the kids at the *collège* won't take him seriously without a properly tied tie.

Tuấn is packing when the door opens. It's Addy.

"They've been repeating the same thing all day," he reports to her. "Higher ground," he says.

"Higher ground," the radio parrots.

"Sebastian says to stay," she tells Tuấn, walking to the bathroom. With the door open, she peels off her waitress clothes. Her black skin glistens with sweat. She smiles at Tuấn and pulls on shorts and a tank top.

She was a friend of his brother's. For a year, he went to the restaurant where she worked the late-night shift. He got off his shift late and ate dinner alone in a booth. At first he thought she didn't recognize him, until one day she came up to him with his credit card and receipt and said, "Well, if it isn't Mr. SBZ himself."

It made him blush. He was never one of the Southern Boyz, and he wondered how far that rumor traveled and how long something like that stayed in the air.

"Let me tell you something," she had said and sat herself down across from him.

I'm in for it now, he was thinking. If she remembered the Southern Boyz, surely she remembered the type of guy he was back then. "People change," he was ready to say.

"I always liked you," she said, "you and your family."

Inside, Tuấn let out a sigh of relief.

"And I wondered what happened to y'all."

"People change," he told her anyway, and they spent that evening, and evenings after, catching up on how much they did change.

They became friends quickly after that.

Now, he wonders what took him so long, why he didn't have his eyes open. They've been together for two years now.

"When's your mom coming?" she asks.

"Soon." He throws more clothes into the suitcase.

Addy walks over. "You're doing it wrong," she says, taking out what he's packed. "Only what's necessary."

The AC is broken. It's stuck on high and it won't turn off. Since the night is hot, the windows fog up. Vinh stops the car, wipes the windshield with his hand. Everything is still blurry.

"Can't we go any faster?" Hương asks.

"I can't see a thing," says Vinh.

It has begun to rain harder, not the sprinkling they've been having all night. It's like a different storm and it sounds like nails falling.

Vinh begins to drive again.

"High-speed winds expected like you've never seen before. Rain, too," says the radio. "Get to higher ground. Stay indoors."

Hương licks her lips and turns up the radio. Though he wouldn't say it aloud, Vinh knows Hương likes emergencies. She thrives on figuring out how to avoid danger, how to stay alive. Once, the news reported an earthquake in California. When Hương got wind of it, she went to the grocery store and bought emergency supplies— flashlights, a portable radio, batteries, a flare gun. "In case we get stuck in the wreckage," she had said. It didn't matter that it was two thousand miles away; she would save them all if it came down to it.

"I feel bad about Bà Giang," says Hương. "She wouldn't come. I tried to drag her. I literally tried to drag her. That's why it took so long. My, that woman's gotten fat."

"She'll be safe. That woman's a survivor," says Vinh.

"That's what she said," says Hương, "but what if she's wrong? I can see it now, the winds blowing the apartment away. They'd find her stuck up a tree somewhere."

"Now that's funny."

"Not if it really happens."

Vinh speeds up. The streets are empty. Everything's closed up. All the buildings have plywood boards covering the windows, the doors.

"Take a left up here," says Hương.

"Are you sure?" asks Vinh.

"Yes, I'm sure."

Ben sits on a bench with a thermos, a notebook, and a pen.

Today, Ben is sure, he will write. But what? He wanted to write about his life here over the last five years (he couldn't believe it, either; it just happened that way). There was plenty enough to write about, several books' worth of stories. About his time with Michel and the other communists. About how the police kicked them out. (Other than a mattress thrown out from the third floor along with a bottle of wine, it was rather anticlimactic, but words could bring it to life.) About struggling in Paris and the various jobs he had—first as a recycling collector (he kept telling Tuấn it was *recycling*, not *trash*, though he didn't seem to know the difference); then for a while he worked as a housekeeper for a lycée; and now he cleaned dishes at a restaurant and wrote articles at night for a website for tourists and English product descriptions for an online clothing company. He was sure he could find something to say about all of this, something of importance.

Yet, if he were honest with himself, everything here was boring. He thought he would find some connection to his father and in that way his past as well. At the very least, he thought he would have a good time and learn to live life passionately, the way the French supposedly do so well, and live it on his own terms.

Yet he had none of these. He had nothing. He regretted his decision to stay with Michel and in Paris. Michel was a kind enough man who once had big ideas. But nowadays he co-taught geography to middle schoolers. How people changed, he thought and wondered if he had changed, and, if so, how much.

But there was no time to worry about that. That was the past. He had to think about the future and what he would do now.

"I'm sure we would've passed it by now," says Hương. "Maybe we should've turned back there."

Vinh steadies the wheel. The wind. He feels the car whipping back and forth. He is unsure if he can hold on to it, control it.

"These houses," Hương says. "They all look the same. Are we even in the right neighborhood?" They must have taken a wrong turn somewhere, but it's too dark to tell.

"Should I turn back?" he says.

"Just take this street and go around the block," says Hương.

Vinh slows down. There are no lights on this street, though there should be. There must have been a blackout.

Before Vinh can turn around, he realizes it's a one-way street and a car is coming toward them. He slams on the brakes but at the last minute decides to dodge it. He feels the wind pushing the wheels, spinning the car. He sees a lamppost, he sees a mailbox, then a wall comes toward him and disappears.

He hears the crash before seeing it, feeling it. The airbags deploy, smash against his face. He feels his teeth biting his cheek, tastes the metal in the blood.

"What happened?" he hears Hương say. "Vinh? Are you okay?" She sounds far away, as if she's outside the car.

He reaches over. There, that's her arm. Here's her elbow. Here, there's blood, warm and sticky.

"Trời ổi, are you okay?" he asks.

"Em không biết. My head hurts."

Vinh squeezes her arm. He realizes the water's coming in. He reaches for the car door. When it doesn't open, he pushes—pushes as hard as he can. It's impossible to open. He pushes harder. Maybe they're in water, he's thinking, but it doesn't look that high. It couldn't have flooded so quickly. He uses his shoulder and tries again. This time the door opens a crack, but it's enough for him to slide through.

When he climbs out, he sees the full damage. The front is smashed in, the windshield cracked. The door on his side is dented, but Hương's door is stuck against a telephone pole. He sees her struggling to open it and rushes over.

"Can you open the window?" he asks.

When he doesn't hear an answer, he repeats himself and leans in closer. He hears her pressing the window button, releasing it, pressing it again.

Vinh pulls at the back door, but, like the other door, it's stuck. He pulls with both hands until it opens but only a crack.

"Can you get to the back?" he asks.

He sees her moving, climbing over to the backseat. She pushes at the door.

"You have to go through the crack," he says.

She says something he can't hear. She pushes again. He pulls. She hits the window.

"Back away," he hears her say, muffled.

He backs up. Hương hits the window with something, but it bounces back.

Seeing what she can't do, Vinh begins looking around for something heavy. He walks several paces before he sees a piece of wood from a tree. He heaves it up, tells Hương to back away, and hurls the wood through the window, which breaks into pieces. Hương smashes the flashlight at the remaining jagged edges and climbs out.

Already, Vinh notices, the water's rising. They must get to higher ground soon. He pulls her up. He sees a bluish bruise on her forehead.

"We have to go," he says. "Somewhere safer."

"But Tuấn," she says. She tries to gather where they are. "We have to get Tuấn," she says.

"We don't have a car anymore."

"His house," she says. She pulls away and starts running.

"Hương!" he calls. Vinh runs after her. He is soaked. He sees the water dripping in front of his eyes. The air, he feels, is getting colder. "We should find shelter," says Vinh, trying to catch up. "Tuấn will be fine."

At the intersection, Hương pauses. "We missed a street," she says. "We must have missed a street," she repeats before running off.

On the radio, the mayor says, "This is the storm of the century." A clip they've been replaying all day. In the background are reporters, clicking their pens, scribbling on notepads. "Mayor Nagin, Mr. Nagin, Mayor Nagin," they all say at the same time.

"It's getting late," says Addy.

They sit by the window even though they both know they shouldn't. Addy presses her face against the glass pane.

"I don't see them. I don't see anybody," she says. Rain whips the window. She can feel the wind on the glass, can feel it bend. She knows it will all be broken when they return. There will be plenty of cleaning to be done afterward. She imagines all the cleaning they will have to do later: sweep up the glass, remove the standing water, scrub and disinfect everything. But they will get through this, Addy is sure. Their families fled their lives in other countries and built new ones from scratch—out here in the swamp. They not only survived but thrived. They come from hardy stock, and this makes her proud.

"Let's get away from the window," says Tuấn.

". . . mandatory evacuation of the city of New Orleans . . ." says Mayor Nagin.

The lights flicker and turn off. The mayor stops talking. The buzz of electricity is gone.

"Babe, are you okay?" asks Tuấn.

"Yeah," answers Addy. *He's a sweet man,* she thinks. Rough on the outside but sweet under that shell. She just had to get to know him and, from there, how easy it was to fall for him. She hears Tuấn stumbling over furniture then lighting up a match.

"Where do we keep the candles?" He walks to the kitchen.

"Maybe we shouldn't wait for them," says Addy.

"What?" says Tuấn.

"I said, 'Maybe we shouldn't wait for them.'"

"They're on their way." Tuấn returns with a scented candle. "I swear they're coming," he says. The flame lights up. He almost looks hurt at the suggestion of leaving without his mother.

Sweet man, she thinks.

The house begins to smell like lavender.

Hương imagines the road is not asphalt but soft, wet soil. Where is Tuấn's house? Why can't she remember it when she needs it the most?

She turns down another street. It's familiar, though it's all dark. All the houses look the same, all duplexes or shotguns. Like when she first arrived.

She can't tell where she is now. The rain makes everything blurry, and her hair becomes wet, heavy, matted. Running, she pulls her damp hair together. Not finding a rubber band on her, she shoves the ponytail down the back of her shirt.

She feels blood rushing to her head, throbbing. The bruise is tender.

Then comes an explosion. She sees it in the air, the sparks like fireworks. She wants to scream but stops herself.

Guns, she thinks. *Guns or bombs, guns or bombs, those must be guns or bombs, someone has a gun or a bomb.*

She imagines hoodlums with baggy pants raiding the city. She imagines tanks driving through the water. She imagines skinny shirtless men in paddy hats, shoeless in the rain.

Then the thought: they need to leave the city now. They must leave and never return. This is her last night in the city, she is sure. She must leave.

But her son.

But my sons . . . Tuấn and Bình. Tuấn and Bình. Tuấn and Bình . . . Say their names. Keep them in your heart.

Ben closes his eyes. And again he sees water. He sees it everywhere. His brother is screaming and his mother—she's screaming as well, holding her stomach. He realizes now it is him in that stomach, him in that belly. So that boy is another boy. He didn't drown. It was another boy.

A man grabs the boy by the wrists. From where Ben watches, the boy sits in praying position, hands together, head toward the sky.

"What are you doing?" a woman yells. It is not Ben's mother, but another. Another mother. Another's mother.

The boat sways violently. There is a whirlpool. It is night. There is only night for miles in each direction. The boy lets out a yelp, but the man shakes him so the boy quiets, his cries sucked into a vacuum.

"Sacrifice!" someone yells.

"He's the youngest," says the man. "He's not losing anything. He hasn't anything to lose."

The woman stands up and moves toward her son.

The man jerks the boy away from the mother's reach.

"Sacrifice!" someone yells.

"Just a boy!" someone replies.

"Sacrifice," another person cries, and before another protest, before another word, the boy is dropped into the sea. The woman disappears into the black.

Ben clenches his hands into fists. He feels something coming up through his throat, something bitter. He looks at his mother and brother. With her hands, she covers Tuấn's eyes.

"Murderer!" someone yells.

"Sacrifice!"

"Just a boy!"

"Murderer!"

"Sacrifice!"

"Just a boy."

With flashlight in hand, Addy walks out the door. Tuấn comes out with a backpack. He throws the flashlight into the bicycle basket. Addy climbs on the seat and sees Tuấn running back up the steps.

"What you doing?" she asks. She feels her heart racing. The storm has gotten stronger. The rain pelts her skin. She pulls on the hood on her poncho. If it floods, she can swim, she thinks. She hasn't swum since high school, but she's sure it's like riding a bike: your body remembers.

"My mom's not answering her phone," Tuấn says. His hood blows off. "She's coming. She wouldn't leave without us."

"But honey, we need to leave." The water is soaking her feet. The wind blows and she can barely keep their bicycle up.

"I'm leaving a note. So she knows."

Addy hears the sound of heavy-duty tape ripping from the roll. She hears this several times until Tuấn is satisfied.

"She'll find us," he says. "Told her to meet us at the Best Western across from Touro Hospital." He gets on the bike and Addy leans against him. He stands on the pedals, presses down hard, and they start moving through the accumulating water.

"That's the farthest I'll go without her," he says.

Sweet man! Addy thinks.

"Tuấn!" she cries. "Bình! It's your mother. We have to leave! We have to go somewhere else. Tuấn! Bình! Where are you?"

Then she sees the sign for Ursulines Avenue and she turns the corner and sees the house, Tuấn's house. She can tell because it's the only duplex painted half red, half blue. The blue side is his side. They took a wrong turn, but they were close all along.

"Tuấn ơi," she yells. "Your mother's here. We have to go. Bão tới!"

She runs up the porch steps and notices his bike is gone. On the screen door she sees the note.

"'Ma,'" she reads, "'meet us at Best Western, Touro Hospital.'"

My boy, she thinks. *He's safe!* She just has to get to him now.

She runs down the steps. "Best Western," she repeats to herself under her breath. "Touro Hospital. Best Western. Touro Hospital." She runs. She will get there, she is sure, if only she'd run faster. But is it this way? She isn't sure. She has to face south. South is where she needs to go to see her boy. "Best Western. Touro Hospital." She picks up her pace, though the wind is getting stronger, the rain heavier. "Best Western. Touro Hospital."

Lightning breaks the sky, and she hears the distinct sound of a tree snapping and falling.

Hương remembers the old man with the beard and a cigarette in his mouth. She remembers running through the jungle, the rain—it must have been raining, too, that night.

Her heart races as she hears the sound of boots behind her. She tries to speed up because someone is out there.

And they are after us. Again, they are after us.

But her sons! Where were they? They must leave. They must leave immediately. Their lives depend on it. But where were the boys?

"Tuấn! Bình!" she cries and picks up her pace, running as fast as she can.

"Hương!" a voice screams. "Stop running!" She feels a hand grab her shoulder and her body spins around.

"Công," she nearly cries out until the lightning flashes and illuminates his face.

"Vinh," she says, panting.

"It's not safe. We have to find shelter," he says, but she pulls her arm, tries to break free. Vinh pulls back. He can't make out if the water on her face is rain or tears. He pulls her even harder, but it feels like the wind is ripping her away. He thinks of trees and their branches ripping apart in a storm. He plants his feet firmly and holds on to her arm tightly. He feels his feet soaked, but he also feels mud. It must be everywhere. Earthy and brown and dirty. He smells it, the mud. He pulls hard until Hương crashes into him and they crash together onto the flooding ground, her back on his front, her weight and the water's weight on him.

For a minute, the only sound is their breathing. They become an island. They become a stranded ship. They are a boat far from shore. He holds her tight. He swears, if only to himself, not to let go.

A loud scream like a battle cry wakes Ben up.

But he's not in Paris anymore. He's back in New Orleans, back in Versailles and the house of his childhood, and nothing is out of place. Except the water.

He's in his room and water is gushing in through the windows. The water is brown and smells like the bayou. It brings in twigs and branches and leaves; it brings in trash—plastic bags, candy bar wrappers, cigarette packs. Before he can think of what to do, he's knocked over and is underwater. He gets up and pushes through to the door, and there, gripping the frame, he's able to steady himself. The water's already up to his waist.

Then, again, the piercing scream. He wades through to the hallway, holding the wall along the way. The wallpaper's peeling. The hung pictures are falling down.

"Hello?" he yells back. "Is anyone there? Mẹ? T?"

He gets to the kitchen, and there the water's bursting through the window, too. But no one's there. Suddenly, the sink explodes with a deafening blow and more water spews up.

The apartment steadily fills with water as he tries to walk to his mother's room. *That's where the scream must be coming from,* he thinks. He can't tell if it's a woman's voice or a man's (*Maybe it's both,* he thinks, *two people screaming in unison*), but he's sure that's where the scream is coming from.

He grips on to the wall and part of it gives. He slips as a wave pushes him back and his body plunges in.

No, he thinks. *No.*

He holds his breath.

Everything under is brown, murky. He tries to get back up, but the water is heavy. He waves his arms, his legs. He must move, he thinks. He tries harder, but it's useless. He feels himself sinking deeper. His heart quickens. He needs to stay alive, he tells himself. He needs to get up. Why can't he get up? He wants to scream—he feels like he needs to scream—but he can't.

And somehow, the scream—the other scream in the other room—gets louder. It's like someone is turning up the volume, and it's all he can hear, this scream.

Sorry, he wants to say, sorry I can't get to you.

And he opens his eyes, and the sun is still shining.

He's in Paris again. He's in the park, lying on a bench under the shade of a tree. Ben feels sweat on his forehead, the beams of sun baking his skin. He stands up and is amazed at the ordinariness of the day. A woman walks her dog. A man talks loudly on his phone. A group of runners jogs by. Like it's any other day.

Vinh knocks on another house door. A car is in the driveway, though under a fallen tree. Someone has to be home. But would they let them in?

"We have to get to the Best Western. Near Touro," Hương tells Vinh. "Tuấn's there." She dials his number and no one picks up. It lets her leave a message, but she doesn't.

"He's safe," says Vinh. "He's found shelter. That's what we need to know. We'll meet him in the morning."

"But—" Hương says.

"We're in no condition," says Vinh.

Then the door opens. It's a silhouette that greets them.

"Who's that?" It's a teenage boy. Even in the dark, Vinh can see the boy's wearing baggy clothes and that his posture is hunched.

"Our car, it crash," says Vinh, pointing out into the road, though the car is nowhere to be seen. They've walked a long way. "Can we please come in, please?" He squeezes his grip harder around Hương's hand. She looks at the flooded street. She imagines Tuấn in a hotel room, sitting away from the window, calling her but not getting through.

If only, she thinks, *if only I can be sure. If only I can hear his voice.*

"*Please*," Vinh repeats.

"Marshall, let them in," says a woman's voice, "before the water comes."

The boy's stance relaxes and the door opens. Vinh and Hương walk in. In the darkness, Vinh sees a short Black woman holding a flashlight. There is also another child, smaller, a girl.

"Come in!" the woman says. She waves her flashlight to see their faces. "Chinese!" she says. She sounds delighted. The flashlight shines on the stairs. "We're staying up there," she says, "if flood-water comes higher."

Vinh pulls Hương in. The teenage boy closes the door, delicately.

———

When the water is up to their knees, they hop off the bike and begin running. They're running as fast as they can, but it feels like they're going nowhere. The water is pushing them back; the raindrops are like BB gun pellets.

But with enough walking, the water subsides and they see in the distance a row of streetlights and houses. The electricity is a sign of safety. They stare at it as they trudge through. A mailbox floats by. A pink flamingo lawn ornament covered in mud goes after it.

Addy falls down and Tuấn comes and pulls her up. She's breathing hard.

"Stay with me," he says.

Even exhausted, she is beautiful. When she nods, he stands her up, and, arm in arm, they walk against the water's current, against the wind. Everything is cold. Everything is freezing.

Tuấn thinks that if he survives, he'll have a cold for a week. If he survives the cold, he will ask Addy to marry him. It seems like a fair idea.

After several more minutes of walking, they notice the water leveling off. Addy falls down to her knees again. Tuấn kneels down beside her.

"Are you okay?" he asks. "Babe?"

"I'm all right," she says, "just exhausted." She leans on his shoulder, panting.

"We should rest," he says, pulling her up. He tries to think. Where exactly are they? He needs to call his mother, tell her their change of plans. "There're houses up there. You see the lights?"

No one sleeps. Not the woman, not her son, not her daughter, not Hương, not Vinh. They pace the attic. They look out the window.

They pace some more. The kids play card games and make shadow puppets with the flashlight until the mother tells them to stop wasting the batteries.

The woman turns on the radio. The radio is saying the same things over and over again: stay inside, get to higher ground, pray for New Orleans, pray. When she has had enough, the woman turns it off.

Hương thinks about Tuấn. She tries to call him, but nothing goes through, not even text messages. But it doesn't stop her from trying several more times. She leaves a voicemail, hoping it will reach him eventually. Her mind turns to Bình. She wonders if she should call him, too, though she knows he's in Paris. She's thankful he's not here, thankful he's safe from all this.

She looks out the window: a black night now that the electricity everywhere is gone. She can't see a thing outside.

She paces around the room, the worry in her restless. She watches the kids, the boy and the girl. They're lying down now. The boy is playing with cards by himself. The girl has a small doll, which she rocks gently.

"Your kids," says Hương. "So good! So quiet!"

"That's because they're stuck in the house with me," says the woman. She claps her hands and laughs. *She's a good mother,* Hương thinks.

"I have two sons," says Hương. "They're away."

The woman's face becomes concerned. "Are they out *there*?"

A car alarms goes off. Lightning flashes in the sky.

"They're somewhere," Hương says. "They're somewhere."

The woman shakes her head, comes over, and gives Hương a hug.

They find a house with a wraparound porch and three floors. Because the lights are still on, they are sure they will be let in. After several knocks and a ring of the doorbell, a man in a red satin robe greets them.

"The storm," says Addy. "There's a flood down there."

"Can we stay for the night?" asks Tuấn.

"Well, come on in!" answers the man. He has a high-pitched voice, a girlish manner. "You two look like drowned rats!"

Inside the house, they stay on the top floor. "Just in case," the man says.

The man lives by himself here, has lived here all his life. Sometimes alone, sometimes not. He shows them a picture of his lover, who died in the eighties.

"When they announced the evacuation, I couldn't leave," the man says. "I just couldn't! I have roots here. I'm a pretty flower. You can't just pluck me out. I'm too pretty!" the man says. He laughs, and his laughter is so infectious, Tuấn and Addy laugh, too.

Together, they watch the news. The water is rising, it says, and it will continue to rise.

They've found safety, Tuấn thinks. They're not out there. They'll find his mother and Vinh in the morning. He hopes they've at least gotten out of New Orleans East. The bayou would've flooded by now. And those trees would have fallen in this wind. He knows the destruction of Versailles is possible, but he doesn't want to think about it.

He calls his mother. It goes to voicemail.

"Ma," he goes. "We're on Coliseum Street at a nice man's house. There's barely flooding here. Give me a call when you get this, okay, Ma?"

They watch the news until it's just repeating itself. There's no new information. They're all just waiting for it to be over.

"What will stop the water? What will get it to stop?" they all ponder aloud.

"Sebastian said we'd float," mumbles Addy, more to herself than to anyone.

"Well, he's got it wrong," says the man. "New Orleans is more like a . . . more like a . . ." He twirls his hands in the air, trying to find a word. "It's more like a bathtub," he says.

The city is like a bathtub. The winds are the hands of a housewife. The water a mixture of tap and cleaning detergent. The housewife scrubs and scrubs. She is sure not to miss a spot. She wants to make sure no one forgets her name when she is gone and how good a housewife she was. She is bitter.

In the morning, there is a loud explosion. It shakes the house, sloshes the floodwaters, moves the earth.

"What was that?" asks the woman. She opens the window. Then she closes it and runs to the stairs.

"Water!" she yells. "There's water in the house!"

Vinh runs to the stairs and sees water gushing in so fast it turns white. He sees a table floating like a raft. Then a vase. Then a floor lamp.

"The window," says Hương. She walks over and opens it. For a second, Vinh thinks she's going to swim away. When she lifts up a leg, he runs to her. Then he realizes she's climbing.

Half of her body disappears from view, and then her legs are gone, too. The girl is next to go up, aided by her brother. He goes up after. Vinh tries to help the woman up, but she wants him to go up first. He obliges and she comes after.

The air on the roof is icy. Vinh looks out and sees all the water, all brown, all flowing like they're in a river, but instead of rocks, there are cars and rooftops.

All of a sudden, Hương screams, "God, oh, God!"

The kids turn her way. The woman gasps and pulls her children toward her.

Hương points out into the distance, not ten feet away from the house. Vinh turns his head, and, to his surprise, there's a body.

The body is a man's, from what Vinh can tell. Dead for a while, probably. The body wears jeans and a long-sleeved plaid shirt. There are no shoes and no socks. For some reason, Vinh thinks he must've had a hat.

The body floats facedown and continues moving with the current until its shirt tangles with the branches of a tree and stops. From the tree branch, it sways. Vinh imagines lungs full of water, lungs full of mud.

Ben walks up the stairs with a tote bag of groceries. He tells himself he should've brought two bags to divide the weight. He's bought more than he should have, but at least they'll be stocked for a couple of weeks. He stops after the second flight, takes a breather. He wishes they didn't live on the top floor in an apartment building with no elevator.

When he gets home, he drops the bag in the front hallway and changes to sweatpants and a T-shirt.

He turns on the TV and begins unpacking. He'll cook something simple tonight, he thinks. Maybe pasta with chicken. For dessert, fresh fruit. He puts on a pot of water, salts it. Preheats the oven.

On TV, a cartoon plays, something with badly drawn animals. He surfs the channels and sees a familiar talk show, something that looks like a British mystery, and a kids' show with puppets. Then he stops on the news. The first thing he notices is that it's New Orleans. Before he sees the text, he knows it's the city of his youth. The surprise, though, comes when he realizes it's flooding. No, not flooding—New Orleans is drowning.

He drops a metal pan. The sound of it crashing to the floor doesn't take him away from the screen, where muddy brown water fills the city as far as the eye can see as people stand on top of houses and cars. The camera zooms in to a woman waving her arms. The clip switches to a video of a strong wind blowing against a tree at night. The tree bends and bends and finally snaps, colliding with a car. A boat evacuates a building. A helicopter hovers over a home.

Ben's heart drops. He sits down. He feels himself getting hot and itchy. He gets back up and opens a window. He turns up the volume and sits back down. The images of New Orleans are replaced with a video of the mayor at a press conference.

"The City of New Orleans," he says, before his words are translated by a French newscaster. *Un ouragan,* the newscaster says. *Catégorie cinq. Inondation. État d'urgence. Levées.* The video returns to collapsed houses and buildings and overturned cars and floating trash islands. People stand in lines and cry, hugging pillows, as if the floodwater hit their homes while they were asleep. *Un désastre complet,* says the newscaster.

Ben's hands shake; his entire body is shivering.

And what of his mother? And his brother? There are no reports of New Orleans East, of Versailles.

He feels cold all of a sudden and walks over to close the window. It shuts suddenly and the windowpane startles him with his reflection.

The oven rings and the pot has boiled over. He turns it off and lowers the volume on the TV. He rummages through the kitchen drawers for an address book. They play the video of the tree and car again. They play the one with the boat and the people climbing off of roofs, holding plastic grocery bags of their belongings. It looks like it could be a different city, a different country, but it's not. It's New Orleans.

He picks up his phone and misdials the number several times until he finally gets it right. The phone rings and rings.

When the rain stops, the sun comes out. Water still flows in the streets, but it doesn't look like anything more than what a heavy thunderstorm would bring. Tuấn and Addy thank the man for his help. He gives them cookies. They thank him again and leave.

Tuấn and Addy walk for several minutes.

"I thought I was going to die," Addy says.

"It's times like these that we realize how short life is," he says.

Because of the debris—fallen trees and electric lines—they take the long way back—up through the Lower Garden District then east toward home. They are walking on an overpass as Tuấn checks his phone. The signal bar lights up the screen. It dings when it receives two voice messages, one from his mother and another from his brother. He's about to press Play when he hears Addy gasp.

"Look!" she says. "Look!"

Tuấn follows her finger and his heart stops when he sees it's all rooftops and people small as ants. "Where's the city?" he wants to ask. "Where's New Orleans?"

The people are waving their hands. They are waving their hands and they are yelling.

They yell and wave their arms for help. But Hương doesn't move. She stays seated on the roof, watching the dead body stuck in the tree. It waves with the current, but it's stuck.

The others, including Vinh, are on their feet. The children tried to spell out HELP with their clothes but had only enough for HE. Now they jump up and down, hands in the air, reaching for the skies. They've seen two helicopters in the last hour, but neither has stopped.

"They're ignoring us," says the girl. "They don't like us."

"We just have to try harder. Jump higher. Scream louder," says her brother.

When they see another helicopter, the two kids try to jump higher, try to wave their arms faster.

"Help!" they yell. "Help! Help! Help!"

"Maybe they don't know we're alive," the girl says. "Maybe that's the problem." She takes in a lungful of air and lets it out: "We're alive! Help us! We're alive!"

The brother follows. "Help us!" they both scream. "We're alive! Help us! We're alive! Help us!"

The helicopter seems to float in the air, then it starts to descend. The kids get excited.

"Finally," the girl says, and does a little dance. The sound of the blades spinning makes everything hard to hear.

"Hương, it's here!" yells Vinh. "It's over, Hương. It's all over."

The helicopter hovers over the house. They let out a rescue basket as a man talks through a megaphone.

"Climb into the basket," he says. His voice is loud, steady, and calm. The megaphone squeals before he continues. "Two at a time," he says, "climb into the basket. Thumbs up when you're ready."

The mother motions for the kids to go up first. The boy rushes to the basket and seats himself. His sister jumps in and sits across from her brother. They both give the thumbs-up and the basket is pulled up. They throw their hands into the air and holler like they're on an amusement park ride.

When the kids are safe, the basket is dropped back down again and the mother rides it by herself. She sits and leans her head on her knees, head turned down to see everything one last time. "Oh," Hương hears her say. It sounds like she wants to say something more, but she stops herself. The woman covers her face with her hands and begins crying. She leans over and waves goodbye to her house.

When the basket is lowered the third time, Vinh grabs on and calls for Hương.

"Hương," he says. "It's time to go."

She hears him, but she can't move. Instead, she watches the body in the tree. It shakes with the water, and the branches scratch the body.

"Hương," Vinh says. He hits the basket with the palm of his

hand to get her to hear. "It's time to go." He climbs in and sits. The basket sways.

Someone has to help the body, Hương thinks. The man must have a family. They must know what happened to him; it's only right. Then she wonders where they were. She imagines them driving away from New Orleans in a mad rush. *Did we forget someone?* they'd ask themselves.

But what if he was alone? What if his family wasn't here in the city? What if they lived far away, scattered across the country? Scattered across the earth? How would they ever know?

The man in the helicopter shouts down in his megaphone, "We have to go, ma'am. Climb in."

The helicopter hovers and bobs up and down as if trying to balance.

"Hương! Do you hear me?" says Vinh. "They're going to leave! We have to go, Hương. Do you hear me? It's time to go."

Eventually, the tree can't hold the body anymore. The shirt rips and the body is released into the water, moving past the house and past another tree.

He is heading somewhere, though Hương doesn't know where.

She looks around and is surprised she doesn't know where she is. South, north, Uptown, Mid-City—with all the water, she can't tell where anything is anymore. She closes her eyes and tries to remember what it had been like before.

"Hương!" Vinh cries. The basket begins moving upward.

Hương stands and grabs Vinh's hand with both of her own. The basket sways as it moves and she holds on tightly, teeth clenched from all the holding, as she is lifted up into the sky, now so blue and now so bright that the roof fades and the trees below fade, too, the same way the shore shrank from view that night so long ago.

She remembers staring out the back of the boat, pinpoints of starlight illuminating the land until it was gone. She was hoping that it would reappear—the coast, the sand and the rocks, the man she loved. *Any minute now,* she kept on thinking, until the sun rose up over the horizon and a woman tapped her on the shoulder.

"You've been up all night," the woman said. She nodded toward the center of the boat, where the others were fast asleep. Hương turned around and saw mothers holding sons, fathers holding daughters, siblings huddled together, all of them far away from home. The woman held on to her shoulder.

Hương held out her hand to the sea—a gesture of grasping or waving goodbye. *But,* she was thinking. *But . . .*

"Time to go," the woman said, this time in a voice softer and gentler.

Hương nodded and clasped her shaky hands together—hands that would, years later, become steady hands, sturdy hands.

Yes, Hương thought in a lull of calm and clarity. She turned around toward the front of the boat. The sun was rising. They were facing east. The water, she realized, wasn't that bad. The waves, you got used to them. With time.

Vinh lifts her into the basket.

And the phone rings as she leans out to look at her city.

Yes, she thinks. She knows exactly where she is now. These weathered buildings. These streets. These waters. All these years.

She flips open her phone. "A lô?" she answers. "Bình? Mẹ đây."

ACKNOWLEDGMENTS

Thank you to the following people and organizations for supporting me, inspiring me, and motivating me during the process of writing this book: Nayelly Barrios, Victoria Castells, Nivea Castro, Rea Concepcion, Cristina Correa, Kristene Cristobal, Katya Cummins, Amy Fleury, M. Evelina Galang, Craig Gidney, Nicola Griffith, Bruce Owens Grimm, John Griswold, Chris Herrmann, Angela Hur, Anne-Marie Kinney, the Knopf publishing team, Lambda Literary, Caitlin Landuyt, Brian Lin, Christopher Lowe, Kristina McBride, the McNeese State University MFA Program, Lori Mosley, Michael Nguyen, Nguyễn Phan Quế Mai, Viet Thanh Nguyen, Haneen Oriqat, Thomas Parrie, Ruby Pediangco, Roseanne Pereira, Julie Quiroz, Nancy Ruffin, Andrea Ruggirello, Matthew Salesses, Talisha Shelley, Erin Elizabeth Smith, Julie Stevenson, Sundress Academy for the Arts, Karimah Tennyson-Marsh, Tin House Writers' Workshop, Jenn Alandy Trahan, and the Voices of Our Nations Arts Foundation.

A NOTE ABOUT THE AUTHOR

Eric Nguyen earned an MFA in creative writing from McNeese State University in Louisiana. He has been awarded fellowships from Lambda Literary Foundation, Voices of Our Nations Arts Foundation (VONA), and the Tin House writers' workshop. He is the editor in chief for diacritics.org. He lives in Washington, D.C. This is his first novel.

A NOTE ON THE TYPE

This book was set in Minion, a typeface produced by the Adobe Corporation for the Macintosh personal computer, and released in 1990.

Typeset by Scribe, Philadelphia, Pennsylvania
Printed and bound by Berryville Graphics, Berryville, Virginia
Designed by Maggie Hinders